PASSIONATE PURSUIT

J. Matheny

ISBN: 978-0-9858166-0-5

DEDICATION

To all who suffered in this war and all other wars.

Also, to the five-year-old grandson of a friend who asked…..

"Why do we have wars to make there be peace?"

❧Chapter 1 – The Ship❧

The threads of fog were dense enough to form a fabric of sorts, screening everything with its veil and preventing even the wavelets from being easily apparent. Without the sound of their slapping against the hull, one could have thought that the ship glided on a sea of glass.

To the young woman standing on the deck, the throaty call of the foghorn seemed eerie and melancholic. She shivered, then pulled the collar of her coat closer and snuggled into its warmth.

It brought memories --- memories of another time, a time when she was not alone, and she rode the wave of that remembering, basking in the glow of its warmth and joy.

They were young, she and Franz, and on their way to France. It was 1936, the days of The Great Depression were beginning to wane, and their families had sent them to Europe for their honeymoon --- and, being in business, to take a first-hand look at the economies…..

Ah, their fathers, the consummate businessmen…..

Enough of that, she thought! Back to their precious time together on board their ship of dreams….. She remembered, so vividly, his hair blowing in the wind on the deck when he'd forgotten his hat. She offered her spare scarf, but he'd invoked the rule of men vs. women's clothing and refused. He didn't catch cold, though --- the steamy encounters in their stateroom saw to that.

Her mind pondered that for a moment, wondering if she could handle the memories of their love-making, then shelved them for another moment --- in favor of feeling his arms around her, warming her from outside instead of from within. Ten years..... Ten long years..... At times, it seemed like a hundred and, yet, sometimes like a minute. He felt so close when she thought of him, that she half-expected to turn and see him standing there with that tender look in his eyes and the slightly lop-sided smile he got when he saw her.

As the memories began to raise themselves, she became oblivious to the fog and let them filter into her awareness. Ah, here was the first night on board their ship.....

Walking up the gangplank was the beginning of their adventure. After waving to the friends who had made the journey to New York to see them off, they giggled at their aloneness and beat a hasty retreat to their stateroom. She remembered how the scent of the flower arrangements was almost overpowering, but, in their youthful excitement, they ignored it completely. She could see the exquisite peignoir set she had brought with her and relived changing into it in the bedroom, while Franz waited, with anticipation, in the sitting room. Finally, he came and knocked on the door to see if she was all right. Then, when she opened the door, just stood there staring at her. Even her beautiful wedding gown hadn't evoked this response.....

It was as though he had been struck dumb --- or maybe he felt that the beauty of the moment was too precious for words to mar it.

Finally, he took her hands and led her to the bed, then seated her and knelt to take each slipper off of her feet. There was something about him holding her feet in his hands that had made her go all soft inside and, suddenly, there was a fire in her private parts that made her wriggle and shiver. Remembering it, she shivered again --- or was it the cold breeze?

He stood, then, and began to disrobe slowly, tantalizing her by taking his time in folding each piece, though he probably was only trying to allay his own nervousness. With each moment and each piece he removed, she became more aroused. When he finally stood her up again and removed her diaphanous, marabou-trimmed peignoir, then lifted the hem of her negligee, she felt faint with the heat radiating from her body.

Lifting it over her head, he slid it off and, finally, surveyed her nude body. He reached out his hands to her breasts and held them, feeling their warmth and the twin pebbles of her hardening nipples against his palms. His own body was responding and he could see that Liz was staring at the rising sword at his groin. He lifted her in his arms and carried her to the bed, then turned down the lamps next to it. He left them partially lit --- he wanted to see her as he made love to her.

They lay there like two alabaster statues of lovers --- not moving --- savoring every moment and, in their innocence, allowing their passion to rise to a fever pitch. Franz stroked Liz' naked body gently and slowly, without knowing how erotic that was or how much turmoil was going on inside her. She had never felt like this before --- on fire and, yet, shivering at the same time. As she wriggled and twisted, she could feel a wetness, slippery and slick between her legs, and fleetingly wondered what it was, but the thought was driven from her mind by her raging hormones and emotions.

Franz took her hand and brought it to his shaft, showing her how to stroke its hardness and feel the softness of the skin. This was no easy task, for his own hormones were doing quite a dance of their own.....

Finally, he stroked her belly lower, placing his hand on her furry mound and, ever so lightly, tickling the hair there.

The Liz of 1946 gasped at the memory of that moment, her own juices flowing now, as she remembered how they flowed then, and went on to remember more --- feeling the arousal of her own body so keenly and having double pleasure in the simultaneous memory of the then --- and that feeling being carried over to the now.

Her mind flew back to the moment of her final arousal, the moment when his fingers slipped into that mound and found the slippery juices lubricating it. His long fingers slid back and forth in their new playground, exploring the terrain and finding the hidden recesses therein, as well as a little button --- rigid and pushing upward close to the top of her mound. This was the most sensitive part of her, he found, and the slightest slipping of his finger across it in the juices emanating from her body, gave her more pleasure than she'd ever known in her life, but too much pressure and her body would jerk like a puppet on a string. She was learning new things by the minute --- as was Franz.....

He'd found her most secret recess and slid into it, with his fingers, on the fluids. It was tight, tighter than he thought his staff could manage, but perhaps if he gently stretched the membranes, his engineer's mind thought..... He inserted another finger and, moving in and out, he could feel the tightness relaxing and stretching. Hopefully, there would be little or no pain when he finally entered her.....

Liz felt as though she had become a snake --- a squirming, wriggling, writhing, snake..... Her body would not stay still and, in her intense arousal, she kept forgetting to stroke Franz' member, then would reach out to hold it again.

Finally, his lips on hers, he spread her legs by rolling between them. Shaft in hand, he gently prodded at the opening between the halves of her fuzzy mound and, gently, he worked his rigid member into it. He lay there, supporting his body weight on his forearms, and waiting for her to get used to the idea of having him inside of her. It did not take long. She was too aroused to put this train in reverse and began to surge forward with her hips --- slowly and gently at first and then firmer and faster as her arousal pushed her. Franz could feel himself building to a climax and, try as he would, could not hold back any longer. His cry of impending completion stimulated Liz to find her climax as well and she bucked him like a real bronco as they finished their dance of love, only to collapse in a tangle of flesh both slippery and sweaty.

It was many minutes before either could say a word --- or move, for that matter.

Gently, slowly, Franz rolled off of her saying, "I suppose we'll have to dress for dinner or they'll think we're seasick....."

The older Liz smiled, remembering his quip and her retort: "If we don't dress for dinner, they'll think we're more than sick....."

She could still see the look on his face in her mind's eye as she one-upped him at his own game of words.....

She smiled. She could still feel his presence so strongly that she knew he must be alive somewhere --- if she could only find him.....

In response to the thought, her mind flew to the interview with the War Department. How shocked she had been to learn that when he disappeared they had classified him as a German sympathizer due to his ethnicity. He was *born* in America, but branded for having come up missing while on a business trip in Europe in early 1939 --- seven very long years ago. Her mind became agitated as she rehashed the memory of that interview and the long years of waiting and hoping. She'd gone to using her maiden name, Hart, to avoid the anti-German prejudices and had made no waves about his absence to avoid coming to the attention of the public --- a public with decidedly negative sentiments toward those of German descent.

So, she had bided her time, waiting for the ceasefire and the treaties, meanwhile researching his itinerary and making plans to visit every place he had been --- in hope of finding him --- or word of him. Her family had been from Alsace-Lorraine, that bit of land which was claimed alternately by both France and Germany, like some bone between two dogs, and she was fluent in both, French and German, as well as English --- hopefully, with those three languages under her belt, she would be able to make herself understood wherever her journey took her..... She also spoke Luxembourgish, but that would not get her very far anywhere outside of Luxembourg.

Marseilles was to be the first stop for the ship and then on to Genoa, Italy, where she would leave it. She had leads in Marseilles to follow up on, but she felt certain that her Franz had gone much further than that, for his last letter was from Germany and her inquiry to the government of the Netherlands had been answered with a curt statement saying that they had no record of his having entered the country. He had not booked his return ticket due to the uncertainties of travel during the time of impending war on the continent, preferring to wait and see what ship was available when he arrived in the Netherlands --- and knowing that he might add England to his itinerary.

She was finally on her way, now, and nearing the path she would follow. She felt an intenseness --- an alertness --- some sort of excitement beyond anything she'd encountered before. She was on a mission and an adventure.... .....alone.

Her family was incensed, to be sure, but these were, after all, the days of women riveters and shipyard workers and, ultimately, her parents had given in. Besides, the war was over and things would surely be safer. They had even helped her to plan ahead and make a few reservations for lodging and transportation. Ever the businessmen, her father and father-in-law had arranged for her to speak with any companies Franz had contacted, if they were still in business, in hopes that she might be able to re-forge the links.....

She sighed at the thought of this, but knew it was fair that she do it, since they had paid for the entire trip --- and first class accommodations all the way.

Holding her coat closely, she circumnavigated the ship via the deck. The wind was not blowing strongly, but there was surely still a chill of winter on the Atlantic. Perhaps the Mediterranean would be better, she mused, and began to fantasize meeting Franz on a sunny beach in Italy..... Oh, dear, enough of that for now, she thought, as she felt her libido rising again.....

At this point, a fellow traveler popped out of a door in a heavy coat and hat. She peered at him through the fog and made it out to be a Mr. Henri, who was en route back to France now that the armistice had occurred.

"Hello," he called to her, hurrying to come alongside, "Are you walking for long?" he inquired, politely.

"Oh, I've been out here for hours," she allowed, hoping he would go back indoors and leave her to her thoughts, but that was not to be. Soon, they were joined by another passenger, and then another --- all taking a constitutional before the evening meal.

Realizing that her reverie was at an end for the time being, she drifted indoors and off to her stateroom for a short lie down before dressing for dinner. Remembering her first night aboard a ship, again, her lips curled into a secret smile.

Liz napped for about two hours before the first bell rang for dinner, then, hurried into a gown, patted her hair into place and, slipping a wrap around her shoulders, made her way into the hall and toward the dining rooms. She met other guests on their way to dinner, as well, and murmured greetings to them while they all ambled in the direction of the evening's repast.

The Frenchman sidled up to her side, hoping to engage her in conversation, but another passenger claimed his attention at the last minute and Liz breathed a sigh of relief. She needed no would-be suitors at this point: her heart was still engaged elsewhere.

She was seated at the Captain's table --- he seemed a bit of a rogue and appeared to enjoy looking at pretty women over dinner (and any other time), whether they had conversational skills or not. For her part, Liz could carry a conversation as well as any other and gave good account of herself at any gathering.

There was a beef roast this evening --- welcome to all after the wartime rationing and meatless days. Liz had suffered little from the dietary deprivations of the war due to the farms and businesses owned by her father, but beef had usually been reserved to the government for the troops, leaving chicken, rabbit, pork, and game for the family.

Conversation at table centered on the armistice, the war, and the rebuilding, as it would for long after the war, but the ladies wondered, out loud, how soon they would see the latest Paris designs and when the men would all be home from the occupation of Germany. Basking in the glow of her reverie on the deck, Liz held up her end of the conversation in a serene and other-worldly manner.

Soon dinner was over and, as a band began playing, couples moved to the dance floor in her dining room. "May I steer you around the floor for this number, Miss Hart?" the Captain asked.

He stood a little straighter and sucked in his tummy on hearing her, "Yes, Captain, of course."

The tune was a waltz turned slow, sultry jazz; one made popular before the war. As they glided across the floor held in the one-two-three of the waltz, he asked, "Will you be sailing with us on your return trip, Miss Hart?"

"No, Captain, I plan to leave the continent via Amsterdam. I have a long journey ahead," Liz answered, then took another tack, "Have you been a captain for long?" Knowing, now, that she would not be available for him to flirt with much longer, he began to talk about his favorite subject, himself, instead of trying to win her favor. She smiled and nodded, encouraging him to continue in this vein, while congratulating herself on her escape from his list of possibilities. After a few more dances, with some of the other guests, Liz retired for the night to the peace of her stateroom. She read for awhile, then showered and crawled under the covers --- ah, how she loved that after the first night with Franz: letting her bare skin slide across the sheets. It always reminded her of their love-making.

As she lay there waiting for sleep to claim her, she thought of him: his teasing, his smile, his hands moving lightly across her skin and arousing her to a passion she never knew was possible. As she thought of him, her hands began to stroke her skin as he had, softly, gently, lightly, arousing her less than his hands had, but pleasurable nonetheless. In time, her fingers found their way to her mound and the slippery crevice therein. The smaller fingers of her own hands traced the delicious circles his had traced there on her firm little button and in her deep, hidden grotto, but her gasps and soft cries of excitement, arousal, and release were heard only by herself.

Afterward, as she lay there lightly pinching her nipples and remembering the delicious feel of his larger fingers doing it, she thought of the cities she would visit in her search for him. Some, she had seen before, on her honeymoon, and she anticipated the memories of Franz in each of them, but others would be new to her and she would have to find other ways to remember him there.

๛Chapter 2 – Gibraltar๛

The day was sunny, with few clouds and, at last, the Strait of Gibraltar was mere hours away. Liz felt a quickening, an excitement in the knowledge that she was moving ever closer to her goal.....

It appeared that the stop at 'The Rock' would be pleasantly warm due to the mild winter climate of the region and she looked forward to seeing the wild, yet somewhat tame, little monkeys called macaques, again. She remembered how ingenuously they had begged for food when the honeymooners visited in 1936.....

And, suddenly, Franz was there in her mind. It made her glow inside as she thought of him --- his gentle personality, his unfailing kindness, his dreams, and his love for her. It drove her forward on her path of discovery and steeled her to the task of finding him, no matter how long or how hard the way. Somehow, within her, she knew that he still alive; he must be alive.....

At 4 p.m., anchored in Gibraltar Bay, the ship ferried boatload after boatload of travelers to The Rock to shop, dine, and tour the enclave. Being a British Protectorate, the English-speaking tourists found no trouble in communicating with the residents and, thus, flocked to the restaurants for the seafood dishes the community was famous for. The next day, at about the same time, the ship would weigh anchor for the Mediterranean and proceed onward to Marseilles.

Liz spoke to a few fellow passengers, but she really didn't want to tour the island with them and, hearing her ambiguity, they left her be. This was their special place, hers and Franz', and she didn't want to overlay those memories with other, newer memories, and run the risk of diluting the ones she already had.

The boat trip was uneventful and in short order she was standing on terra firma, as her father always said. She wandered along the cay, watching the fishermen unloading their catch, and enjoying the warmth. She thought of touring the botanical garden again, but decided to walk through the town instead, watching the bustle of tourists and wondering how the shopkeepers had felt about being evacuated, during the war, to other parts of the British Commonwealth. She thought about their shops and wondered how they had managed to survive, without income, in a new environment --- and who had taken care of their property while they were gone. Indeed, things looked a bit seedier than they had 10 years earlier....

As she rounded a corner, she saw a small café --- one they had visited that spring --- and memories came flooding back with all of the emotions of that time. The suddenness of it hit her before she could adjust and, without warning, the tears came tumbling down her cheeks and wetting her immaculate rayon blouse. She let them run for a few moments before reaching for a handkerchief and wiping them away. The release felt good --- too many tears pent up in her, not falling, because she'd had no confirmation of what had happened to him.....

She walked, and as she walked, she thought --- deep, soul-wrenching thoughts. What if she didn't find him? What if she found him, but he was unable to recognize or remember her? These, and other worries, plagued her, but in the midst of letting them assert themselves, something within her rose up like a cobra waiting to strike and dared the worries to challenge her. She *was* the master of her fate and the captain of her soul. The war had made her strong, as it had so many women. Her countrymen had paid a huge price, but they had emerged victorious. They were a force to be reckoned with --- her and her country. She knew that she would continue forward and that nothing would stop her as long as she had breath in her lungs. Somehow that power had come from the depths of her being and asserted itself. There had been a shift so major that she almost didn't know herself.

A different Liz met the boat when it was time to go back to the ship that evening.

೨Chapter 3 – The Ship --- Again೪

Liz woke to hear and feel the ship getting under way. Must have slept through breakfast and lunch, she mused..... No wonder, after poring over maps all night and into the dawn.....

Being on a ship was a different world --- she could begin to understand the beliefs, of ancient cultures, wherein the dead were ferried to the nether regions in some sort of otherworldly state of being. It seemed so befitting, that journeying on a current, rather than making one's own way.....

She lay there, in that early state of awakening, musing on this and other matters philosophical as the ship's vibration and muffled noises brought her more and more into awareness.

Finally, hunger got the better of her and, throwing the covers off, she began the task of dressing in order to go in search of breakfast. In less than 20 minutes, she sallied forth from her stateroom.

Late luncheon was still being served, she found, due to the numerous passengers who had either stayed on shore all night or imbibed too freely of the ship's libations after walking about in the sun the day before. A few looked the worse for wear, she thought, as she walked to her table. No one was using the table, so she thought she would be lunching alone, but a girl in her late teens came and asked if she might sit with her. Table-hopping was not customary, but since she was alone, Liz consented and they began a lively conversation.

The girl, Rose Maitland, was traveling with her parents and, finding herself the only one of her age group on board, she had selected Liz, who seemed more youthful than a woman in her late-twenties, to talk to. They chatted pleasantly over luncheon and Liz, drawn out, began to speak about her husband and the few years they had been together before his trip.

"But, I don't understand why he left you at home when he went on his trip?" Rose questioned.

"Oh, I didn't want to stay at home!" came the quick reply, "He simply wouldn't hear of me going with him when a war seemed to be in the offing. My parents and his sided with him and, other than stowing away in his baggage I couldn't see any way to get around them. Unfortunately, he only took one small trunk and his briefcase and I couldn't fit into either of them, more's the pity."

"Didn't you feel awful when he left?' Rose asked, in her innocence of propriety.

Un-offended by the youthful faux pas, Liz said, "Of course, dear, I was devastated. I felt as though my heart, my reason for living, had gone. I stayed in the bedroom for days, but then I came out and began to read and paint. He sent me cards and letters as he traveled, and I felt less afraid for him bit by bit, …..as I received them, but still, the newsreels were bad and everyone seemed to have such a sense of gloom and foreboding. ….And, of course, they were right, weren't they?"

Touched, Rose patted her hand saying, "Oh, but I'm certain you'll find him," and, then, with that certainty of youth, "You must!"

Liz smiled at this ingenuously absolute certainty, seeing herself in her mind's eye as a teen, but only said, "Yes, I will, Rose, I will," knowing that Rose, having not been tried by the misfortunes of the world, would not understand her trepidation. "And, what of you?" she countered, successfully leading the conversation in another direction.

Her question led into a vivacious litany of the joys of being old enough to go to dances and talk to boys, picking out one's own clothes, and what Rose would like to do when she was older.

Before luncheon was over the ship was fully underway and, within a short time, Gibraltar faded from sight as they headed for their next port of call.

Liz walked the deck with Rose for awhile, enjoying the sun and fresh air, while listening to her chatter and remembering her own youth. It seemed so far away, so long since she was that girl with no cares or worries. It took a girl like Rose to help her touch in with that person again, that person who had nearly ceased to exist when she got the news that Franz was missing. She remembered that day as she nodded and smiled at Rose, not fully hearing what had been said, but politely continuing the mostly one-sided conversation.

There had been a telegram from Luxembourg asking if he was delayed and still planning to visit, because he had not arrived on the appointed day. A few days later, another came from Brussels asking the same..... When they contacted the U.S. Embassy, they were told the government believed he had defected while in Germany.

Bad enough to be missing, but to be thought a traitor as well! It was too much, much more than she had told Rose. For many months, she wouldn't leave their beautiful little house, preferring to be alone in her misery, pretending that he would be home any day. Then, finally, when the war began, and certain that Franz had been killed or taken prisoner, she decided to do work in support of the war effort as a volunteer. Their families had money, as well as she and Franz, so she didn't need to earn any, but in working to raise funds for the Red Cross and the USO, she was able to find the antidote for the numbness she felt. It wasn't a 100% cure, but it went a long way.

Rose broke into her reverie with, "Do you know how to drive a car? My father won't let me learn. He says that it is for men to do, but my friend Sally's sister, who is married, drives one. Father says that only loose women drive and that decent ones hire a taxi."

"Ah, yes," Liz said, under her breath, "Parents!" Then, more loudly, "But, why would you want to drive when you are so pretty that you'll have every young man wanting to drive for you?"

Rose smiled with a glow, saying, "I hadn't thought of that. Am I really pretty? Mother says that if I smile too much I'll get wrinkles and what little looks I have will go out the door."

Poor child, thought Liz, as her mind saw her own gentle mother's face.

Eventually, it was time to go indoors and play cards, visit, or take a nap before dinner. Liz opted for the nap, but lingered for awhile at the railing, gazing at the huge open expanse of water on all sides of the ship and remembering the honeymoon they had experienced, --- imagined Franz at her side at the railing, with his arm around her, blocking the breeze and warming her in more ways than one.....

Finally, she returned to her stateroom, but not to sleep. As she lay there naked on the bed, she could feel his hands on her, stroking her everywhere, arousing her to a fever pitch, then letting her settle down, and beginning all over again. Their lovemaking went on for hours and her memory of it did, as well. Her own little hands touched all the places that Franz had touched, and just as intimately, finding them equally as responsive .....and wet. Her own sighs and moans evoked the deepest of her memories and, when she was finally still, her juices flowed between her thighs and onto the sheet beneath her. Yet, even in this completion, this fulfillment, she ached for more, for his staff to be within her, sliding deeply back and forth, as her hands couldn't do.

Her thoughts were interrupted by the dressing bell signaling that dinner was in the offing and, after a few more moments devoted to her memories, and her body, she slid from the bed and, grabbing a robe, headed for the bathroom.

Half an hour later, showered and dressed in an evening number of slinky cream satin, she left for dinner. In the dining room, the tables were filling and there was a buzz of conversation. Heading toward the Captain's table, she slipped into her seat and took stock of her dinner companions. The Captain had not yet arrived, but some of the others were already seated and having a glass of wine. As always, men engaged her in conversation and, within moments, the table had become quite lively with the bantering of conversation.

There was only one married couple at the table tonight, the Captain having a predilection for the fair sex, but there was the requisite number of guests for the table to be "even". The Captain came in after the meal had begun, excusing his lateness with the information that he had been working over the wireless with the Port Authorities in Barcelona to secure their preferred berth.

She didn't dance with him that night. In fact, she didn't dance at all, preferring to sit and visit, or rather to listen in on other conversations, in a detached manner, only halfway taking in the information.

She smiled as Rose waved to her from the dance floor, looking delightful in a satin gown of a pastel shade of her namesake. She remembered the delight of having Franz' arms wrapped around her as they danced and it made her feel whole, both then and now, and she smiled, thinking of her bliss and of the joy Rose was experiencing.

It was late when she finally opened the door to her stateroom and made to ready herself for the night's sleep --- and it was hard to keep the memories away, to push at them and hold them back --- and did she really want to? Wasn't it better, this reliving, than holding the loneliness within? She wasn't certain.

While she lay there, she thought of their time in Barcelona.....

As they ate in a restaurant near the shore, the honeymooners were enchanted with the view of sandy beaches and breaking waves. Truth be told, they were also enchanted with each other. Their hands kept touching and the connection between them was as though electricity was flowing through their veins.

She remembered how Franz could hardly wait to get her back to their hotel and make love to her, tripping on the last stair as they raced upward and slightly skinning his knee. No matter, she thought, it didn't hold him back.

As they locked the door behind them, he was already pulling at his clothing and then at hers, greedy for the pleasures of their union. She didn't stint him, for her arousal was a match for his, and she began helping him in his task. .....in no time at all, they were as naked as the day they were born and had tumbled like two children into the bed.

Unlike children, however, they had other things on their minds --- no innocent wrestling match would suffice. Franz lifted his bride up to sit on his belly and began caressing her body, with special attention paid to the breasts so handily placed in front of him. She could feel his manhood tapping against her buttocks and low back as his movements at her front made that shaft bob about, tapping whatever it came in contact with. Each time it touched her, she felt a jolt of arousal and hoped that he felt it as well. Meanwhile his hands were busy, kneading her breasts and pinching the tiny nipples which hardened and stood up proudly.

She reached behind her and managed to catch hold of his manhood, as it bobbed near enough, which caused a jolt for him, as well as a groan of pleasure. Turn about is fair play, went through her mind, but was quickly forgotten as she savored the effect it had on his hands. She let out her own sounds of pleasure as his fingers found her little button and began to push it and slide in the slippery wetness coming forward from her secret recess. Tightening her buttocks, she lifted her hips and leaned back a bit, so that he could move his hands more easily between her nether lips and pleasure her.

Then, suddenly, he stopped, and said, "Let's let it build again after a minute." She complied and their breathing became more normal again, but shortly, very shortly, they were at each other again, like a pair of snakes writhing around each other.

Again, they built up to a passion --- this time she lay next to him and they kissed long and deeply, legs entwined and pelvises grinding toward each other. Franz' long, slender fingers finding her wetness and gliding into her hidden parts on it, opening her, preparing the way for his own shaft of delight......

Finally, when it seemed that they could bear no more pleasure, he laid her on her back and, spreading her legs apart widely, inserted himself into that tunnel of ecstasy so hidden from all view but his. As he entered her, she moaned, a hot, hot sound of passion with a rasping note to it, and shoved her hips forward toward him to meet his thrust. With each thrust of his hips, she met him halfway, faster and faster, breathing in gasps and groans, until, finally, she moaned, "Oh, now, Franzl, now. Yes, yes, yessssss. Yes!"

Franz, felt her hands clutching his back, his arms, anything she could reach, in the release of her passion and increased the tempo as they spent their passion, extending her orgasm as his own overtook him. As the waves passed over and the seas of their lovemaking became calmer, he held himself within her, wanting to stay there for eternity. Finally, slowly withdrawing, he collapsed beside her and reached to hold her breast, but fell short of the mark and had no more energy, for the moment, to even lift his hand.

Liz lay on the ship's bed, much as she had in that hotel in Barcelona. Naked, she held her breasts, tracing the nipples as he had. The remembering had given her the same wetness as the original event. She slipped her fingers into her wet, furry mound, sliding them back and forth, and feeling the same sensations as when he had done it so long ago. The pleasure became almost unbearable --- her head throbbed, her hips pumped back and forth, writhing from side to side as though she were trying to free herself from bondage, but the only bondage here was her arousal. Higher and higher her hips rose, meeting her fingers as they bored into her and slipped back to slide lightly across that tender button. At last, her stifled groans, and other sounds, came gasping through her lips as she finished in a massive spasm of pleasure.

Without even thinking, she rolled over, pulling the covers over her, and fell into a deep, deep sleep.

ঔ Chapter 4 – Barcelona ঔ

The sun of the Mediterranean latitudes warmed her as she
stood at the railing watching the port of Barcelona grow ever
closer.   Apparently, the Captain's communications with the
Port Authority had proven successful, for he looked pleased
when she saw him ---probably happy with the berth they
would pull into.

They would stay here a day and a half and she felt very light-
hearted --- she would see a few of the places she and Franz had
visited on their honeymoon just before the Spanish Civil War
began.   At least he didn't stop here on his trip in 1939 --- the
hostilities didn't end until a few months later --- so she
wouldn't have to scour the city for information.

It took awhile before the ship made port and docked, so
eventually she tired of the sun and retired to her cabin to wait.
She spent the time reading the guidebook from their
honeymoon trip, though it was 10 years outdated, reasoning
that it would have the places they had visited included in it, at
least.   She eventually went to the dining room for a light
luncheon and, then, waited on deck with the others for
permission to disembark. Some carried small cases with them,
if they planned to spend the night in town, soaking up local
color --- and liquor --- but she intended to return to the ship.

Soon enough, they were descending the gangway for the shore and heading to the waiting line of ageing taxicabs. Some were pretty dilapidated and she avoided them, but found one which looked to be in fair condition and asked to be taken to the Church of the Sagrada Familia. As she rode through the streets, she was surprised that they seemed familiar to her after so many years.

When they arrived, she paid the taxi driver and then asked him to pick her up there at 7 o'clock. It was then that she turned and looked at the church, which had been over 50 years in the making and was still unfinished. There were no differences that she could see. As she turned toward it, it was as though the 10 years had fallen away and she felt that, if she waited, she would feel Franz' hand at her waist, urging her forward toward their sightseeing tour. Shaking her head to clear the scene, she knew that he wasn't there --- but, the feeling had been so strong.....

She observed the church from every angle, sitting on benches that she had sat on with Franz, stopping to admire the architecture at just the points they had, and almost hearing his engineer's voice describing the technology involved in its design and construction.

She passed much of the afternoon in this pursuit, then sought a restaurant for dinner. She was in luck --- quite near to the church, she found a small restaurant they may have patronized and feasted on fresh fish fried in olive oil and served with a lemon larger than her fist which had been cut in quarters, tomato wedges, fresh bread rolls, and a glass of brandy. The cost was the equivalent of a few pennies.

Afterward, she walked through the streets looking into the stores and admiring the buildings until she returned to the place where the taxi had dropped her off. She was surprised to see him waiting there and greeted him with a smile. As they returned to the ship, he spoke to her in broken English, telling her of the hardships of the wars --- the one in his country, as well as the world war. He was old enough to remember the First World War and talked of it as well --- pragmatically, as though nothing else ever happened.

She asked him if people sometimes disappeared in wars. Looking keenly at her, he answered, "Much times in the wars, Senorita. Much people no find after the war civil," pointing downward to indicate right there in Barcelona, as well as, where their bodies were to be found.

Liz nodded with a pursing of her mouth to indicate that this was sad. His eyes said that he understood and he nodded his head.

Soon they drew up at the quay and he handed her out of the car. She took a few coins from her purse, then took a few more and gave them to him. He looked at the amount with surprise in his eyes, then looked up and saw her nodding. He understood that her generosity wasn't charity, but a thank you for sharing his observations with her. Touching his forehead in a half-salute, he nodded and turned to leave, but Liz stopped him, saying, "Would you pray for my husband at the church?" She held out a handful of coins to him and saw his hands come up and shake back and forth in the universal sign of 'no'. She said, "Oh, no. This is for the church. Please take it there for me when you pray."

J. Matheny

Suddenly understanding, he nodded and beamed at her, then, promised to pray for her husband and to bring the money to the priests for the building fund. He watched as she walked up the gangway, thinking how young she was to be a widow.

On board again, she retired to her room with her thoughts and her memories. This night she didn't feel so amorous. There was a more bittersweet feeling to her mood...... She couldn't quite put her finger on it, but she felt a certain amount of sadness. Perhaps it was the unfinished church, or the recent civil war, or even perhaps that she was moving closer to the possibility of knowing what had actually happened to Franz......

ᔆChapter 5 – The Trip to Marseillesᕉ

Though passengers were still able to go ashore, Liz didn't feel up to it and spent the day reading. She was minimally conversational at meals, just listening to the conversations swirl around her. In any case, the dining room was only half full for many had taken the option of spending the night in town, seeing more of the sights, and buying more of the inexpensive Spanish wares.

By evening, the ship was underway and she made it an early night, retiring almost immediately after the dessert dishes had been cleared. The Captain, looking concerned, asked if she was feeling well and she answered that she was fine, just a little tired from walking so much the preceding day, before leaving the table.

Back in her stateroom, she sat at the writing table and began a letter to Franz. She would never send it, because she didn't know where to send it, but she simply had to write it, to release the pain of his not being there, to tell him how she felt, to communicate somehow.....

Dearest Franzl, she began, *I visited the church in Barcelona yesterday. It looked almost the same as when we were there together. I suppose that's no surprise since they've had this civil war and certainly little progress in the construction --- though it could have been destroyed.....*

I stopped at Gibraltar as well. What a surprise to find that they had all been evacuated during the war and had just returned. Things looked a bit run down --- I suppose that the troops garrisoned there didn't bother to keep the civilian buildings up.....

Next we will sail to Marseilles and I will see if I am able to find anyone who spoke to you when you were there. Surely, there will be someone who has seen you and can let me know if you went onward.....

My dearest love, I miss you so terribly that I cannot find words to describe it. If you are no longer alive, and I don't want to believe this, please find a way to give me a sign. If you are living, please help me to find you. Whatever it takes, please help me.

I love you now as I did from the first. Never forget that. I love you no matter what has happened --- even if you have been wounded and are deformed or nearly dead. You are my heart, my soul, my reason for being,

Try hard to stay alive, my dearest, because I am coming.

With Loving Devotion,

Liz

Once she had gotten the words out, she could cry and cry she did --- long and very wetly until, finally, she slept.

By morning she had regained a good portion of her zest for life and her outlook wasn't so glum. Knowing herself, she knew that her happy nature would override the blues rather quickly.

She slipped out of bed, showered and dressed, then, headed for the dining room. This would be a busy day, she felt --- better have a good, hearty breakfast.

As she rounded a corner, she almost bumped into Mr. Henri, who was going in the other direction. He began with, "Excuse me, madam; I did not expect to see you. Are you going ashore or dining?"

"Oh, I'm just ready for breakfast," Liz replied. "Are you going to look at the sights?"

"Hmm, yes, I plan to go ashore, but I would like very much to show the beauty of Marseilles to you, if that pleases you," he managed.

Quickly realizing that a guide who knew the lay of the land would be handy indeed, she asked, "Oh, you know Marseilles?"

"Ah, oui, I know her, having lived in the city for some years before the war," he replied.

"Then, would you be able to help me see if the contacts my husband made before the war are still conducting business --- or even alive? I do so want to trace his path to see if I can discover what happened to him," she said, with pleading tones in her voice.

Mr. Henri, a Frenchman to the core, could not help but be touched by her plight and agreed immediately to help her in her search, while showing her the city as a bonus. "I shall meet you in the lounge in 45 minutes, madam," he said, "Better take a wrap against the wind."

Her heart feeling as light as a feather, Liz nearly flew to the dining room. She ate, but could not have told anyone what she had eaten, for she was thinking about the places she needed to visit: two manufacturers --- and a private entrepreneur, wanting to know more about airplane engines.

In 45 minutes she was on her way into the lounge, dressed elegantly, but businesslike, in a tailored navy blue jacket and skirt with creamy white blouse. On her arm was a ¾-length lightweight wool coat in the same shade of navy blue and a matching hat was in her hand --- insurance against the evening air, should they tarry.

Mr. Henri stood up when he saw her enter, amazed at the transformation from lovely lady to beautiful business woman. He had no doubt at that moment that, if her husband still lived, she would find him and that, if he was dead, she would know how and by whom.

"Are you ready?" she asked, pleasantly.

"Oui, oui, madam. Vous êtes enchante," he answered.

"Et vous êtes un flatteur, monsieur Henri," she retorted.

He was surprised that she spoke French, but didn't let it show as he took her arm and walked her down the gangway.

"Let us go to a cafe for coffee and we will plan our day," he said.

Liz nodded and showed him the list of companies and individuals that she hoped to contact --- with the few he surely would have known being at the top of the list.

"Hmmmm," he began, "We shall go to the City Offices after our coffee. They will know which businesses are still operating, for they must report to the tax collector. Then, I believe we can attempt to contact the individuals through the telephone company, since you have some telephone numbers and addresses….."

Liz was amazed at how quickly he saw the problem and organized it into manageable parts, just like her Franz. Of course, he knew the city and, also, he didn't have his emotions tied up in the search, she reasoned.

It was a short taxi ride to a small, but clean, cafe --- virtually undisturbed by the bombings of the war or the German occupation from 1942-44. They sat at an outside table with a faded umbrella that allowed intermittent sunlight to warm them. Mr. Henri pulled a map of the city he'd procured, on their ship, out of his pocket and unfolded it, pointing out the City Offices and the telephone company to her. It didn't take them long to decide to go to these first and leave the individuals until later or the next day; prioritizing the names. After half an hour of coffee and a shared pastry, they were ready to descend on the city officials. Mr. Henri asked where the nearest cab stand was and the owner pointed up the street.

Their task was still greater than they had anticipated in spite of Mr. Henri's organizational skills. The city offices were crowded and had little seating. Liz' knowledge of the French of the far north of France did not always help her with French as it is spoken in Marseilles and she was glad of the help of Mr. Henri. In the hours they spent there, they were able to discover that some of the companies she was looking for had been nationalized or turned into military departments, which would make her quest very difficult to research. Others had disbanded or been bombed. It looked as though she would be most likely to find help through individuals, after all.

In spite of the disappointment she felt, there was a sense of accomplishment and forward movement and she relished that and held it to her heart, knowing that it was the first step that every journey begins with. Liz felt undefeated --- and she had met a friend --- Mr. Henri.

Although the day was waning they went to the offices of the telephone company to seek information on the list of names she had. Most were no longer at the same addresses and only one of the others had telephone service. Since there was only the one, they decided to search him out at the old address and continue on the morrow if they found he no longer lived there.

Another taxi was readily obtained at the City Offices and they were carried to the address of Mr. Alphonse d'Croixville. As it happened, this area of Marseille had suffered damages in the war, and, apparently, only a smattering of telephone lines had been restrung or reconnected, for few of the buildings were being lived in by anyone with money. The driver managed to find his way to the address they gave and, seeing the quality of their clothing, was willing to wait for awhile as they searched out Mr. d'Croixville, hoping that he would receive a good tip.

Though the man's home was on the 3rd floor of a building that was partly in ruins, the stairs seemed solid and they were able to reach the apartment. The woman who opened the door was disheveled and looked at them suspiciously. Too well-dressed for this neighborhood by far, she judged.

Liz asked for Mr. d'Croixville and the woman laughed, saying, "He no longer lives here. He escaped when the Germans were rounding up the Jews in this district. He knew that his fancy education and business connections wouldn't save him from them. Lucky for him that he escaped --- they took the rest to Poland to be killed. All that is left of him here is his desk."

"Could I see it?" Liz ventured.

"Of course! But if you offer too little, I won't take the offer," said the slovenly woman, as she showed them into the apartment, misreading their interest.

Liz opened the drawers one by one, hoping with each one that she would find some evidence of Franz having met with this man. Finally, in the last drawer, she was rewarded. There was a small, plain notebook and on a page near the back she found his name with a date and time, the very date he would have been in Marseille. There was a little bit of cryptic writing after his name, but it made no sense to her. Perhaps, she thought, it was engineering matters..... The checkmark through the date made her think that Franz had been there and it lifted her spirits immeasurably. Mr. Henri concurred with her thoughts, but wondered aloud where Mr. d'Croixville had disappeared to.

They returned to the ship, later that evening, in time for dinner and, with her lighter feeling, Liz threw herself into the conversation at her table. The Captain noted that her mood had lifted and attributed it to the afternoon she spent with Mr. Henri.

Later, as she slipped into bed, Liz thought about the day and how helpful Mr. Henri had been. He reminded her of Franz with his neat and tidy thoughts and his ability to size up a situation. Ah, then came the thoughts of Franz, and she fell asleep thinking of the notebook and wondering what the cryptic marks could mean.....

❧Chapter 6 – Marseille, the Next Day❧

Liz spent a lazy morning in her room, looking through the notebook and musing about the elusive Mr. d'Croixville. She had remembered to ask for a breakfast tray in her room, so there was no need to go to the dining room before lunch. As she nibbled, she wondered when Mr. d'Croixville left Marseille. Could he have left with Franz? She flipped through the notebook, which seemed to be a record of his appointments, each with cryptic notations, looking for dates and found that there were none after his notation of Franz' appointment. Of course, she suddenly realized, this could be because he began a new notebook.....

Somehow, though, the thought that he could have gone with Franz or followed him, seemed to linger in her mind.....

Eventually, she felt a longing to be with people, then, dressed, and went to the dining room. The meal had already begun, but with some passengers not yet back from shore, it was a rather laissez-faire event. She looked for Mr. Henri's face, but he was not to be seen. Fleetingly, Liz wondered if he'd gone ashore again, but the Captain's voice commanded her attention.

"I said, how are you doing today, Miss Hart?"

"Oh, I am quite well, sir," she replied.

"You took your breakfast in your room," he noted.

"Oh, I walked so much yesterday..... You know how it is --- exercise always gets to your muscles the next day."

"Yes, yes, I know --- happens to me every time I go rowing."

"You didn't tell me you enjoyed sport," Liz bantered, hoping to get him back on his favorite subject.

He took the bait firmly and began telling her about his school days.

Eventually, two of the usual occupants of the table, a young beauty and an older man of great means, interested in becoming her 'good friend', arrived simultaneously from opposite directions. The spell was thus broken and the Captain, ever ready to appreciate beauty --- and to cozy up to the wealthy --- began anew.....

It was then that she saw Mr. Henri enter the room. Their eyes met, but, rather than coming to her table, he made his way to the one he usually sat at. She felt herself wishing that he had come to talk to her at least --- with so many chairs available.

After lunch, she went to the lounge for a game of cards and he came in as well, trailing her by a few minutes. It was then that he finally came up to her with, "And how is the lovely Miss Hart?"

She looked up at him and asked if he would like to join the game, but he told her he had no patience for card games and asked if she would like to accompany him in a stroll about the deck in an hour. Seeing no reason not to, she agreed and he left for his cabin.

The card game was diverting --- a few heated hands of pinochle. She was on the losing team and, when she got up to leave, nobody seemed to mind having a different player enter the game.

She picked up a wrap in her room, then went to the deck to meet Mr. Henri. There were few people there, but she could see more on the pier returning from their forays into Marseille. As she looked landward toward them, Mr. Henri startled her by whispering in her ear, "Let us go to the other side of the ship --- we are too visible here."

Why on earth would that worry him, she wondered, but complied, and when they got there, she asked him what the remark meant.

"Miss Hart, just because the war is over does not mean that all is well or calm," he answered. "I went back to the house of Mr. d'Croixville on a hunch and people have been asking about you. You have been watched. Why, I wonder?"

Liz opened up and told him the truth --- all of it. She didn't know exactly why she trusted him, but she did. It surprised her, because she had planned to be rather incognito during this trip, but nonetheless, her secret was out --- at least with him.....

When he had heard it, he looked at her very seriously and said, "You must tell no one of this. You do not know who might wish you ill or even abduct you --- if not for this information,

43

for a ransom. Wealthy young women do not travel alone. If we travel in the same direction, may I provide escort?"

Stunned, Liz didn't know what to say, but managed to stammer, "I think that would be all right."

"So, what are your plans? Where do you go?" he asked.

She thought for a moment and said, "To Genoa and Milan, then on to Switzerland, to Stuttgart, Heidelberg, and Frankfurt in Germany, to Luxembourg, Belgium, and lastly Amsterdam. I don't know if it will be necessary to go to all of the cities if I find news of my husband, but I had planned to take a ship at Amsterdam either home to America or to London for a visit before going home. How the trip plays out is fully dependent on whether I find news of him and what that news is."

Mr. Henri nodded his understanding and, putting the back of the fingers of his left hand in front of his mouth, he stood there for a few moments in thought. "You will seem to be alone --- and I a fellow traveler," he concluded.

"And, do we begin this charade now?" Liz asked.

"Ah, yes, I believe that it would be best. Do not fear, ma petite, for I will be watching to see that no harm comes to you," he said, with great feeling in his voice.

"Perhaps we should not be seen too much on the ship," she ventured.

"Certainement! Vous comprenez!" came his reply.

And, thus, the two parted company --- ostensibly.....

Liz went back to her stateroom and waited for the dinner bell, knowing that she must play a part and act normally --- a young American woman visiting Europe on a grand tour.

As she waited, she looked through the notebook again to see if she had missed something or if any of the cryptic markings would seem clearer to her. It was then that she noticed a faint, but definitely legible fingerprint where someone (the owner?) had apparently had a leaky pen and, getting ink on his thumb, had transferred it to the paper when he turned the page.

It was at this moment that the bell rang and startled her into dropping the book and, when she leaned forward in her chair to pick it up, she was amazed to see that something had fallen partially out. She picked the notebook up carefully, thinking that a fragile page had come loose, but found, instead, that this paper had slipped out of the cover, which had apparently been slit to make a secret compartment. The paper had been folded in half and she opened it to see what was so important that it required hiding.

To her surprise, it was filled with cryptic symbols like the ones she had seen her husband write --- scientific symbols --- and nothing more. Deftly, she refolded it and slid it into its repository within the notebook cover and rose to dress for dinner, then, remembering to hide the notebook, she slipped it into the midst of a group of travel books provided by the shipping line in a small bookcase at the back of the desktop.

The dining room was full, due to the voyagers having returned from Marseilles, and all were chatting animatedly about their experiences and the bargains they had found. Liz slipped into her place at the Captain's table and began a conversation with the gentleman on her right --- he had sojourned overnight in Marseilles to partake of the night life and had many interesting stories to tell. Her light, tinkling laughter was a delight to his ears and he waxed very eloquent, in spite of the occasional frown from the Captain in his direction.

Many lingered over coffee, and the tempting dessert selections, to listen to the adventures of those who had spent more time on shore, exploring the city and the numerous delights of its shops and restaurants, before they retired to the lounge with its smaller tables and dance floor --- or to their cabins.

Liz stayed late, enjoying the conversation and dancing as the ship began making its way toward Genoa, where she would disembark.

It was quite late when she finally opened the door of her stateroom and, without even turning on a light; she slipped out of her clothes and between the silky sheets of her bed. Too tired for fantasy, she fell into a profound sleep.

༄Chapter 7 – Genoa ༄

Liz only awoke when she felt the shudder of the ship as it slowed to accept the tugs which would push it into Genoa's harbor. At first, she felt disoriented, wondering where she was and what the vibration was, then remembered that she was aboard ship and that this was her last day there --- next, Genoa, then Milan.....

She sat up, then made to get out of bed and looked around her at her now well-lighted room. The drawers had been emptied out and everything was on the dresser or the floor in front of it. The clothing she had hung in the closet was tossed across an armchair and her luggage was opened, with everything out of it, as well.

If she had been wider awake, the shock would have alarmed her more, but, being in the process of waking, she was still trying to make sense of what she was seeing. Finally, she understood and went to look for her jewelry. Amazingly, it was all there. What kind of thief leaves jewelry, she wondered, then realized that perhaps it was not *that* kind of thief and went immediately to the tiny bookcase of travel booklets. There, between the books was the notebook, still intact, and as she felt inside the cover, she ascertained that it still held its secret cargo.....

Now, she wondered, should she make a fuss or simply begin packing the clothes. Since reporting the vandalism would take hours, time she didn't want to waste, she decided to remain silent and slip away into Italy as planned.

The packing went more rapidly than she had anticipated and she was ready to leave the ship before lunch had even been served. She had not made reservations in a hotel, nor had she purchased a ticket for the train to Milan, yet, but she would ask the cruise director to do that for her. Perhaps, she mused, it might be better for the hotel concierge to direct her in purchasing the train ticket.....

As she sat down to lunch, she was pleased to see that the fish she had seen the kitchen boys carrying back to the ship from the quayside fish market in Marseilles was being served up. Some of the passengers had asked for poached, others for fried. She opted for the fried, since it was usually firmer.

The dining room was crowded again, since they were only just docking and no one had disembarked. She glanced at the table where Mr. Henri usually sat and saw him chatting with an elderly woman next to him, then remembered: better not stare.

Luncheon passed uneventfully, the ship docked, and, since the telephone lines would not be connected here, the cruise director referred her to half a dozen hotels and suggested she take a taxi to them in the exact order she had indicated, until she found accommodations at one. She was able to help her with information on the rail schedules to Milan and other European cities and Liz, with a handful of brochures, returned to her stateroom, ready to forge ahead. As she made to enter the room, Mr. Henri passed her in the corridor and handed her a note with a finger to his lips, tipping his hat politely as he continued on his way.

Once inside, she unfolded the slip of paper and read:

Meet me in the lobby of the Genoa Bristol Palace Hotel at 3 o'clock. Yesterday, I made you a reservation there. H.

About 20 minutes later, the steward she had asked to help her with her luggage knocked on her door. In a few moments, he was wheeling her belongings through the corridors toward the deck and the gangway with Liz following in his wake. He brought the cart down the gangway and onto the dock where a long row of taxis waited for fares, behind a makeshift barrier funneling the departing passengers into the queue for their passport stamp. In no time at all, the luggage was stowed in the trunk of a likely one and Liz tipped the steward as he handed her into the back seat. As they left the dock, Liz said to the driver, "Hotel Bristol Palace," and he nodded his acknowledgement.

It was only 2 o'clock when she arrived at the hotel. The doorman quickly summoned a bellboy who deftly trundled her luggage into the hotel and up to the desk for her, then waited patiently as she checked in. "Your room is number 315, madam," the clerk informed her in English only slightly accented, as he handed her bellboy the key, "We hope you enjoy your visit to our hotel."

Soon, she was following the bellboy into the elevator to her room on the 3rd floor. He graciously opened the door, allowing her to enter before he brought in the luggage, which he removed from the cart and placed on the folding luggage racks provided before handing her the key. Liz tipped him generously for his efforts, having read of the poverty which followed in the wake of a war. He smiled and handed back half what she had given him, saying, "Too much." She made a mental note to give it to him when she checked out.....

At 3 o'clock sharp, she entered the lobby and, seeing Mr. Henri reading a magazine, sauntered in his general direction nonchalantly, as though looking for an interesting periodical on one of the lobby tables. Finally, she selected one and prepared to sit in his vicinity, but she dropped it and he graciously bent to retrieve it, while managing to pass her another note.

She sat in another chair a little more distant and facing away from the desk, then opened it and read: Walk to the desk and ask where you may find a good restaurant in the area, then leave the hotel, go to the right, walk two blocks and enter the restaurant on the corner. I will follow in 5 minutes, walk in the opposite direction, circle the block and meet you in the restaurant.

After pretending to read the magazine for a few more minutes, Liz yawned, then got up and went to desk. "Where may I find some good restaurants?" she asked the clerk.

"Oh, madam, there is one to the left and another to the right. Both are good, but the one to the right belongs to my aunt and she is an excellent cook. It is called Aida after her favorite opera."

She appreciated his honesty and went to the right as she would have done, in any case, had not Mr. Henri told her to. A few blocks down, she found the restaurant and, after reading the menu card on the stand outside, she entered. She asked for a corner booth, far from the windows, saying the sun hurt her eyes and, once ensconced, Mr. Henri entered and found her.

They sat and talked for almost 2 hours as they partook of an appetizer --- by Italian standards. For them it was a full meal – luckily luncheon on the ship had been fish, a light meal compared to red meats. Being the mid-afternoon, when many restaurants closed, they had the restaurant almost to themselves and, in the booth, they were nearly invisible.

Liz asked many questions about Franz and didn't mention what she had found in the notebook. He answered everything she asked with a forthright honesty that she admired. She found herself liking him very much. He seemed to know that someone was trying to see if she had any information, but either he didn't know what information or he wasn't comfortable with divulging it. Then, she asked him, "Why would someone search my stateroom on the ship last night and leave all of my clothing out --- so that I would be sure to know they had done it?"

If her intent had been to shock him, she had certainly succeeded. He seemed to stop breathing as he stared at her for a moment, then asked, "Was anything missing?"

"Oh, no, nothing at all, but it was rather disconcerting."

"I can imagine," he murmured.

"But, what of you? You haven't told me very much about yourself. Why have you returned to Europe?"

"I left somewhat after the beginning of the war. The danger here seemed too great to me and I sought a safer place to reside. Now, however, things are returning to a more sane state of affairs. I feel that there will soon be a surge in commerce, industry, even research, and I wish to be a part of it."

"Are you sure that you want to help me to find my husband? It may take some time?" she asked, hoping that he would say yes. When he did, her face glowed with delight and he thought, looking at her, that this was a woman one could easily fall in love with.

He told her that he would research the names and companies she had given him and meet her the next day at noon in front of the Doge's Palace. Should she not arrive, he would go to her hotel at 2 p.m. and wait in the lobby, a wise precaution, she agreed, citing the search of her cabin.

Liz agreed to meet him the following day and left him in the restaurant looking at the names.....

❧Chapter 8 – Genoa, Search Begins – With Help❧

When she returned to the Bristol Palace Hotel, Liz began to unpack and make herself at home. This could be a stop of a few days or more and the wrinkles needed to hang out of her clothes. She looked at a few critically and decided they could use more than a hang-out. The wools were fine, but the rayons were looking a bit crumpled. Well, tomorrow would tell.....

After reading the travel brochures for a few hours and nibbling on some fruit from the bowl in her room, she decided to go to sleep and get an early start the next day.

As she lay between the sheets, thinking about the events of the last few days, some things began to fall into place, but others were still a mystery --- such as, who had ransacked her room?

The following day, she would meet Mr. Henri at the Doges' Palace, a place she remembered well from her honeymoon. Being there would be nothing like her visit with Franz, though. She moved into the memory of that day: the sun, their love, and the romance of seeing a palace. They hadn't stayed in a hotel that time, so they went back to the ship and to their stateroom. Her body throbbed with the memory of that night --- their night of love --- and her hands stroked her breasts, her belly, and lower. The scene played in her mind as though in a movie.....

Trying to ignore his pounding heart, Franz lifted her slip over her head as she held her arms up, then pulled her close for a moment, to feel the warmth against his skin. Tenderly, Franz cupped her breasts with his hands, rubbing his fingertips across the nipples until they were hard, as hard as pebbles, then held his palms against the pebbles and slowly, ever so slowly and sensually, slid them in small circles, the rigidity arousing him until his breathing was ragged. He asked Liz if he could make love to her in a voice which had become heavy with his need. He was hard, so hard that it felt as if a saber straight from the forge, hot and ready for action, was pressing against her now naked belly. He could feel her nipples pressing against his skin, making little spots of heat where they touched. His head dipped and he brushed his lips across hers --- just a hint of a kiss to awaken her mouth for things to come.

Franz' hands caressed her body, sometimes only fingertips or only palms, giving way to the whole hand --- lightly, to tantalize, then firmer to build the fire. He kissed her nipples, taking them gently between his teeth and making them tingle --- making her whole body tingle.

Liz did the same, and more, as she reached for his rigid staff, that shaft of bliss and fulfillment. Firm and erect, it pointed in her direction, asking, nay begging, her to hold it, caress it, fondle it and let it touch her. It said, "You are the one! And, NOW is the time!" --- in pantomime, if not in words. She obliged it, giving it the attention it desired, first allowing her fingertips to lightly brush the silky skin making Franz shiver, bringing it, and him, to the point of no return. Those tiny hands coaxed groan after groan from Franz as they played 'fingers walking' along its length, alternating with little squeezes from time to time. He so wanted her to take his member into her mouth, to kiss and lick that part of his anatomy into a climactic frenzy, but at the same time wanted the sensation to linger, to stay at that sub-climax where awareness of the sensation is keenest. He wanted Liz to feel it, too, to experience her own pleasure as well as his; to rise on that tidal wave with him and partake in the intensity of the shared explosion together.

Finally, trembling both with emotion and with physical arousal, Franz laid her back against the pillows and parted her thighs as she wiggled with the heat of her desire, unable to be still. His throaty voice whispered, "May I be inside you?"

Liz breathed, "Yes --- oh yes," as the sensations playing through her body overwhelmed her senses.

His kisses were deep and sensual as he arched above her, then entered her secret doorway, sliding slowly and unhindered into that private recess with his firmness and feeling the slick, tight, warmth enfolding him. No kisses, now --- he needed more air, for his body demanded it to fuel the rhythm he'd begun. His hips, gently swaying front to back, picked up speed, then slowed to savor, resuming the pace to maintain the high point without spilling over --- yet.....

Liz' body was writhing with the ancient rhythm of love and need, pleasuring itself as it pleasured Franz, two bodies with one course, one mind, one goal --- satiation. Up and up they rode this wave, higher and higher until, finally, though they almost wanted the journey to last forever, the pinnacle was reached. Their muscles began to twitch and tense with the goal in sight as Liz' body arched upward and, her arms around him, held them bound tight to one another while the roller coaster ride peaked, then descended, and their bodies relaxed to bask in the afterglow of their heated encounter. Franz lay atop her supporting himself on his forearms without withdrawing. The weight was a welcome one to her as he maintained that connection, a pressing feeling of oneness with something greater, like take-off in an airplane. Finally, he rolled to the side to lie next to her. Energetically spent, he almost fell asleep as she pressed her warmth to him.

Franz' hand brushed her breast carelessly, as though it had no energy to lift itself to hold her and she snuggled yet closer to him, feeling a connection intimate beyond anything she had ever known. He would feel it, too, when the lethargy lifted from his frame --- that knowing that they had met before in some faraway place in time.

They were one, now and forever, as they had been since time immemorial.

Hours passed and, in time, the cabin began to grow light again, though the few candles they had lit earlier had sputtered and gone out long ago, their wicks drowned in the melted wax. The lovers were still asleep on the wide bed, the covers askew, naked in the frail morning light, with limbs entwined.

Franz was the first to stir, but Liz was the first to open her eyes and survey the room. As they scanned, her eyes lit on his chair and the hastily thrown undergarments it held. She smiled with pleasure and drew a breath, then sighed a contented sigh. Little tingles were dancing through her being and centering in her hidden recess. She clenched her thigh muscles and wiggled. It didn't go away. She clenched tighter, but it only succeeded in enhancing the sensations. As she clenched and released the muscles, it was as though the beauty of the night was happening all over again --- she could feel the heat rising in her loins and knew her body wanted him, wanted Franz inside of her sliding back and forth in that secret hollow.

She slid her hand to his side, then up, and to her amazement, his staff was truly stiff enough to hold up a tent. She touched it gently and he moaned softly as he slept. It was not a pained moan, but an mmmmm..... Hoping this was his body's consent to her touch, she held his manhood in her hand to feel the pulsing of its magnificent life force. It seemed to grow even larger and taller as she held it, until, finally, she could hold back no longer. Leaning forward, she touched her tongue to the tip where a tiny hole was apparent. The appendage jerked slightly, but seemed to swell toward her lips, inviting her to taste again. So, she did. Her eloquent tongue found a new fascination: the skin of this shaft was as soft, nay softer, than the silk of her undergarments. She slid her lips along its length, feeling the silkiness as a sensual pleasure against her almost-as-soft mouth. Slowly, she began to nibble at it, little pretend nibbles along its length and breadth.

As she played, she could not prevent herself from doing something she had never heard of: she opened her wet mouth and took the tip of that shaft inside it. At this point, a dozing Franz became fully awake and lay there afraid to move for fear she would stop. Fortunately, she was unaware that he was no longer sleeping and continued her explorations. As she held him in her mouth, her little hands were busy, feeling other parts, stroking the warm fur beneath his shaft as well as that surrounding it. As she did this, the shaft seemed to rise, to thrust itself in further, then recede. She grasped it round its base with both hands, then, to steady it, and began to suck gently, first at the tip, then holding it deeper in her mouth with the tip touching the back of her throat. She pulsed her tongue against it and felt it swell within her mouth. This was fun, playing with this new toy, fun that made the place between her thighs pulse with a strong rhythm, sending sharp little tingles down to her toes and upward to her breasts and nipples. Her body began to writhe as her mouth made love to Franz, her juices dripping across her legs.

She was barely aware of Franz' hand sliding up her leg until it found her slippery opening, and his fingers entered. Her back arched and her mouth opened to let out a moan of pure pleasure, but she was back at his manhood almost as quickly as she had let it go. In her excitement, she was sucking and licking alternately, squeezing him rhythmically with her hands and moving her hips up and down against the finger he held inside of her as well as the ones that cupped her own furry mound.

At first, when Franz began to groan with the power of his impending orgasm, she was afraid, thinking she had hurt him, and almost sat up, but his hand urged her head back to its post and she realized that this was pleasurable to him as well as her, so she continued with her lips and tongue until he was spent in a way as strong as the night before. Her own peak had been lesser after the fear that she had hurt him, so she lay next to him and slid her own fingers around in the juices between her thighs. This felt good, so she continued as she lay there musing on the new things she had experienced.

Eventually, Franz came out of his fog and, seeing what she was doing, moved her little hand aside and took over its work. Slowly, he slid his fingers around in circles, touching the hard little pebble at the apex of the opening as often as he could. If he touched too firmly Liz would jump with the shocking pleasure of it, so he slid his fingers feather-lightly back and forth in the slippery juices as she breathed harder and harder and wriggled more and more, muscles alternating between relaxing and tensing. As he slipped his fingers into her secret cave from time to time, he could feel its pulsing and it aroused him once again. He bent his head to her furry mound and licked and teased the lips which lined the center division, then found the little button with his tongue and began to suck gently on it. Waves of pleasure charged through Liz' body. She had felt nothing like this in her life and the sensation was almost too much for her to bear as his tongue brought her to the longed-for release again and again.

He waited until she had come to the top of a peak of pure all-encompassing pleasure before he entered her and, when he did, it sent shock waves through both of their bodies. The pleasure of bringing her back up to the top was a stimulant to his manhood and his energy as he pumped his hips back and forth with a vengeance, seeking to bring them both to the same wave they had ridden the night before. There it was --- the wave --- he could feel it, and knew by the sounds she was making that she was there with him, riding high and being ridden well. This time, the orgasm was beyond what they had experienced the first time. Sweat pouring off their skin, they came apart where they had joined, juices spilling onto the sheets beneath them. Both fully spent, they collapsed into sleep as deep as the sea they had been riding.

Remembering the love-making of their honeymoon, Liz, stroked those parts that Franz had stroked, arousing herself to a passion even beyond the remembering, for she was feeling it as well as remembering. Her fingers slid across the little button, now wet with her juices, and the lightest of touches was like electricity making her body jerk. That very lightness did more than hard pressure --- it teased and made her tingle. The muscles in her legs tensed and released over and over as she slid across that button. Finally, in a rising rhythmic culmination the climax came so hard that it took her breath away for a moment and she gasped as she rocked with the sensation. As she subsided from the ecstasy of the wave, she had only one thought: AGAIN!

Her fingers began playing and stroking, gently, almost imperceptibly at first, then, as the super-sensitivity abated, more enthusiastically, as she thought of Franz' fingers inside of her as she stroked her little button, until, once again, she rose to the peak she had been seeking in an orgasm stronger than the one she had experienced prior.

Rolling on her side and curling in a ball, she put the fingers of her right hand inside of her warm, fuzzy, juicy, secret place and fell into a sleep so profound that she didn't awake until late morning.

℘Chapter 9 – Genoa, the Search Continues℘

Liz awoke with a start as the morning clouds broke, sending sun pouring into her room and onto her face. Oh dear, she thought, it's after 10 a.m. and I haven't even bathed or breakfasted..... She could see immediately that the day would be a busy one.

Quickly showering to clean herself after the night before, she slipped into a blouse which had almost given up all of its wrinkles, and the blue wool suit she had worn in Barcelona, on the off chance that Mr. Henri would have someone for her to meet and question.

Downstairs, in the hotel's adjacent restaurant, she ate a light breakfast: eggs poached in milk, toast, and American style coffee with thick cream. At about a quarter past 11, she asked the doorman to find her a cab, and soon she was on her way through the winding streets of the city to the Doge's Palace. With the destination nearly 4 miles distant, she had begun early enough to allow for the unexpected.

Liz arrived a few minutes before the appointed time and waited in front of the Doge's Palace, busily looking through a brochure and appearing, to all intents and purposes, to be an ordinary tourist.

At exactly noon, she saw Mr. Henri ahead of her, also reading a brochure, and waited for him to approach. Her wait was short and he came to her pretending to ask a question about the brochure in his hand, then whispered, while pointing to his brochure, then at the building, "I have put a list of people to visit, in Genoa, and question about your husband, inside the brochure. Sadly, it is very short, for many have died. Now, drop your brochure and I'll trade when I pick it up for you. Then, you go on the tour and I'll pretend to continue examining the building's architecture."

When, the exchange was made, she purchased her ticket from the docent and waited for the tour to begin, wondering why he didn't tell her where to meet him next. Ah, well, she reasoned, perhaps, he would give her a sign or send a message.

The palace was beautiful and she remembered seeing it with Franz; how they were awed by the beauty and ornamentation. She was glad, however when it was over so that she could find somewhere nearby to buy a cup of coffee and eat a sweet roll while she looked at the information Mr. Henri had given her. As always, near tourist attractions, there are such shops and she found one easily, bought her coffee and a sweet called palmiere, a treat of filo dough cut and rolled to look like palm leaves, then, baked with sugar and cinnamon --- though this one was mostly sugar and very little cinnamon.

Liz sat and enjoyed her afternoon treat as she read through Mr. Henri's brochure until she came to his note, lightly stuck to a page. On it were only 2 names and addresses. If memory served her, she had seen one of the streets not too far from the hotel, but the other would require a map.

Later, when she procured a taxi to return her to the hotel, she watched for the street and counted the blocks from the hotel: only 6 and in the direction of the restaurant they had eaten in yesterday --- she could do that quite easily. So, it was that she asked the taxi driver to take her to the address, first, instead of the hotel.

The building was old, not harmed by bombs, at least not visibly, but it had an air of age and neglect. Liz rang for the concierge and, after many moments and many noises, was rewarded with the face of a middle aged woman in the window of a first floor apartment. The woman opened the window and asked, in Italian, what she wanted. Liz answered in English that she was looking for Signor Bienvenuto. The woman disappeared and came to open the door, inviting her into the building in extremely broken English mixed with Italian. Pointing to the stairway, she indicated 2 fingers and then 4, 24….. …..apartment 24. Liz nodded, saying, "Grazie, grazie…." and shook the woman's hand, then started up the stairs.

She knocked on the door of apartment 24 and waited. It took awhile, but the door eventually opened, first a crack and then more. When the opening was about the width of a hand, she could see that there was a man behind the door.

Cocking her head to one side, she asked in English, "Are you Signor Bienvenuto?"

"Who wants to know?" he asked with an accent, but was obviously schooled in English.

"The wife of Franz Tischler," Liz answered. On hearing this, the hand reached out, grabbed her arm, and pulled her into the apartment; while the man's other hand closed the door.

He looked her up and down, sizing her up, then asked, "What d'ya want?"

Liz lowered her eyes and said, "To know what you know about my husband --- if you have seen him, heard from him, know of him..... .....at any time since 1939....." After a few minutes, she looked up and found, to her surprise, that the man in front of her had tears running down his face. Startled, she gave a little shiver, then waited for him to compose himself and speak.

"I..... I saw him in 1939...... He talked to me about helping..... .....the economy..... .....by doing business with his company; about stop..... stopping a war..... ......with strong business ties," the man stammered..... "He never contacted me again, after I saw him leave on the train..... and I thought it fell through or..... that maybe he got killed in the war. My company was nationalized, so I could not have participated..... in that way, ...but perhaps I could have helped him as a consultant."

The man sat there silently and Liz sat silently with him, each thinking their own thoughts and weighing their own burdens. Life was not always easy, but it was always full of experiences, both sad and happy, and all brought learning. Each came to this conclusion in their own way, and when their eyes met, they knew this, somehow, through some process of thought transference.

Liz stood up, saying, "It's time that I go. She thanked him for his help and told him that at least she knew now that Franz had come as far as Genoa. Then, she asked, "Do you have any money?" and reading the look in his eyes, said, "Here, take this and use it well, where it is best suited," handing him a small wad of bills. "And, please, remember to say a prayer on his behalf --- and contact his father if you have any more information. He will know where I am as I progress."

Again, his eyes began to tear. She took his hand and held it between hers for a moment, then quietly let herself out as the tears flowed down his careworn cheeks.

With a pensive look on her face, she walked back to Via Xx Settembre and turned toward the restaurant she would stop in, before continuing on to the hotel. As she walked, she looked in the shop windows at the wares. Once they had been swollen with goods, but now the pickings were much slimmer --- the city was certainly trying, but had not rebounded from the war --- yet.

It was only a matter of minutes until she stepped over the threshold of 'Aida' and, since she had arrived early, the desk clerk's aunt was there to greet her instead of being up to her elbows in pasta --- back in the kitchen. "Ah, la signorina Americana," she said, with a beaming smile, upon Liz' entry.

Liz didn't correct the dear lady on her marital status, lest she think that Mr. Henri was her lover and they were having a tête-à-tête, but reached for the menu she was handed and took the waving hand to mean she should select any table, since all were currently empty. She opted for the same booth they had occupied the previous day, due to its lack of visibility from the entrance.

As she ate the seafood stew she had selected, she remarked to the clerk's aunt, who had come to sit with her and visit until the customers began arriving, that it reminded her of cioppino, which she had eaten in America with the same dense, crusty, toasted bread she now held in her hand.

"Ah, yes," the aunt said, "Is Genoese fisherman in Santo Francisco who invent cioppino --- some fish, calamare, crab, mussel, tomato, oliva, garlic, basil..... My brother, in California, he send me list how to make..... In Livorno, 120 km from here, is made almost same since 300 years."

As Liz ate, she enjoyed listening to the pleasant lady's discourse on everything that came to her mind; in a quaint version of English she had learned, mainly from her nephew, to help her with the tourist trade. She found herself liking the forthright, unassuming lady and hoped that she would see more of her while she was in Genoa.....

Although the proprietress pressed her to eat more, when the cioppino had dwindled to a few empty mussel shells, she was too full for anything more substantial than a dessert --- cannon-shaped puff pastry filled with a creamy pudding, topped with whipped cream and sprinkled with toasted almond slices and ground cinnamon..... She finished every bite and ordered another dessert --- something akin to fruitcake --- to take back to her room for a late snack, ...or perhaps breakfast.....

As the customers began drifting in for dinner, she paid her check, said good-bye, and headed in the direction of the hotel.

With a full stomach and her second dessert in a confectioner's box made of thin cardboard, she entered her room.

Not quite in the mood for thinking about her search, after her visit with Signor Bienvenuto, she pulled out a few slim volumes she had brought along to read on the trains, for she anticipated traveling. Choosing one, she returned the others to her suitcase and sat in the large, plush easy chair in a corner of the room for a good read, but somehow she couldn't concentrate on the book. Her mind kept jumping from one thing to another: so many thoughts, so many threads, so many possibilities, and no Franz, yet......

She took out her list of possible contacts, looking at the many names, including the ones she had crossed out due to their deaths --- or their disappearance --- and realized that, if they continued to be eliminated at this rate, she'd probably have only 20 or so to talk to. Well, she consoled herself, she had established that Franz had made it this far, at least, and Bienvenuto had seen him off at the train...... That was something. She would still see the other person still available in Genoa, a Mr. Ruiz, but wondered if there would be more information of any use, now that she knew Franz had left.

Having dealt with all of that, she decided to try again to concentrate on the novel in front of her...... Again, her restless mind wouldn't leave her alone and she found herself wondering when Mr. Henri would pop up again --- and where and how......

Finally, she decided to see if she could sleep and took the book to bed with her......

✎Chapter 10 – Genoa, the Other Lead✎

Having fallen asleep, over the novel, at an earlier hour than usual, Liz was up and bathing at 8 a.m. Eager to get out into the city and speak to the other lead, as well as revisit some of the sites she and Franz had enjoyed together, she didn't linger in the water, though it was tempting, as she rubbed the soap over her body, fondling herself and rubbing her fingers over her hidden button in the process..... Mentally, she slapped her hand and said to herself, "Tonight, Liz!" then slid her fingers over it a few more times for good measure and found that she couldn't wait until evening.

She leaned back against the porcelained cast iron and pinched her nipples until they were literally singing with joy, squeezing her breasts from time to time and feeling the tension build in the parts still under water. Finally, she slid her hands down to those nether regions and began to play there. Two tiny hands caressed, rubbed, and entered her most private places, using the lubrication of the water, as well as her own flowing juices to facilitate penetration and bring her the most pleasure.

As she felt her orgasm rising in her, she slowed to allow it to subside and then rebuild, and found herself biting into a washcloth to keep from crying out each time it built to an almost finale. Then, when she could take it no more, and the sensation was at its greatest height, she continued sliding across that little button and felt every muscle in her body begin to spasm in waves. She bit hard on the washcloth, holding back the scream she knew was building to avoid alarming guests in the adjoining rooms.

At last, her vagina convulsed for the last time and her thighs squeezed together over her right hand, tightly, as if to keep it a prisoner of her lust, then fell apart, allowing her to withdraw it.

She felt almost too relaxed to stand, much less walk around looking for the lead she wanted to question, but, after washing away the excess juices, and not allowing herself to succumb to the sensation again, she managed to stand up, exit the tub, and dry herself.

By 9:30 she was on her way down the stairs to the doorman for a taxi, having eaten half of the second dessert from the night before as breakfast.....

He smiled when he saw her, thinking her quite the nicest American he'd encountered, and held the door for her as she entered and closed it once he saw that she was completely inside.

Giving the address to the driver, she leaned back in the seat for the ride, for this address was further out in the suburbs. She'd have to ask the taxi to wait for her or risk not having a ride back.

After a little more than 45 minutes, they arrived at their destination --- a more rural area, with fields. The driver's English was no prize-winner, but he nodded, knowing that she had nowhere to go and would have to take his taxi back --- happy that he would be earning money without expending any gasoline as he waited.....

This was an individual house in a suburban village setting, she saw as she walked up to the door and, then, knocked. She knew that there was someone home since, as she waited, she could hear the normal noises of a family through open windows. Finally, after a few minutes, she knocked again. This time, someone came to answer almost immediately --- a boy of about 10 years --- who spoke a small amount of English. He explained, with a smile, that the teacher was sick, so all of the children in his form were home for the day. Liz smiled back and asked for her potential lead, a Mr. Ruiz. In response, the boy turned around and hollered, "Abuelo, abuelo, una mujer bonita esta a la puerta! Come, grampa!"

When he saw that his grandfather was coming to the door, he turned to Liz, and with a dazzling smile filled with perfect white teeth, said, "This is my grandfather, Senor Ruiz. He is old now and his ears do not work much, but his head is good."

It was Liz' turn to smile at the earnestness of the boy and he responded with another view of the so perfect teeth. When his grandfather came to the door, seeing a beautiful woman, he showed her into the parlor and seated her in the most comfortable chair, then drew another close so that he could hear her better.

Noting his preparations, Liz began in English and found that he spoke it, but his hearing was definitely not that of a young person. Still, she pressed onward, explaining her search and her hopes as he nodded over and over.

Then it was his turn to talk and he began quietly and slowly, saying, "My dear, I am an old man, grown older in this terrible war and my ears have been damaged by the noise of it! However, I still remember..... .....and I still think. I remember your husband: a young man and serious, ...but able to laugh. He wanted to make contracts with my company --- a company that is now gone, fallen to the bombs and financially ruined by the cost of this war. Un fiasco!" He punctuated the exclamation with a gesture of his hand, as though to wave it out of existence, paused for a moment to breathe, then continued, "I didn't hear from him again and I supposed he heard of my misfortune or, perhaps, was killed in the war like so many I knew. First, the private war in Spain, then Mussolini, and finally, that rotten scum, Hitler..... I wish I could tell you what you are seeking, but I don't have the answer. If you find him, though, tell him that I will work for him for free if he needs a good engineer in Genoa and that I will travel if he can pay my expenses, for I have nothing left and am consigned to living with my son and his family in order to survive."

Listening to his words, Liz' heart nearly broke and silent tears streamed down her face, falling on her once dry blouse in a torrent and wetting it thoroughly. Her growth was continuing exponentially, as she interacted with these people who had suffered so much and lost so much, and she assimilated their stories of pain and deprivation. She felt that, somehow, life was preparing her for something --- something very large.....

Her hand went into her purse and brought out a wad of bills as large as the one she had given to Bienvenuto, then pressed it into Senor Ruiz' hands, folding one over the other to indicate he must keep it. Then, she found words coming out of her mouth that didn't seem to be her own, "Senor Ruiz, I am going to write a telegram to my father and my father-in-law and ask them to begin thinking how they can give you a job right here in Italy or in another country, if you wish, to help with the rebuilding in a different way than cleaning up broken buildings. People need more than new houses and streets, they need engineers and they need companies that can provide good jobs for them."

Lost in thought, he had been unaware of her tears, even of her pressing the money into his hands, but when she began to speak, he heard every word and it broke him out of his reverie. He looked into her eyes and said, "You are your husband. That is what he said when he was here: 'companies that can provide good jobs for them'. This is truth and he knew it."

Then, he saw the money in his hands and tried to give it back to her, but she folded his fingers over it and said, "No, Senor, this is for you. It is a small gift to repay the large gift you have given me and you may share it with your family."

The old man's wrinkled face broke into a beatific smile at the mention of his family and, as his lips parted, she could see the same teeth his grandson had in his own mouth, giving him a look of being a much younger man and bringing a glow to her heart.

When she left, he walked her to the gate and held the taxi door for her, waiting until she was comfortable before closing it. She rolled down the window and squeezed his hand one more time, before the driver pulled away from the house and turned the car around.

The ride back to her hotel was a quiet one. The driver hummed to himself and she gazed out at the scenery --- looking at it, but not really seeing it, and lost deep in thought. She had meant what she said and now she would have to sell the idea to Franz' father and her own, as well as be their inspiration.....

She wondered if she had it in her, but then answered herself with the knowledge that it would be a tribute to Franz whether he was alive or dead and it would help those he respected.....

True to her word, she asked the driver to find a telegraph office before taking her to the hotel and, true to her word, she sent a wire to her father to let him know that she had seen 2 of Franz' former business contacts and that an idea had come to her that she wanted to discuss with him soon and gave him the name of her hotel in Genoa.

When she finally reached her hotel, she was so emotionally drained that she asked the desk clerk to have some bread and cheese sent up to her room soon and she retired there to wait. It seemed that she had been there no longer than a few minutes, when the knock came on her door. She opened it to discover Mr. Henri standing there. He quickly stepped inside and around her to stand behind the door, lest another hotel guest pass in the corridor.

Putting one finger to his lips, he indicated she should be silent until the door was closed, then pushed it to and turned to her, saying, "This is good: you have visited both of your leads. Was the information helpful? No, no, a rhetorical question," he said, holding up his hand to still her as she drew a breath to tell him what she had learned. "I am only here for a few moments to give you the information you will need for your trip to Milan."

With this, he handed her a folded train schedule and, ear to the door, listened to see if anyone was in the corridor, before opening it and stepping out the door in one deft movement, then closing it behind him. Nonchalantly, he walked down the hallway and descended the stairs.

In her room, Liz opened the railway schedule and saw that a time had been circled and a date written beside it. A hotel name had been written next to that and a note:

Be at The Parco delle Basiliche, near the Basilica of San Lorenzo, at noon the day after you arrive in Milan.

Another knock on the door startled her. Thinking it to be Mr. Henri again, she opened it quickly and almost fell into the plate of bread and cheese a bellboy was carrying. "You ordered food, madam?" he asked.

"Oh, yes, I almost forgot. Over there on the dresser, please....," she mumbled at him as she searched in her purse for tip money. "Thank you."

"You are very welcome, signorina," came the lilting reply, once he saw the size of his tip.....

༐Chapter 11 – Last Day in Genoa༐

Liz awoke the next morning to rain coming down on the windows and decided that it was an in-bed day. She had no more leads here and didn't want to set out for the station on a rainy day, but, fortunately, Mr. Henri's note had specified the following day for her departure date.

At about 2 o'clock the rain stopped and the sun came out. Encouraged, she decided to see if it looked like the rain was truly over and, perhaps, she might leave the hotel. Indeed, when she was ushered through the doors of the lobby into the street, she could see not a cloud in the sky and set out for 'Aida' in hopes of seeing a familiar face.....

The clerk's aunt was there, talking with the few patrons who had ventured out after the rain. She beamed at Liz when she opened the door. "Ah, the Americana....."

Liz was a little embarrassed by the attention, but sensed that the woman's heart was genuine.

"What will you eat, today?" she asked.

"What do you recommend?" Liz replied.

"I have fresh meat ravioli with marsala sauce, gnocchi with roasted garlic, and the dessert you like so much, ...before --- with the cream and cinnamon."

"Oh, yes, I will have that," Liz quickly agreed, smiling, "And a cup of coffee Americano with the dessert….."

"Rapido," the clerk's aunt said to her hovering waiter --- and, to Liz' surprise, the food appeared on her table in mere minutes.

She savored the food --- hot, ethnic, and pungent. Then, she lingered over her coffee and dessert, licking her fingers free of the whipped cream and cinnamon with all the delight of a child. Finally, she put the last of the topping in her coffee and managed to eat the pudding-filled delight with greater ease.

The clerk's aunt came and sat with her for awhile, as she often did with others in her shop. Liz wasn't used to this, but apparently it was not unusual in Italy, so she relaxed and enjoyed the conversation. The lady was very proud of her nephew and told Liz that he wanted to go to school to become more than a desk clerk. Liz smiled and said that he seemed to be an intelligent young man, which brought an answering smile to the face of his doting aunt.

Eventually, Liz had eaten every morsel of her dessert and made ready to settle the bill, when a baker's box appeared on her table. Calling the waiter, she asked, "What is this?"

"Ah, signorina, a gift from my mother," he replied.

Liz opened the box and found more of the dense, fruity cake she had bought before --- enough to see her along her journey, …..another day. After wrapping it back up, she left enough for the bill and more on the table, then made her way back to the hotel.

Knowing that she would be leaving in the morning, she packed her clothes and, when she was done, sat down with a book for a bit of reading before bed. By 8 o'clock, unable to keep her eyes open, she crawled under the sheets and fell into a deep sleep.

In the dream state, she heard Franz speaking her name, at first, then saw him from a distance --- stretching his arms toward her and calling to her. It was as though, he couldn't leave where he was and come to her, no matter how much he wanted to. She couldn't seem to make herself go forward, either, and her feet felt like she wore shoes of lead.

She awoke twice during the night, but always went back to the same dream: Franz calling her name and saying how much he loved her, how much he needed her, and how much guilt he felt for leaving her alone so long. Then, she heard him say something she didn't understand, "Lisbet, look for me near the angel." Her sleep was fitful, and less than restful, but she slept.

ꙮChapter 12 – The Train to Milanꙮ

The sun shone through the windows of her room brightly, waking her early. She had not rested well and she lay in bed for a number of hours after she awoke, trying to make sense of it all --- both the dream, or was it dreams, and the words.....

Finally, she simply had to get up and prepare for her trip to Milan, so, dragging herself from beneath the covers, she showered and dressed, then put all of the last minute things in her luggage --- nightgown, hairbrush, and so on.....

Studying the map, she saw that it was only a 70-mile trip, so it shouldn't take more than a few hours, even if she was booked on a local instead of an express. She was to leave on the 12:15 train. Good! She should arrive in time to find her hotel and have dinner before making up for the sleep she lost the night before.....

As she checked out of the hotel, Liz spoke to the desk clerk and told him how much she appreciated his aunt's restaurant and her company at dinner..... When he smiled, she said, shaking her finger at him, "And go to school --- you will never regret it."

His face looked startled and, then, he smiled again. "You have been talking to my aunt!"

Liz grinned and nodded as she turned to leave.

At the train station, she hired a porter to bring her luggage to the baggage check-in, but found that on this local run, they preferred that the passengers see to their own baggage in the overhead racks and the baggage car was only a convenience allowed passengers going to a further destination. Fortunately, she had not taken large trunks like some travelers she had met…..

The trip was, indeed, no express, but at least the second half had fewer tiny towns and they sped along the rails toward Milan. The countryside was beautiful in this latitude even though it was only nearing early spring. The little villages and small towns seemed to be quaint, slow-moving, and inviting…. The war damage still evident, of course, was located more in the larger cities and areas where there were factories --- of what use to bomb a field on purpose and waste the ammunition?

The train pulled into the main Milan Station at a few minutes after 3:30 --- a bit late, she judged by the conductor's frown, as he stood there looking at his watch. Liz found a porter and, wheeling her luggage out to the front of the station, he selected a taxi for her. Once inside, Liz told the driver that she wanted to go to Hotel Pierre Milano.

The ride was pleasant in spite of the damaged buildings still visible. Italy had little or no money for rebuilding --- that would have to come later.

Her hotel was quaint. There were restaurants in the vicinity and Liz made a mental note to ask which ones were the best when she checked in….. In no time at all, the driver had brought her luggage into the hotel and a bellboy was taking it up to her room while she followed in his wake. She had asked the desk clerk about restaurants and he was less helpful than the last one. Fortunately, the friendly bellboy had some suggestions….. Thus, it was, that she ended up in a small, but cozy restaurant a few short blocks from the hotel…..

She was early for dinner, but having experience with tourist's habits, and needing the money, the restaurant treated her well. She ordered ossobuco (veal shanks in a gravy), and the trimmings (vegetables, dense, chewy Italian bread, and dessert). This would surely hold her until tomorrow, she thought.

No friendly proprietress here, but the waiters were polite and helpful --- especially for a pretty American tourist…..

Her meal finished, she returned to the hotel, relishing the thought of a good night's sleep. She must be up early to meet Mr. Henri the next day…..

By the time she entered her room, Liz' brain was screaming for sleep --- and she gave in to it without a moment's hesitation…..

❧Chapter 13 – Milan☙

By morning, Liz was set to rights and woke up feeling as though she could take on the world. Her meeting with Mr. Henri was for noon and the park was only about 6 blocks east of the hotel --- he had chosen well….. She looked at her map and saw that she would be able to sightsee as she walked to the meeting. Intrigued by the concentric rings of streets (or rather, boulevards), she opened the guidebook in her room and found that they were the sites of the ancient walls of the city as population growth and threatened sieges forced them ever outward. This sounded interesting, she thought…..

Ten o'clock found her already dressed, and walking on the Via Edmondo de Amicis toward the park. She took her time, looking in the store windows and admiring the wares, then, stopped at an intriguing café and ordered coffee and a roll --- enough to see her through to lunch. The sun shone brightly and she sat by the window, enjoying the warmth of the day. Finally, catching a glimpse of the clock over the cashier, she saw that she would arrive just 5 minutes early if she left at that moment, so she paid her bill and headed toward the park.

Enjoying a leisurely walk was not on the agenda at this point --- she was conscious of the time and made straight for the

Basilica which the park was named for. As she had
anticipated, she arrived a few minutes early, so she spread
out a shawl she had brought on the ground and sat on it near
the entrance to the Basilica, then, opened one of her
guidebooks to read, feeling confident that she need not
watch for Mr. Henri, for he seemed particularly adept at
finding her.

A few pages into the book, a shadow fell over it. Looking
up in mild annoyance, she saw Mr. Henri standing there
looking down at her. "Aren't you afraid of a sunburn," he
asked.

Holding back a retort, she took his offered hand and allowed
herself to be assisted to stand. Picking up her shawl and
folding it, then stowing her book in her purse along with it,
she asked, "Have you anything for me?"

"Ah, yes, as a matter of fact, I do," came the reply. He
pretended to point something out to her in his guidebook and
then pointed to the Basilica, as though he was enlightening a
tourist, in case they were being observed. She quickly
understood and pantomimed asking him if she could buy his
book, which he finally allowed and, leaving her with the
book, went to the Basilica for a tour.

She wondered how to proceed at this point and decided that
she could seek out a shadier spot and look through the book.
Still within sight of the Basilica's main entrance, she sat and
read, thumbing through, nonchalantly, until she found the
small sheets of paper he had inserted.

There is only one lead for you, here, but he is a very good one. Dr. Tomas has an estate in the countryside outside of Milan. It can be reached by taxi in about 30 minutes. The address is on the next sheet along with other important information. You need not make an appointment --- he will be expecting you tomorrow for lunch.

Leave for Bern the following day on the 4:15 train. In Bern, you will be met, at the train, by a Frau Berger, who takes in boarders for long or short terms. She will have a room for you in the old city, and will make you comfortable. She is also a cook of some repute and you may eat at her table or at one of the fine restaurants. She is only one of your leads; the other is Mr. Lorenz, whose address she will give you. You will arrive on Friday and leave on Monday at 2:30 for Zurich.

In Zurich, you will check in at the Romantik Seehotel Sonne in Kussnacht am Zurichsee, about 10 minutes from Zurich. You will be contacted. H.

She pretended to sneeze, then found a handkerchief in her purse and, after patting her nose with it, managed to incorporate both of the small sheets of paper into it, surreptitiously, and ease them into her handbag.

So, she would not meet Mr. Henri until at least Zurich..... Strangely, she felt almost a sense of loss --- they had become partners in the search for Franz with her depending on his expertise.

As the afternoon wore on, she walked back to her hotel, first stopping to buy a pair of walking shoes she had seen in a shop window, then, stopping for a late lunch at the restaurant she had discovered the day before. Their blue-plate special was brasato, a beef, wine, and potato stew, so she ordered it --- and a plate of various cookies to nibble with her coffee, richly augmented with cream.

Carrying the bag of cookies she had bought and her new shoes, she returned to the hotel.

Not much to do, that night, so she decided to read for awhile. As she lay on the bed reading, she began to think about the Basilica and the time she had seen it with Franz. Oh, what a rascal --- he had pushed her into every corner and alcove he could find to steal kisses and squeeze her tempting parts..... As she thought about it, she remembered how it made her feel: the tingling of her body, and the excitement of her emotions --- that he was so daring. He made her feel irresistible and wanted and loved as they played and teased in their private way. His eyes glowed when he looked at her and she felt as though a light turned on in her that must be obvious to everyone.

She began to feel that glow and it was as though Franz was there with his arms around her, touching her, kissing her, and stroking her skin. This was more than fantasy --- it was as though she could feel it, really feel it. Her thighs became heavy with the emotion of it, and she felt desire growing in her groin. Her heart was pounding and she could feel hands on her breasts, squeezing them the way he did and pinching the nipples to arouse her.

As she began clenching her thighs together, her secret place began to throb with a hunger to feel him inside of her. Liz rubbed her hands on her little button, but it was not enough, so she inserted her fingers in the hidden recess and slid them back and forth as Franz had. This helped, but it was still not enough, so she lay there, sliding across the slippery button with her middle finger and feeling the sensation of Franz being inside of her, and pushing in and out, as though his ghost were there with her. It seemed a little bizarre, but she was not in a position to critique that thought, for her body was writhing and working itself toward an orgasm almost without her volition.

She circled the button with her fingertips and began squeezing it like Franz had squeezed her nipples --- oh, the sensation! Then, she pulled on it lightly and found it brought on more. Her breathing was ragged as she worked herself toward that completion, that rising to the top of the rollercoaster, then plunging down at breakneck speed to the sudden stop where you could still feel the vibrations pulsing through your body.

Her finger dipped to bring more of her juices forward again and slide on the button, which was swelling and protruding, becoming harder like a miniature penis which would never ejaculate. Oh, if he were only there to suck on it as he had before. She wanted to feel that as much as feeling him inside of her.

Suddenly, her orgasm was upon her and she shuddered over and over, jerking like a marionette on a stick, totally incapable of stopping the wave from rolling over her, overcoming her, and pleasuring her. Liz lay there, for a moment, too weak to move... Then, she pulled the covers across her without even bothering to slip between the sheets.

❧Chapter 14 – Dr. Tomas❧

Liz arrived at the estate of Dr. Tomas at about noon. The taxi driver agreed to wait for her, even though it would be quite awhile and, as she left, he moved to the passenger side front seat with his feet in the driver's seat.

She was greeted at the door by a buxom Italian lady who brought her to the sitting room, where the doctor was reading. "Ah," he said, when his housekeeper had left, "Madam Tischler, is it not?"

"Yes, Dr. Tomas, I am Lisbet Tischler. How did you know and what do you know of my husband?"

"Ah, calma, calma, a question must be answered before you ask another….."

"I'm sorry," she said, "It's just that I worry so about Franz….."

"Yes, I understand your distress. I knew who you were, because I know our mutual friend, Mr. Henri. As for your husband, I have not seen him these 7 years --- not since 1939, when he stopped on his journey to speak with me about collaborating on some research in the field of airplane engines --- at least the hydraulics portion of them. I never heard from him again and presumed that his firm dropped the issue, solved it, or lost a contract, although it did seem a little strange that I never heard from him at all….. But, then, with Mussolini and the war and all, mail often was lost --- the bombings, you know, and the blackshirts….."

He continued, "I corresponded with a colleague in Dusseldorf, Herr Nachtigal, who said Franz had never arrived there at all. This was, or course, before the war started officially in September with the invasion of Poland. We didn't know for certain all of the cities he had planned to visit, so we couldn't determine where he had disappeared with any certainty. I suspect it is most likely that it would have been inside Germany, for who would want to kidnap or kill him elsewhere?"

Shocked into silence by the word "kill", Liz sat and thought for a moment, then said, "What you say makes sense --- although the Germans *are* daring enough to kidnap someone and carry them across a border….. But, if they knew that his itinerary included German cities, why would they bother? Unless, perhaps, they needed or wanted him immediately….."

Dr. Tomas looked pensive for a moment, then said, "There was a time, just before the war, when it was rumored in intellectual circles that they were having problems with the hydraulic systems in their submarines….. I wonder….."

They both sat there in silence for quite awhile, each deep in their own thoughts….. This mutual reverie was interrupted by the announcement that luncheon was being served in the sun room.

Liz was enchanted with the sun room --- another name for a garden room or orangerie. So many beautiful plants! Light came through the windows in the cooler months and warmed beds of river rocks, which then gave off their heat at night so that tender plants never became too cold. Many of them were homes to espaliered fruit trees and orchids..... The doctor, however, was very proud of his early strawberries.....

As they ate the lovely luncheon, his cook had prepared, Liz and the doctor spoke about their respective lives and how the world might change now that the war was over. They found agreement on many points and Dr, Tomas quickly grew to respect his young guest's mind. It is usually thus with people who agree with us..... .....very seldom, when they don't.

"So, you travel to Bern, next?" the doctor interjected into the silence, of a lull in the conversation, as the meal began to take its effect on them. "Berger and Lorenz, I suppose....."

Startled, Liz blurted out, "How did you know?"

"Oh, we intellectuals and engineers all try to keep track of each other, my dear," he said. "This is one reason that his disappearance has been so troubling. It makes us wonder how we missed it, perhaps through complacency or thinking that it was due to poor war communications --- and we wonder now who may be next....." He paused for a moment, then said, "I suppose you'll be going to Heidelberg."

Liz' jaw dropped open and she quickly closed her mouth.

Seeing this, he ascertained the accuracy of his words and said, nodding, "It is not the same, but this will pass and the Nazi reforms will be re-reformed by a Council of 13. See Weber, Professor Alfred Weber. He is a good man. See also, Frau Herta Schreihart --- if you can find her."

"You..... you know so much," Liz stammered, in spite of herself, "I feel as if I know nothing and others know all about me --- and about Franz....."

"Oh, my dear, don't trouble yourself with worries," he said, patting the back of her hand, "We don't know everything, just these few things of where Franz has been --- and, of course, his desire to bring peace through commerce and technology, because it is the desire of all humanitarians to see populations prosper."

Liz felt considerably calmer --- it must have been his hand patting hers, just like her father often did.....

They talked for awhile more --- about the war and the horror of the disclosures coming out, as well as the new United Nations group being formed. Liz asked, "Do you think there will ever be a United Europe?"

Dr. Tomas thought for a moment, then answered, "I believe that it is possible, but it will be fraught with petty jealousies and cultural judgments even if it comes about. We have spent too many centuries approving only of each other's cuisine and resorts...." Smiling, he winked at her and patted her hand again.

She smiled at him and, as he saw that glow, he wished that he were 40 years younger.

Hearing a clock chiming in a distant room, Liz asked him what time it was. He startled her with the answer: "Half past four o'clock."

"Then, sadly, I must take my leave of you. I have kept my taxi driver far too long," she said.

And, thus it was that he showed to the door, and remained standing there under the lintel and waving as the driver started the engine and eased down the drive --- then turned, finally, to go inside and seek the comfort of his sun room once again.

Liz, ensconced in the back seat of the taxi, allowed her brain free rein --- to wonder what kind of network this was that knew so much. Engineers? Spies? Masons? She ached to know the answer, but doubted that it would come easily --- if ever..... Then, her internal dialogue put in its 2 cents, saying, "Just be glad that they're helping you and not the other way around....."

Meanwhile, her taxi continued toward the city and she began to see the lights of evening twinkling in the distance and coming ever nearer.

This had been a very long day in many ways, both emotionally and philosophically --- Liz was sure that she would sleep soundly.....

ᔐChapter 15 – Onward to Bern᪬

The day dawned gray and dismal --- clouds threatening rain --- and the air had turned cold.

Liz decided to attempt to find breakfast before she packed, so, dressed in her warm coat, she brave the elements for a block to a little café she had seen. It was open and tourists were eating --- she became one of them.....

After her breakfast, which was nothing like "continental", she hurried back to her hotel with a bag of rolls baked with sausage and cheese in the center to carry her though the day --- lest the dining car, if one existed, was full.

Once indoors, she began her task of packing, once more. This time, she wore the new shoes she had bought --- much more suited to the constant walking, on cobbled or damaged streets, and left the stylish American shoes in her luggage. Finally, with everything ready to go, she sat down with the book she had put in her purse, and began to read. It was a novel she had purchased to while away the time on the train, if it became boring, and it did its job quite well, for it was 2:30 when she looked up again. Better go now, she thought.....

She called for the bellboy and within a few minutes he was there, carrying her luggage down the stairs, then, asking the doorman for a taxi and waiting as she checked out.

Soon, she was on her way to the station, knowing that she would be early, but better that than wait for the rain to begin again and be late. This train allowed her to check her luggage --- the trip was over 150 miles and certainly not within the local area. So, she carried only her purse and a valise containing the sausage rolls --- with the notebook tucked into a hidden compartment.

The train was already in the station and waiting, so she was allowed to board early, and she sat and read until she heard other passengers boarding. The first group was a family: father, mother, and twin boys of about 12, apparently going on a ski holiday. More passengers entered and it seemed that the slopes must still be in full season, judging by the number of skiers in her car.

Reading was impossible with the boys talking about their trip, so she spent the first few hours looking out the window as the day waned. The train wound in and out of and around picturesque Italian villages and then Swiss dorfs, leaving the cloudbank behind. And, as the now-visible sun began to set, more and more lights twinkled in the twilight of the evening. The boys became quieter, as children often do at dusk, then ate some sandwiches their mother gave them and soon fell asleep. Feeling hungry, Liz opened her valise and took out a sausage roll, curling up in her seat to read while she ate.

The book was absorbing and she didn't hear the announcement that they were nearing the Bern station, so she had to scramble to put the book away when the train began to slow down.

The parents of the twins had awakened them and, with sleepy eyes, they followed their parents off of the train. Soon, the passengers were all streaming toward the immigration booths to have their passports stamped or their identification papers verified, before they moved on to collect their baggage and arrange transportation.

Liz moved along with the group and, as she walked to the baggage claim window, heard a woman ask, "Fraulein Hart?"

Liz turned quickly and saw the perfect grandmother figure --- a woman who turned out to be Frau Ana Berger. "Are you looking for me?" Liz asked.

"If you know someone named Franz, I am," came the answer.

"You are Frau Berger?"

"Yes. Shall we gather your baggage?"

"Oh, yes. Do you have a vehicle or shall we need a taxi?"

"My brother, Hans Hausner is waiting for us with his car. I will only address you as Miss Hart, because he knows nothing of your search, my dear."

Liz nodded her understanding.

They redeemed Liz' luggage from the baggage clerk and soon it was on its way to the street on a porter's cart. In hardly more than 10 minutes it was in the car, along with the ladies, and thence to Frau Berger's comfortable home, a short distance away.

Frau Berger's brother spoke with her in Swiss, which Liz understood only a bit, due to its French and German roots, and she made out that the gist of the conversation was that his wife's arthritis was acting up.

The ride was shorter than Liz expected and soon she was ensconced in a chair in Frau Berger's private sitting room in front of the fireplace, where a healthy fire and steaming mugs of cocoa were taking the chill out of their bones.

After a few tiny sips of the hot liquid, she asked Frau Berger how she knew Franz.

Frau Berger began, "Oh, please call me Ana, Lisbet. Franz did. He is a good boy, that one. He came to visit Herr Lorenz and stayed here in my house. He knew I am a widow and insisted on paying double, so I gave him more meat and extra strudel --- to be fair. My brother took him to the train when he left for Zurich, but before he left we had many conversations about the possibility of the coming war and about the world in general. I believe that we agreed in our philosophies."

"I suspect that you did," Liz ventured…..

"Yes, yes, it was so," came the affirmation.

"How long was he here?" Liz asked.

"Only 3 days," came the response, "And, then, he was gone. His energy was so strong that it seemed to linger in the house for days --- as if he was still here and not on the way to Zurich. He talked about you --- how beautiful you are, and kind --- he loves you very much." She smiled at this, thinking of her own days of young love.....

"Did he say anything about where he planned to travel?" Liz prompted.

"Yes, he said he would be traveling to Stuttgart and Heidelberg in Germany --- also Luxembourg and Amsterdam. He asked questions about Dusseldorf, Frankfurt, and Brussels, too, but he didn't say he would go to any of them."

Liz frowned. "Those are all cities we discussed before he left, but he didn't seem to be..... I wonder if he changed his mind after he sailed..... Hmmmm....."

Ana was still smiling about her memories, but managed, " He didn't sound very positive about Dusseldorf....."

At this point, Liz remembered that Ana was supposed to give her the address of Herr Lorenz and asked her for it. "Ah, yes, I have it right here," she said, heading for her writing desk. She pulled a drawer all the way out of the desk and reached at the back of the opening for something --- a small, thin, book the color of the raw wood interior of the opening. Taking a bit of paper, she wrote it down for Liz and handed it to her with a serious look, saying, "Don't lose it --- and destroy it when you leave him. You should go tomorrow;

my brother has the day off and can wait for you. Sunday he goes to church and won't drive."

With everything settled, she replaced the book behind the drawer and slid it back into its place. Then, she began to ask Liz the usual conversation questions --- about America and her trip. She had never traveled outside of Europe and not even much there, so she had an avid interest in America, asking if Liz knew any movie stars and if she seen the Grand Canyon. Liz had to disappoint her on one score: she knew no movie stars --- not even an "extra", though she had been within touching distance of a few more than once. At this disclosure, Ana went to the desk again and, opening a drawer, lifted out a scrapbook.

"See, I've got pictures of them all," she confided. "If you like, I can give you some."

Liz reminded her that she was on a journey in which she must travel light and Ana nodded her head in understanding, sympathizing with her for not wanting to add extra things to pack.....

They chatted about the pictures of the stars and the movies they had starred in for awhile longer, as well as other things that ladies share --- cooking and recipes and such --- but, the hour had grown late.

Finally, when she saw Liz' head nod, she said, "Oh, my, look at the time and I haven't even taken you to your room. It's on this level next to mine. I save it for family or friends."

Before long, Liz had been cozily tucked into a deep feather bed with a thick, fluffy down comforter. She thought she felt like a baby bird must feel and her eyelids simply refused to stay open one more minute.

❧Chapter 16 – Bern, Herr Lorenz❧

Liz slowly struggled back to consciousness from the deepest sleep she had ever known. Between the altitude, the brisk climate, and the sensation of floating in the midst of a lake of down, she almost wanted to stay asleep forever. She lingered, not wanting to give up one moment in her haven, but the bright sunshine streaming through the window drove sleep away and forced her, at last, to forsake the warm, cozy retreat, no matter how tightly she squeezed she eyelids together.

Finally, she opened them and looked at the window. What she saw was enchanting --- windows made up of many small panes of, perhaps, 6"x 8" pieces of glass. The sunlight was glowing white and dust motes in the air picked up the light, shining in their turn.

This made it easier to forsake the warmth of the down and she quickly changed into her clothes to hold her body heat. Looking at the clock, she saw that it was almost 9 o'clock and decided that it was time she looked for Ana.

Ana was waiting for her in the sitting room, having already prepared her other guests' breakfast and set it on the sideboard in the dining room. "Come, my dear, breakfast awaits you and you shall eat well….. We have quiche, fresh bread and sweet rolls, hot cocoa or coffee with fresh cream, and hot cereal if you wish it."

She showed Liz into the dining room and introduced her to the only guest remaining, a Signore Giuliano, who came at the end of winter each year to see the early spring flowers of the Swiss countryside. He ate quietly, listening to the ladies conversation and enjoying his quiche enough to take a second slice. After a bit, he left to seek the flowers beginning to bloom in the Alpine meadows among the patches of melting snow.

Liz and Ana visited over the coffee and sweet rolls, but, eventually, Ana's brother, Hans, knocked on the door and whisked Liz away to visit Herr Lorenz. The ride was not too far, some 30 minutes through the beautiful city and countryside, and soon she was walking up to his door. He was a hospitable man and asked her to bring Hans in for a bit of strudel and rich coffee in the kitchen with his sister, Hannalore, while he and Liz talked. Hans gladly agreed.

After hanging her coat, Herr Lorenz led Liz to a small study of sorts with a desk, a few comfortable chairs set at right angles with a table between and a pleasant fire in front. He indicated a chair and she sat down, as did he.

"Und so?" he began.

"Sprechen wir auf Deutsch oder Englisch?" she asked.

"Oh, English is fine by me," he said, with a wave of his hand and a nod of his head.

So, Liz began her story by asking the questions she had asked the others, "Did my husband visit you, Herr Lorenz?"

"Ach, dear child, call me Kurt. And, the answer to your question is 'yes'. He visited me in 1939 --- that was before the war..... It was spring, if I remember, but later than now. There were more flowers --- and less snow..... He came to talk about good trade agreements being the way to prevent wars and wanted me to help him with that and with research on some airplane hydraulics. I work more with dams and water, but the principles are the same, you know. He said that he would contact me, but once he left, pfffttt," he said, with a wave of his hand, "No more news of him. I thought that someone else got the government contract he was hoping for, so he had no need of an old man anymore."

"Did he tell you where he planned to visit while he was on this trip?"

"Yes, yes, he did..... He was planning on speaking to some of his colleagues --- or maybe only one..... .....at Heidelberg University. You know, they were taken over by the Nazis during the war..... Some say even much earlier."

"Was there anywhere else he mentioned?" she asked.

"Yes, he said that he had thought of going to Dusseldorf, but the man he wanted to meet there could meet him in Frankfurt, so he would be able to save some train fare and time. He spoke of Luxembourg and of visiting relatives there, as well..... An uncle or great-uncle, I believe..... Ach, perhaps a cousin....."

"Yes, those were to be some of his stops," she said. "So, it had not changed, except to eliminate Dusseldorf. And, did he tell you anything else?"

"Well, yes, it was a little bit strange….. He told me that he thought someone had been following him, but that he had changed trains suddenly, and they didn't seem to have followed him here, to Bern."

They both sat quietly in front of the fire digesting what Kurt had just said. He, wondering if he should not have divulged it and concerned that he had worried her. She, with her mind going a mile a minute, remembering the so obvious search of her ship stateroom in the harbor at Marseilles and her secretive contacts with Mr. Henri.

As people often do, when having followed their thoughts to a conclusion, they both began to speak at the same time, then each offered the other the opportunity to speak first. She wanted to hear what Kurt had to say, first, but he was a gentleman of the 'old school' and would not hear of it. So it was that she began…..

"I wish to tell you something, Herr Lorenz," and, at a look from him, "--- uh….. Kurt. When I was on board ship, in Marseilles harbor, my stateroom was ransacked. Nothing was taken that I could tell, so I don't believe that it was jewel thieves or such. But, I had been to see a Mr. d'Croixville in Marseilles, only he was no longer living there. I came away with a notebook and had placed it with some travel brochures, so it apparently went unnoticed. I found that it had a note stuck in a pocket slit into the cover and the note had strange marks and symbols on it."

"What kind of symbols," he asked.

"I don't know," she answered, "Just symbols….. I have the note with me if you would like to look at it."

"Yes, I would," he agreed, standing up and going to his desk, where he pulled a magnifying glass from a suede-lined wooden case.

She took it from her purse and handed it to him as he sat next to her again. He squinted through the magnifying glass at the small document, making little sounds of hmmm and mmmm as he looked at each part. Finally, he said, "My dear, this is an interesting document. It is a combination of things understandable --- and codes. Whoever created it is a genius or a code-breaker. They may be the same thing. I can tell you that it contains engineering symbols; however, they mean little or nothing to me without deciphering the rest. May I copy this and work on it after you leave? I would keep it hidden and safe --- and will let you know if I am able to decipher it."

Liz had concern written all over her face and Kurt had enough age to be an easy reader of faces. She stammered, "I….. I don't know," afraid to part with this one thing that seemed to pose a link to Franz.

Kurt understood and proposed, "Think on it and I will visit you on Monday morning at Ana's. It is my day for shopping so it is no trouble. If you decide that I may copy it, there will be time."

"Oh, yes, Kurt, that would be good," she said, with relief.

There was a knock on the door of the study and Kurt's sister came in to announce that lunch was ready and that Hans would be eating with them.

As Liz sat down at the ornate wood table, she fleetingly wondered why the Europeans ate such heavy meals at lunch and often a mere snack for dinner. For four people, the table seemed to be groaning with its offerings: brook trout, potatoes, sweet and sour cabbage, pickled beets, and fresh bread. They ate, but still had room for a cup of rich, strong coffee and large slices of the flakey-crusted strudel that Hannalore had baked that morning.

Finally, it came time for Hans and Liz to leave. The good-byes were said and Kurt winked at Liz as she left --- a secret signal to her that he would see her on Monday morning. She nodded and waved, acknowledging their arrangement, knowing that she would ultimately agree to let him copy the document.

Hans' car sped back to the old city portion of Bern on its peninsula, almost ringed like a moat by the river Aare. As she looked at the river, Liz wondered if the Swiss had held off intruders this way….. It would have been handy…..

Though it was late in the day, this afternoon she decided that she would look in the shops for a bit, since they might not be open on Sunday. Sunday could be for sightseeing, she mused, and Monday for her meeting with Kurt and, then, off to the train for Zurich.

Now that she had seen her two contacts, she felt a little bit keyed up and didn't think it could be attributed to the coffee at lunch. It was more a sense of having completed her research here and wanting to be going to the next place.

They reached Ana's house and she was told that supper was at 7 o'clock, so she should be back before then; also that it would be dark already --- so Ana strongly hinted that she might want to be back earlier. The sweet lady was so tactful.....

Liz walked for a long time --- and comfortably --- in her new walking shoes. The buildings were still beautiful and, yet, many were quite old. There were a number of fountains and bridges as well as the municipal buildings and museums. It was a lovely center city with many apartment buildings and homes, as well, and its suburbs spreading out in every direction across the river and also away from the peninsula. Ana had told her that at least 1/3 of the land of Zurich city was dense forest and she believed it, having seen some on the drive to Kurt's home. All in all, a lovely place to live, she decided.

By the time she returned, there still plenty of time to clean up for dinner and to help Ana set the table. They would be 6 for dinner: Ana, Liz, 2 boarders and 2 temporary roomers --- all of the latter, men.

It was a lively company. The men were all bachelors, all well educated, and all enamored of Liz from the moment they saw her. Ana smiled --- one of those indulgent smiles that mothers have when they see their daughters being the center of attention --- of a group of eligible men..... Liz was her own vivacious self --- one of the traits that drew Franz to her --- and the gentlemen ate it up like candy that they

couldn't get enough of.... The smile never left Ana's face --
- and when her young cousin who acted as kitchen helper
came in with the coffee and dessert --- fruit tarts this time ---
a look passed between them that said they both were aware
of how much the men liked this charming and intelligent
American.

Later, when everyone else had retired to their bedrooms,
except Liz, who was ensconced in a chair in Ana's sitting
room, Ana said to her young cousin, when she went to the
kitchen for more cocoa, "See how the men admire an
educated woman? You must continue with your schooling,"
shaking her finger at her. "You could be the same with a
little polish and verve. Who knows how high you might
marry, then?"

Liz, blithely unaware of all of this, stared into the fire like
some gypsy woman, as though asking it for answers to all of
her questions. The warmth made her fall into a meditative
state somewhat like a light trance and she thought she saw
Franz and was sure she could hear him saying her name and
asking him to come to her --- in French. The sound of his
longing was almost unbearable to her and she came back to
her senses and her awareness of the room --- and the cocoa
on the table by her side. Ana, who by then had returned to
the room, asked, "Were you dreaming, Liz?"

"No, no I don't think so," Liz answered. "I was just
dozing."

The two of them talked for awhile longer, then Liz went off
to her room to sleep in the featherbed and lose track of
everything in the serenity of that ultimate comfort and

warmth. As she sank into the buoyancy of the feathers, and with the down comforter above her, she thought fleetingly of Franz, but without regrets even, saw his face fade as the power of the bed took over.

ᏕᎧChapter 17 – Bern, Sunday᎙

Liz woke early again, surprised by her urge to spring from under the heavenly covers and dress for breakfast. It must be true what they say about fresh, mountain air, she thought as she combed her shoulder-length light brown hair in front of the mirror….. By 7:30, she was in the kitchen with Ana, sipping from time to time from a steaming cup of coffee on the counter, and helping to prepare breakfast for the boarders. She showed Ana a favorite of her own --- thinly sliced apples or pears on toast, with or without butter.

Oh, I will miss this one when she's gone on, thought Ana…..

Breakfast was a festive meal --- none of the boarders needed to rush off to work or school. They all would do as they pleased, but Ana and Liz were going to church at the Swiss Reformed Church on Zeughausgasse in the old city, dating from the 12th century. Liz was excited to see the architecture and had never been to a religious service of the Swiss Reformed Church, so this would be a new experience as well.

She was not disappointed in the church's architecture at all. Not a staunch churchgoer, she visited many churches to observe services and to admire the architecture, especially of older buildings. This one had stood for about 800 years and that was a noteworthy feat….. The service was orderly and, though the minister waxed long in his sermon, she enjoyed it for the most part, especially the singing.

Afterward, they walked by some other old churches in the vicinity, the Cathedral of Bern on Munsterplatz, begun in the early 15th century, and the Church of Saint Peter and St. Paul, dating to the mid-1800's, during the American Civil War. Both were more grand and glorious than the beautiful simplicity of the older building, but she preferred it for that --- and its age…..

By the time they returned, in the mid-afternoon, they had built up quite an appetite for the roasting goose Ana's cousin had been basting in the oven --- as had the boarders, who had been lounging in the dining room over their coffee for the last hour or so….. Ana and Liz removed their coats and patted their hair in the foyer mirror before entering the dining room and the gentlemen all stood up when they saw them.

Ana said, "Sit, sit, be comfortable," and flapped her hands to let them know what she meant. As a group, they sat on cue. It amused Liz, but she managed to hold her giggle in rather than risk embarrassing them.

Ana indicated that Liz should stay and entertain them while she gave the goose a final basting and helped her cousin to get the meal into serving dishes. Liz complied, enjoying the company --- and the attention as well --- of these four gentlemen. They talked about interesting things, not just what their neighbors were doing or the economy.

It seemed like mere minutes had passed when Ana appeared in the doorway with the goose on a bed of rice cooked with mushrooms. Her cousin followed, with a tray of serving dishes filled with viands fit for a king. When she had put them on the table, she went back to the kitchen for more and, when they were all unloaded, Ana invited her to eat with them. She quickly went back to the kitchen with the tray, washed her hands, patted her hair, and picking up a place setting, returned to the dining room to slip into a vacant chair.

The conversation was enjoyed as much as the excellent food of Ana's establishment. As she listened to the talk swirling around her, Ana thought what a wonderful thing it was to be involved with the young, for it keeps one's mind active. She looked at her young cousin, sidewise, and saw that she was gaily laughing and holding her own in the conversations. This pleased her --- the girl had taken her admonishment to heart. Who knew but that one of these four might someday be a suitor? Or, perhaps, someone of higher status still..... Her eyes half-lidded, she thought of how high this girl might reach and was pleased with herself for sponsoring her --- and with Liz for being a fortuitous example.....

They had been at table for more than an hour before anyone called for dessert. Now, it was the cousin's turn to truly shine, for she had made a dark chocolate cake containing preserved cherries from the last season and poured a sweet sauce made with Kirsch liquor over it all. As she entered, bearing her treasure on a cake plate, she was treated to a hearty round of applause..... She smiled from ear to ear and that smile told it all to Ana….. Confidence in her woman-hood! A must-have for every woman.

All of them lingered over the sweet treat of the cake, drinking coffee with fresh cream and sugar, a la Suisse….. But, now, with their bellies full and their sweet tooth sated, they were a very mellow group. Ana and her cousin took the food to the kitchen, then cleared the table, but Ana shooed the girl back to the dining room to visit and put the food away herself, stacking the dishes in the sink to be washed later. Now was the time for alliances, not clean-ups…..

She returned to the dining room and asked them to retire to the great room, much like a living room or parlor. There, the young people found a game to play called The Landlord Game, a game where money was earned through buying and renting out properties on a game board and all joined in the play on a card table, while Ana sat in a chair, crocheting a new scarf. Ah, how they reminded her of herself and her husband…..

In time, the winner was named and they all drifted into chairs to listen to music on the record player. One of the boarders found some records of classical music --- opera, some Chopin, and a little Debussy. They listened to the Chopin, raptly, the sweetness and lightness of the music for ballet, Les Sylphides, seeming like a perfect ending to their perfect day. Eventually, as the hour grew late, they said their goodnights, each going to their own room, except Ana and her cousin, who finished in the kitchen. Liz went off to sleep instantly, once her head touched the pillow, a sleep so deep that she didn't even hear the wind howling outside.

❧Chapter 18 – Bern, Monday☙

Morning had broken and Liz lay there in the obscenely comfortable featherbed, looking up at the ceiling and thinking about how much she had enjoyed the time she spent here. It would be hard to leave and if she had no Franz to search for, maybe she wouldn't have --- at least not for awhile. It had given her something she had lost through his disappearance and long absence --- the lightheartedness of youth..... A precious commodity, too easily taken from us..... It is one of the worst parts of war --- that it takes our innocence away --- she decided.

Finally, she took off the comforter and went to the window. The howling wind had brought light snow flurries and now the sun had come out and was shining on the dusting of new snow and making it glisten like diamonds. Its beauty enchanted her and she could hardly tear herself away to do her packing,

By 9 o'clock, she came to the table and Ana, who strongly believed that people should not eat alone --- especially guests --- sat with her as she breakfasted on mushroom and egg quiche with her coffee. She could tell that there was a stillness in Liz and asked if she wanted to talk.

Liz opened up to her and talked about what she had been thinking and Ana, patting her hand, said, "I understand, my dear, I understand. I lost my husband when I was younger, not so old." Liz nodded her head and a shy smile tickled the corners of her mouth..... Ana saw this and smiled back, saying, "That's it, we must live onward and, happy is better than sad. They would want us to be happy."

Liz suddenly remembered that she had told Kurt that she might let him copy the notes from the d'Croixville notebook today. As she had surmised earlier, she would allow it. Perhaps he could make some sense out of it, after all. By this time, it was closing on 10:30 and the ladies were on their 3rd cup of coffee. Liz began to walk to her bedroom to retrieve the note when the bell at the front door rang. The ladies exchanged glances and Liz, already up, went to answer it.

"Good morning, good morning," Kurt Lorenz exclaimed when he saw her framed in the doorway.

"And to you, as well," Liz said. "Please come in."

He entered and she took him to the dining room to say hello to Ana and wait there as she retrieved the paper.

When she returned, they were deeply engrossed in comparing notes on the whereabouts of friends since the war. It had not touched Switzerland so harshly as many of the countries in Europe, but there were some who had fled to the United States and other countries or to their summer chalets in the very high mountains --- away from the Nazis and the war. They turned from their coffee and conversation to her as she re-entered the room.

Ana said, "I'll go and make more coffee for us while you talk," and left the room, after refilling Liz' cup, which finished off the pot.

Kurt smiled at Liz and she began to talk to him, saying, "I feel that it would be all right for you to copy these characters and see what you can make of them, but please don't show them to others, for these are still uncertain times."

Kurt nodded and said, "Exactly the advice I was going to give you, my dear. These are indeed uncertain times and, though the war is over, do not believe that all of the Nazi sympathizers are gone. No, they have merely shifted their faces in another direction. Have caution always. You trusted me and I am worthy of that trust, but it could as easily have been otherwise....."

Liz felt admonished and rightly so --- she *was* trusting. She had not experienced the war here, or any other war, in person. She would be more careful from today on. Meanwhile, she gave him the note to copy, which he finished just as Ana, was bringing in the fresh pot of coffee.

He offered to take Liz to the train station, but Ana's brother was already coming to get her, so he bid them good-bye after another cup of coffee and a slice of Ana's apple strudel, which she had brought out with the coffee. As he departed, he took Liz' hands and said, "If you should find that husband of yours, I hope that you will come and visit me before you return to the United States."

Hans came and took Liz to the station on time after she bestowed many hugs and promises on Ana to return. As Liz boarded, she turned to look back at the white fairyland and said, to herself, I'll be back. That is for certain.

The train to Zurich was full of tourists who, deprived during the war of travel, were making up for lost time. While there were a few vacant seats for the 90-mile trip, she noted that there were not many.

It was nice to ride in the daytime --- one could see more, though the 'more' here happened to be very white this day. Liz made the best of it and watched the tourists --- most, people with high hopes of skiing the slopes. This train had a dining car and she wandered back to it after awhile, since she had eaten no lunch and did not know what accommodations she would encounter in Zurich. In the dining car, there were few travelers, most having eaten before the trip. However, there were enough that no table was empty and she must sit with a stranger, a man, who looked out the window the whole time. Finally, when no one was looking, he slid a piece of paper toward her and she recognized his hand --- this was Mr. Henri! His disguise was so good that she could not recognize his face! And, she had the forethought to not stare at him, lest she break his cover.

He had just finished his meal, it seemed and soon his dessert and coffee were finished as well. He departed with a tip of his hat to her, ostensibly a polite stranger.....

After dinner, she made her way to the restroom and, locking the door behind her, she pulled the note out of the napkin she'd used to shift it to her purse and read it at last

You will be met at the station by Karl Berger, Ana's brother-in-law. You will stay with him and his wife for 2 nights and continue on Wednesday morning to Stuttgart on the 10:25 train. You will be met there by a Mr. Henning who will be a lead, but who will also take you to Mr. Jaeger, another lead. You will spend 2 nights with Henning and his wife, then go on to Heidelberg on the 10 a.m. train. You will be contacted.

H.

Liz sat there stunned at what she had read. So many places so fast..... Well, she hadn't thought it would be a picnic..... She slipped the note into her coin purse to keep it safe --- too many directions to memorize with certainty.

She returned to the dining car for dessert and a cup of tea. Soon, they would pull into the Zurich train station and she would meet Ana's brother-in-law..... She sat and enjoyed the view and the food --- until the other passengers began to get hungry and drifted in. At that point, she made her way back to her own car and read until the announcement that they would be in Zurich soon.

At the Zurich station, she was, indeed, met by Mr. Berger, a nice looking man with kind eyes. Ah, Ana must have loved her husband if he was thus.....

He drove her home to meet his wife, another Ana almost, who gave her cocoa and cookies and put her to bed early, for all the world like one of her children, with the words 'the mountain air is tiring'.

Liz' fingers had a mind of their own, though, and they pleasured her as only Franz knew how to do, slipping and sliding between her lower lips as easily as if they were greased. As she felt her passion rise, she thought of Franz and their love-making, his body heavy on hers, a good heavy, making her feel his power. Eyes closed, she smiled and increased the tempo of her fingers as they pleasured her in the one way she could duplicate.

As her muscles clenched and strained toward her ecstasy, the fluttering of tiny orgasms rippled through her loins. Her hips swayed from front to back, in a rhythm she had so enjoyed with Franz inside of her, and so loved to feel with the man she adored. Their connection was special, so hot, so satisfying, that she could not imagine any other --- ever. He had to be alive!

As she reached her final peak, she bit down on the down comforter to stifle her moan of completion as the waves of orgasm rippled through her vagina and the sensation ran down her legs. She could not move and, soon, she slept.....

Ꮗ Chapter 19 – Zurich, Tuesday Ꮗ

This day dawned bright, but it was not the same as Ana's house. The featherbed was there; the down comforter was there; but she knew there was no Ana in the kitchen.

As she lay there, she thought of what Kurt had said the day before --- be cautious --- and wondered what had made her so trusting of Mr. Henri, a complete stranger. After thinking on it for some time, she decided that it was his gentlemanly demeanor, coupled with the fact that he had brought her successfully to so many of the people she was searching for. It was as if he were her guardian angel and, somehow, she felt, deep inside, that he could be trusted.

Having better defined her thoughts about him, Liz got out of bed and, after bathing and dressing, went in search of the dining room.

"Ah, there you are!" she heard from the kitchen when she found the adjoining dining room. It was Ana's sister-in-law, Gabi, who called out, "Are you hungry?"

"Yes, I am," answered Liz.

"Then, come and help me with the breakfast." Gabi said.

Liz gladly pitched in and soon they had porridge, sweet rolls, and coffee on the table.

Ana's brother-in-law, Karl, was not so outgoing as she was: he ate quietly and if it were not for Gabi's occasional remarks, there would have been no conversation at all. Liz felt it was a little somber and she wondered if Ana's husband had been like this, too.

After breakfast, Karl asked her to come into the sitting room and speak with him. Expecting him to be as taciturn as he was over breakfast, she was surprised to find him more talkative. "So, you are looking for your husband," he said.

"Yes, I am. Did you meet him?"

"Yes, I did meet him. He was traveling, like you, on the way to Stuttgart and he stopped to spend the night here. It was not a long visit, but we spoke and he told me of his dreams for the future. He also talked about you. He was sad to be so far away from you, I think. You are not married so long....."

"Three years, almost," Liz answered, looking wistful.

Karl noted the look and said, "You love him very much, no?"

Liz' eyes began to water and she choked out, "Yes."

"There, there, little one, you will see him again. I am sure of it."

"Are you?" she asked.

"Yes, I truly believe that you will find him."

Then, she began to ask the same questions she had asked the others about Franz and where he had said was going. The answers were the same and she now knew that he had gotten as far as Zurich. Apparently, there was no more information to be had. So, she asked if they would take her on a sightseeing adventure.

Neither knew what to make of this, but they obliged her. The snow was not too deep and much had already melted, so the going was not very difficult for the car. After showing her many old buildings, they lunched in a small restaurant and then took her to the Swiss National Museum, a favorite with tourists. She was intrigued with the architecture, but the collections were even more exciting --- ancient stained glass and painted furniture, even old coins and wooden panels and other religious artifacts. They were all entranced with the vastness of the collection and the age of so many of the objects.

Finally, the museum was ready to close and they had to leave. Liz wanted to get a good night's sleep, for they would have to leave early to make the 10:25 a.m. train, so she was glad that Gabi was able to heat up some sausages and serve them with sauerkraut and hot potato salad.

They visited for awhile, but the outing in the fresh air had tired them all and they made an early night of it, knowing that it would be an early morning.

Liz lay there in her bed, dozing, but waking again. Finally, she settled into sleep and only a short time had passed when she woke up knowing that she had seen Franz. At first, she thought he was there in the room, but then she began to wonder if it had been a dream. It had been so real. She had seen him and he was calling her name and speaking to her in French, but why in French --- again? She somehow managed to find her way back to sleep, but it was not as restful as the night before had been.

ᔐChapter 20 – Zurich to Stuttgart᙭

By 8:15, they were all in the kitchen --- with Liz' luggage waiting by the front door. Gabi was busy making breakfast and brought each of them a bowl of soft-boiled eggs mixed with rye bread toasted and torn into small pieces to soak up the yolk. Of course, the usual hot mugs of coffee appeared, as well, anointed with rich cream and sugar. At home, Liz usually drank hers black or with a little milk, but the Swiss way was certainly good --- even the chocolate they sometimes added.

They talked about the museum and the wonderful things they had seen. Karl and Gabi, not usually in the habit of going to cultural places, had been surprised by their own interest once they began to tour the collections. Liz was pleased that their conversation sounded as though they might have found a new pastime and she asked about the other museums and galleries in Zurich to stimulate their interest.

As she and Karl left for the train station, she impulsively hugged Gabi and told her that she looked forward to seeing her again. Gabi smiled shyly, surprised by her earnestness, and Liz, seeing it, smiled broadly and hugged her once more.

The snow of the day before was almost gone and the trip to the station went smoothly. Liz, looking out the window, as they drove to the station, knew that she would return here as well --- so many beautiful things to see and collections to explore.....

At the station, while a porter loaded her luggage on his cart, Liz thanked Karl again for the information he had given her --- which had let her know that Franz had come as far as Zurich. She pressed this point upon him, because she wanted him to know that even this small information had helped her in her quest.

He took her hand and bowed over it as a gesture of respect, then said good-bye and went to move his car out of the temporary parking zone. He waved as he moved it and she nodded her head in acknowledgement, both hands full by now with her purse and the bag of refreshments that Gabi had insisted she take, then turned to catch up to the porter who was already wheeling her belongings toward the ticket counter.

Finally, with the ticket in her purse, there was nothing to do but sit and wait for the train to arrive and the announcement to board. As she waited, she pursued her hobby --- watching people in public places. Many were easy to figure out --- the young families on spring holiday, the students, the businessmen, even the woman dressed in black and holding a handkerchief to her eyes from time to time. There was one man, however, who didn't fit any of the usual categories. It was as though he had put an invisible shield around him and she found him a mystery.

When her train pulled into the station, disgorged its departing passengers, and made the call for boarding passengers, she noted that he stood up and walked to the same train. She allowed him to board ahead of her so that she could choose a seat away from his vicinity, preferring to watch him at a distance.....

True to the schedule, and with an attention to detail and exactitude as precise as the clocks the Swiss had for so long been famous for, the train pulled away at exactly 10:25.

As they gathered speed and the countryside, now with only patches of the recent snow lingering here and there, began to move by faster, she watched out the window, where she had been lucky enough to find a seat. So beautiful, her mind said --- almost aloud.

She enjoyed the clackety-clack of the wheels on the rails, the vibration of their passage, and the feeling of being in a time capsule, of sorts, heading to a distant place with a group of people. It reminded her of H.G. Wells' book, The Time Machine, because it made her feel as though time had been compressed --- when she could move so rapidly from one location to another.

Musing this way, and watching the beautiful countryside passing by her window, she fell into a contemplative state and felt a knowing that Franz still lived, a sense that she could feel his energy. She could hear him calling her name and speaking to her, as though from a great distance, and she sat there listening for a long time, wondering why he kept using French, but never thinking to ask him while it was happening.

The trip was only about 130 miles, though there were many stops, the first being for identification at the border.

Passengers came and went as the train stopped in cities and towns along the way. This was certainly a local, not an express, but she didn't mind --- it made the time pass more interestingly. She ate from Gabi's package of food along the way: sandwiches, cookies and other pastry, a bottle of spring water, and even a leftover sausage.

In the late afternoon, it was her turn to step down from the train. She hurried into the station from the platform and looked for a porter. Then, she saw the man she had seen getting on her train in Zurich. He had left the train here, as well. It made her feel strange.

As she neared the baggage claim office, she saw a man standing with a card in his hand. Written on it was "Hart". She was startled to see her name, but somehow knew it was for her, so she went up to him and asked who he was looking for --- he said, "A Miss Hart. Are you she?"

Liz answered in the affirmative and, after hearing that this was the anticipated Mr. Henning who would put her up and take her to Mr. Jaeger, they found a porter and claimed her luggage.

Mr. Henning was an older gentleman, looking a bit like Santa Claus without the beard and the 40 extra pounds around the tummy. He was also the essence of gentlemanly politeness and treated her as though she were a rare and precious jewel.

When they arrived via taxi to his home, near suppertime, she discovered that he treated his wife in the same deferential manner, so it must be his way of interfacing with women in general.

Frau Henning was just as much a dear as her husband. She embraced Liz and asked him to take the luggage upstairs for her, then pulled her into the dining room and sat her down at the table. It was to be just the 3 of them, Liz could see, by the place settings.

Frau Henning quickly brought her a glass of wine and said it would help her to recover from her journey. Liz asked if she could help in the kitchen, but was denied that privilege with, "Oh, no, Heinrich, my husband, would never allow that --- you are a guest and he will want to talk with you."

"Who will want to talk with her?" called a voice from the hallway.

"You, Mein Liebling," his wife called back.

"Ah," he said, coming into the dining room, "And what does the world's finest cook have for us to eat tonight?"

Liz was not surprised to see a glow coming from the world's finest cook as she beamed at her husband and said, "I have cooked hasenpfeffer, your favorite. And, dumplings, sweet and sour cabbage, and cherry strudel with the cherries I preserved last summer."

"Oh, you make my mouth water! Wait until you taste this, Miss Hart!"

Liz smiled widely. These two were of the same cloth as Ana and she felt right at home.

The dinner was a delight --- both the food and the conversation --- and, after eating her fill of both dinner and dessert, she was refused the honor of helping to clean up the dishes and told that it was time for her to talk with Heinrich over another glass of wine. So it was that their conversation began.

He asked, "You are looking for your husband, is it so?"

Liz answered that she was.

"You want to know if I met him," he began, "Yes, I did --- in 1939. We knew that the war was coming, but it had not happened, yet….. He was traveling to many cities and…… …..consulting with engineers and company owners, …..talking about commerce for peace. When I did not hear more from him, I thought that …..perhaps the Nazis did not like his ideas and arrested him."

"Thank you for letting me know that he got this far. It means very much to me and this way I can go forward to the other cities until I find out where the chain is broken," she said, with tears in her eyes.

Ever the gentleman, Heinrich pulled out his handkerchief and handed it to her, saying, "I am sorry to see your tears, but I am happy that I may have helped you."

"Yes, yes, you have helped so much."

Frau Henning came in at that moment and said, "Ah, I see that it is time for no more wine. Gut, we switch to hot milk with schnapps. You will sleep well."

Liz had to smile at her grasp of the situation and her candid solution. Heinrich smiled, too, saying, "Mama knows best."

This brought a chuckle from deep within Liz and an echoing response from Heinrich, though he really didn't completely understand why she was chuckling, just that her soft laughter made him feel happy.

At that moment, in came his Frau with one glass of the warm milk, enhanced with a liberal dose of his best schnapps. "None for me?" he asked, pulling a long face.

She laughed, "Ach, du! Of course, I will make one for you, too, but you may need to help her upstairs and for that you may not be drunk."

Now it was his turn to say. "Ach, du! I am never drunk with liquor, only with love --- for you...."

She laughed and almost spilled the milk as she was handing it to Liz. Liz, hearing their banter, felt like laughing, too. What a congenial pair, she thought as she sipped the warming beverage.

It was not long before Heinrich was seeing her to her room and showing her where the amenities were. His duty done, he left her and headed downstairs for his own dose of the libation. By then, she was so sleepy that she could barely undress. Her fingers felt like sausages and the buttonholes seemed to have shrunk. In the end, she pulled the blouse over her head, slipped out of her skirt, underclothes, shoes and stockings, and crawled, naked as a jaybird, beneath the thick down comforters and the featherbed. In spite of the outer chill, with the schnapps and milk warming her from within, she fell asleep without a moment's hesitation.

⤳Chapter 21 – Stuttgart⤳

The day dawned gray and dismal --- somehow it made everything seem much more somber and depressing than it actually was. Fortunately, Liz had a large cache of buoyancy to keep her spirits afloat. Also, fortunately, so did the Hennings. When she went down to the kitchen, Frau Henning was already making pork sausages with fried potatoes and toasted rye bread. Liz could smell the coffee and asked if she might have a cup. Her hostess said, "Of course, there," pointing it out, "is where I keep the cups and the cream is in the window." Liz smiled --- she had not seen anyone keep milk in-between double windows since she was a child visiting her aunt in Boston. The double windows were meant to keep the heat inside in winter, but they worked marvelously at keeping milk and such things as cold --- or colder than --- any icebox, or even a refrigerator.

As she stood there sipping her warm brew, she asked if she could help, but Frau Henning had her every action down to a fine science and needed no help --- or distraction --- in creating her culinary miracles. So, Liz watched --- and learned --- how it was done.

Soon, Frau Henning said, "My name is Frieda, you know, Heinrich always forgets to tell people. So, now, we take the breakfast to the table und ess!"

Liz smiled, then helped her to dish it onto the platters and take it to the dining room. Heinrich, coming into the room, commented, "Ah, what smells so wonderful?"

Frieda answered, "Sausages from Herr Mauer's farm. His is the best."

Heinrich lit up like a cherub and quickly sat down. Liz retrieved her cup of coffee from the kitchen and brought out the coffee pot as well, while Frieda trailed with the cream and sugar.

While Heinrich was not of a religious nature, he couldn't help but comment on how wonderful it was to have good food, well cooked, and pleasant company to eat it with, to make life worthwhile --- as he beamed beatifically at the two ladies. Frieda beamed right back at him and Liz smiled at their loving interaction after so many years, thinking, this was how she wanted it to be for Franz and her.....

The thought tugged at her heart and she felt a little pain at the uncertainty, for a moment, then banished the thought that he might not be alive out of her consciousness and into oblivion, where it belonged, with a vengeance. Her Franz was alive --- she knew it and until someone showed her his body she would never doubt it again.

When they had finished their breakfast, he and Liz boarded a streetcar to travel the 12 or so blocks to their destination --- in case the gloom was presaging rain --- and it was about 11 a.m. when they reached their destination, an apartment building looking a little run down from the toll of time and the war. The hauswart, a janitor, was washing the front steps and said to go in, since she had seen Heinrich before. The apartment was on the 3rd floor and it was an interesting experience ascending the broad, elegant, marble staircase after seeing the shabbiness of the exterior. Liz wondered, aloud, if this had, at one time, been an elegant home and been turned into an apartment building. Heinrich looked around him as they stepped into the hallway of the third floor and said, "Perhaps. It could be. It was a fancy address at one time. This is a very old building, much older than it looks."

Liz smiled. To her eyes it looked pretty old, indeed.

Heinrich knocked on the door, then, after a minute or so, he knocked again, whispering to Liz, "He's a little hard of hearing at times."

Finally, a quavering voice behind the door asked, "Who is there?"

Heinrich replied, "Henning!"

"Ach, ich hab' vergessen!!!" came the reply.

The door opened immediately and a gnome stood there. Well, not exactly a real gnome, but he could have passed for one easily: shorter than Liz by a head, large pointy ears and nose, fingers long and boney, and body diminutive. The gnome, who turned out to be Herr Jaeger, invited them to enter, then closed the door, locked it, and went quickly before them to tidy the chairs he offered them. He had been using them to sort some papers; he told them by way of explanation.

He offered them tea, which they accepted, due to his earnestness in wanting to be a good host. Then, as they waited for the tea water to boil, they began to talk, first of mundane things, which so often lead into conversations which are to be of great import, and then of greater ideas. They discussed the war and its impact on the world --- shortly into this, the gnome served tea and cookies; very nice cookies called Sand Tarts, which consisted of two rather plain cookies, sandwiched together with raspberry jam. They were so delicate they would have fallen apart if not for the jam.

As they enjoyed their tea, they discussed further the implications of the war on the world and the individual countries, involved or not --- though its impact must have been felt to some extent almost everywhere.

Finally, after visiting for nearly 2 hours, Herr Jaeger said to Liz, "You wish to know about your husband, yes?" looking at her for confirmation.

"Yes, I do --- anything you know, even if it doesn't seem important to you," she replied without hesitation.

"Let me see..... It would have been 1939..... in the spring..... like now..... no, a little later..... He came to see me about a number of things..... business..... addresses of some friends..... and about the war..... I believe, yes, I believe that he was asking on behalf of your government --- not by what he asked, but by the way he asked it..... It seemed too detailed for a businessman to ask or to need to know. It surprised me."

Liz was startled. This was the first hint that Franz had been in Europe at the request of the government. But, which branch would it be? They all acted independently of each other back before the SSO began in 1940. She plied him further, with, "Do you have any thoughts on which branch of the government he could have been working for?"

Herr Jaeger's diminutive brow furrowed as he thought, trying to pull up elusive memories from 7 years earlier. "I do not believe that it was one of the military services, my dear..... because they are more rigid..... in their actions and more uniform-like in their attire. When soldiers are at the swimming pool, it is as though they have on an invisible uniform. Do you understand?"

"Yes, I think I do," Liz answered; remembering the many friends of hers whose husbands had come home and couldn't seem to relax into civilian life.

"So," continued Herr Jaeger, "I believe that, perhaps, it is the Department of State or some other civilian government department. I cannot discount it, but he does not seem to be the type for industrial espionage. He is a very astute man, intelligent and perceptive --- and good --- a good heart, a kind heart."

The tears sprang forth as she heard this beautiful tribute to her husband and then she reached into her purse for a handkerchief to dab at her eyes. "Yes, he is a good man, Herr Jaeger," she found her mouth saying, "He is all that you say of him, perhaps even a spy for the government, but I don't know that or even know how I could find it out..... Do you?"

Herr Jaeger pinched his nose to stifle the beginnings of a sneeze, then continued where he had left off, with, "The Department of State seems to me to be the most likely one here. They are not good at standing behind their spies, either, you may be warned. Very concerned about image, those guys. I think they even lie to themselves. I will listen very closely to what I hear in the future about him or about their spies who have been discovered. I am no Nazi, be assured, but it is still disconcerting to see spies watching even the benign governments --- those who were neutral."

Then he turned the discussion to the present, with, "Now, you will be going next to Heidelberg if you are following his path. Be certain to take every caution. The Nazis were very entrenched there, even before the war, and, though they have cleaned house, some still are hiding there, behind their degrees. Perhaps it is your husband's visit there that has caused him to be called a defector. I am surprised that he would go there on business."

"Well, he didn't actually plan to visit the University, rather individuals….," Liz said.

"Yes, yes, I see, but even to go into the vicinity….. do you see what I mean?" Jaeger asked.

"I understand," she said, "I will be careful --- very careful," remembering Marseilles and the ransacking of her cabin.

During their visit, she had come to respect Herr Jaeger's intellect and no longer saw him as a gnome --- or, at least, not a foolish one…..

Heinrich and Liz returned to the apartment the same way they had left --- via streetcar --- at almost 3 o'clock. Frieda was delighted to see them --- she had been basting the duck in her oven for them, hoping it wouldn't go dry, but she needn't have worried; it was still juicy and succulent, and the roasted root vegetables were exactly done as well. She had made fresh bread and some bakery to round out the meal. Afterward, they sat and visited as they had at every meal in this house.

Liz enjoyed their company and would be sorry to say good-bye just as when she had said it to Ana. These would be lifelong friends, she felt.

In her musings, suddenly, she heard the name Franz enter the conversation and was right in the thick of it immediately, with, "Franz?"

"Yes, Franz Prater, a neighbor down the street. He brings us fish from time to time. I said it was a shame he had none yesterday, so I had to cook a duck."

"Oh, I'm sorry, my mind was wandering and I thought you meant my husband," Liz said.

"I think you are a little tired, my dear, perhaps a nap until supper?" coaxed Frieda.

"That sounds good. If I don't wake up, just let me sleep until morning, but remember that I must meet a 10 o'clock train….."

Liz went up to bed and this time slept in her nightgown. Indeed, her belly was so full with the excellent duck and vegetables, to say nothing of the baked goods, that she knew there was no need for supper.

This evening, when her thoughts turned to Franz, she didn't feel like remembering his hands on her body --- or, at least, not enough to conquer the lethargy of a very full belly --- rather, she concentrated on the times he had been calling out to her and felt that energy getting stronger. She had been remembering their love-making, because that had made her feel he was still alive, through the vitality of that life force, that procreative power, but now, though that was wonderful, she could feel it though his calling as well. Somehow, she sensed that he felt her coming closer and closer to finding out where he had disappeared and that would lead her to where he was.....

And, as she drifted to sleep, she could hear him calling again.

❧Chapter 22 – Stuttgart to Heidelberg❧

With her train leaving at 10 o'clock, Frieda made certain that Liz was awake at 7 a.m. to eat a hearty breakfast and pack her belongings. She hated to see her leave, but knew that some things must be.

She had asked a neighbor whose brother drove a taxi to bring it around at 8:45 to insure her arrival on time.

Meanwhile, Liz must have a bag of food for a snack. It was only about 65 miles to Heidelberg, but who knew how soon she would eat…..

Liz left on time for the station, with the neighbor's brother and Heinrich in the front seat of the taxi --- two stalwart men to see her safely into the station. Frieda hugged her and cried a little --- as did Liz, but she knew she would be back --- someday…..

It did not take long to make the journey to the station --- 20 minutes or so --- and the taxi waited for Heinrich's return when he helped her find a porter to take her luggage to the baggage check office. Once found, Heinrich gave her a bear hug and said good-bye. As he turned, she could see tears on his eyelashes and said, "I will come back some day soon to visit, you know."

He turned back and taking both of her hands in his, said, "Frieda will be so happy!"

"I will, too," she answered. Then, he hugged her again and left with a smile spread across his face that made his cheeks look like two rosy apples.

She watched him leave the station and went to see if the train had arrived, yet. It had not, so she bought a newspaper and began to read, little noticing that a man had taken a seat on the bench next to her. Without looking at her he said, softly, "I will leave a note inside of a handkerchief on my seat when I leave. Pretend it has dropped from your pocket, then take it with you. Read the note on the train."

In 10 minutes, or so, he left and she pretended be looking for her handkerchief in the pocket of her coat, then picked up the one he had left, a dainty one edged in crocheted lace, dabbed at her nose and put it in her pocket.

Shortly afterward, the announcement was made that her train had arrived and passengers were leaving it. About 5 minutes later, the announcer invited the departing passengers to climb aboard and find their seats. Liz picked up her purse, the newspaper, and her bag of food and joined the throng.

She found a seat next to the window and was happy that she would be able to watch the countryside slide by. The day was partly cloudy rather than the dark, dismal gray, of the day before, and it gave a much happier look to the scenery. As they pulled away from the station, her eyes even caught a momentary ray of sunlight, looking like something from a painting, in one of the churches in Bern.

After a bit, she asked the lady next to her to watch her seat, offering to share some of the bakery she'd left in the bag with her, while she used the powder room. The lady smiled and agreed and Liz was off to a bit of privacy in which to read her note. Luckily, no one was using the facilities, yet, and she didn't have to wait. She opened the note with the greatest of curiosity and read:

You will be met at the station in Heidelberg by Frau Herta Schreihart. She will have a room for you and she is a lead. While there, you will meet Prof. Alfred Weber, an economist and lecturer at Heidelberg University. He is a lead and you can trust him and Herta as well. You will spend the weekend there and leave for Frankfurt on Monday at 1:00 pm.

When you arrive in Frankfurt, you will take a taxi to 22 Schifferstrasse, where you will be provided a room for the night. You will ask the taxi to wait and, once you have taken your luggage to your room, you will proceed via the taxi to The Blue Note Restaurant, which address the driver is sure to know. Mr. Froehlich will be waiting there for you. He is a lead.

On Tuesday morning at 11:15, you will leave by train for Luxembourg City, Luxembourg. It is a journey of about 150 miles --- longer than the others --- and, depending on the amount of stops it makes, it may be late evening when you arrive. There is a room booked for you in the Pension Moselle and a taxi driver will be waiting at the station for you. You will be contacted. H.

Again, so much that she couldn't remember it all, but it did cut down on the amount of times they had to meet....... Into the secret compartment in her compact it went and, after using the facilities, she returned to her seat. The lady who had saved it for her was very happy to visit with her and share her gifts from Frieda and they passed the next few hours in conversation and in looking at the beautiful spring scenery.

The ride was indeed short, merely a few hours and she was there. Waving good-bye to her temporary friend, she stepped down from the train and almost into Frau Herta Schreihart, who was waiting there.

"Komm' mit mir," she said.

"Sind sie Frau Schreihart?" Liz asked, echoing her German.

"Ja, ja….."

When they had moved away from the other passengers, Frau Schreihart said, quietly, "We will pick up your baggage, now, and go to my house. Speak German in front of others."

Liz obliged her at the baggage claim and with the porter, until the luggage was safely put into the Frau's car and they were on their way. "Why the German," she asked.

"We do not want you to stand out here. The University was a Nazi machine during the war and there may be some of that lingering even with the denazification. Be cautious when you speak for the walls may have ears…..," came the answer.

Liz thought for a moment --- this rang true and she knew she must be watchful. She and Franz had not traveled as far into

Germany on their honeymoon due to the unrest they felt brewing --- and, to an extent, she could feel that unrest still, as the Nazis and the Nazi sympathizers were ferreted out.

It was not long before they arrived at Frau Schreihart's home, a two-storey country house, with enough room for flowers, a vegetable garden, and a number of chickens. The barn had become a garage, she saw, as the car entered it.

Her room was beautiful and she thanked Frau Schreihart, who told her it was her pleasure to have her as a guest, and said that Liz must call her Herta, which she promptly did. Herta next asked her when she would like to meet the Professor and Liz deferred to her judgment. Thus it was arranged that she should meet him the next day --- in the afternoon.....

Herta and Liz spent a very pleasant evening discussing world events and the details of the war from Herta's perspective. Eventually, Liz asked the questions she had asked the others, but Herta put her off, saying, "Let us do this tomorrow either when you meet the Professor, or afterward."

Liz said it would be fine and, after eating a light dinner of over-wintered vegetables from Herta's garden and fresh eggs, they lingered for a bit over tea and coffeecake. Liz finally admitted she was tired and Herta walked with her to her room to put out an extra pillow from the linen cupboard.

Liz bathed, then climbed into the huge featherbed naked after seeing that it had two down comforters on top of each other. As she lay there, pensive and open, she remembered one day, one very special day, that began in their garden at home, a day when Franz made love to her. As she remembered it, her fingers began to stroke her breasts, then her flat belly, and more.....

The day was warm and sultry, one of those days that sometimes occur in the summer in inland valleys or near large bodies of fresh water. Liz was walking among the trees in the orchard, wearing a diaphanous dress of printed lawn and picking fruit here and there as she saw likely specimens for the table. Thus, by the time she returned to the drive, she had a rather heavy basket on her arm. It began to slip a bit, and as she bent over to set it down so that she could rearrange it, a peach fell out, then another..... In her haste to get them back into the basket, she failed to notice that someone had come up behind her and she nearly jumped out of her skin when a hand slid up under her skirt and touched her posterior. Straightening, she turned abruptly around and came face to face with Franz.

He smiled, a laughing smile, and she had to smile back. It was impossible to do otherwise with this man who she loved so much.

He put his arms around her and kissed her deeply, savoring his invasion of her mouth and the smell of her skin. His hands rubbed her back and lowered to her buttocks, gripping them firmly as he pressed against her.

Liz' arms were around his neck, as she opened the energy of her being to him. Her fingers found the little bits of curl in his hair and stroked them, letting the feeling seep into her awareness as silently and sensuously as a fine vintage.

He kissed her neck and the spot between her breasts, nibbled at her ears, and felt the lava begin to rise in the volcano of their passion for each other.

This wouldn't do, not here on the drive, he realized, and he held her away for a moment, then picked up her basket and strode toward the house. Liz, startled, stooped after a moment to pick up her errant peaches and hurried after him, wondering what was up.

When they reached the house, he opened the door and ushered an out-of-breath Liz who had, by this time, caught up to him, into the house, then set the basket on the nearest chair and, taking her hand, fairly dragged her off to their bedroom upstairs.

Once inside, he closed the door behind them. Then, he began to undress her --- first with his eyes, then with his fingers and hands. As he savored each element of the denuding of her fragrant body, he planted little kisses wherever he had bared her flesh. First, as always, the skirt must be raised for him to see and touch the tender skin of her thighs, stroking lightly to raise her ardor --- and his.

Then, turning her around, he must see her bottom, stroke it, and make her gasp as he reached between her legs to cup her front from behind with his hand and trail one finger through the center of her mound and into her hidden recess for a skinny dip.....

He kissed the back of her neck --- little butterfly kisses, as light as air --- to make her pant and arch her back toward him. He put his arms around her, then, to reach beneath her

J. Matheny

uplifted dress and cup her breasts, pinching the nipples lightly between his fingers.

Liz was gyrating her hips without volition as he touched her --- each sensation bringing a new eroticism to the act and an increased heat to her body --- and his.

Her hips were beating a steady tempo of forward and back by this time and he knew that this could not go on forever. It was time for her to begin taking off his clothes.

He turned her back around and kissed her again, then lifted the dress completely over her head and tossed it on the floor. She had not been wearing anything under it, so she stood there in front of him naked from head to shoes. He lifted her up onto the bed and, kneeling, removed them, set them aside, and, spreading her legs, slid his fingers into her slippery recess for another dip..... She gasped at the sensation, and thrust her hips forward to meet the welcome intrusion, once, twice, three times, before he pulled back and stood up.

She began unbuttoning his shirt, then reached the belt and fly of his trousers and opened them in turn, sliding the pants down to the floor, then pulling his silk boxers down as well. She raised her head and took his manhood, standing high and proud, into her mouth and suckled it. It was his turn to gasp and, shrugging his shoulders, he allowed the shirt to slide onto the floor.

 Liz, sensing what was coming, scooted toward the middle of the bed as Franz slid out of his shoes and stockings, but he had other plans. Grabbing her by the ankles, he dragged her to the edge of the bed and turned her bottom up. Holding her breasts in his hands, he entered her from behind as she laid there, half on and half off of the bed. Another gasp --- and a groan of pleasure, of benign conquest, and acceptance of it, from Liz.

Franz was busy --- hips plunging forward and back, Liz' slit at exactly the right height, and both hands fully occupied….. Liz wanted to do more, but knew that her time would come in more ways than one…..

Their orgasm built --- the fire was very hot this time. Franz squeezed and squeezed those ripe breasts and finally shot forward, pushing her further up onto the bed as he finished.

Ultimately, after many minutes, he pulled out, and, with her inner sanctum quivering and her legs shaking, Liz turned around and got off of the bed, urging him up onto it. He laid back, legs hanging off of it from the knees down. Now it was Liz' turn. She leaned over him and began to lick him clean, then mouthed his saber in its flaccid state.

Amazingly it began to rise again, like some tower of old, straight and tall, imposing as a fortress. "I don't think you'll get it to go again so soon, love," he said. But, this wasn't her aim. She merely meant to pleasure him with her mouth as much as he could stand. He had no energy left to squeeze her breasts, but that was no matter. She continued her gentle suckling and teasing and it did pleasure him --- an afterglow of the act of loving passion they had just experienced, a reinforcing of their oneness and their love.

The Liz of 1946 lay there remembering the feelings, remembering their connection both in body and in mind --- a connection so strong they barely needed to talk at times. This was it, she thought, this was the thing about them that was driving her forward on this journey --- she would find him through this connection, this oneness and, secure in the knowledge of how it would happen, she fell asleep and began to dream of Franz.

❧Chapter 23 – Heidelberg, Saturday❧

As she drifted out of sleep and into full consciousness, Liz knew that she had dreamed of Franz and remembered some of the dream. She lay there very still, reviewing it for fear of forgetting. He was in a hospital and he was lying on a bed. He could see the nurses and doctors walking by the room. She wondered if this was now or in the past, but no definitive answer came forward, though it seemed that she was to find him through sensing him, his energy, and thus, his whereabouts. It gave her a renewed sense of purpose --- and of hope and belief --- as well as being an awakening, perhaps a rekindling, of an ability she remembered from childhood.

So many times --- almost always --- when they played hide and seek, as children, she went immediately to his hiding place. Finally, he would refuse to play, so she pretended not to know where he was and looked everywhere but his hiding place. Then, he would emerge, holding his arms high, and triumphant in his ability to hide from her. She never told him that she had cheated to let him win.

And, wasn't this exactly what she had been doing, now? Looking everywhere he might have been, gathering clues, moving toward his energy slowly enough to build the excitement….. She faced the day with fresh eyes. So, now, she would be a real detective --- a hunch-player. She would meet with Professor Weber today and see what he had to say.

As her mind went out of 'think mode', the country sounds were filtering into her consciousness and she could hear that the birds were singing songs of spring's arrival in a tree outside the window of the country house. She went to look and saw Herta in the garden, feeding her chickens as she let them out of their nighttime enclosure. Five, was it, no, eight.....

She remembered the chickens she and Franz had raised as children: so many different varieties --- theirs were truly integrated. The rooster was a proud Rhode Island Red and he was king. The hens were White Leghorns, spotted Dominickers, apricot-colored Buff Orpingtons, Araucanas with green legs (they laid blue or green eggs!), even slender black ones that looked like big crows, and many other varieties.

It was fun growing up together as best friends and, ultimately, lovers. They had a closeness that so many couples didn't have --- shared memories, going back nearly to the cradle.....

She smiled as she thought about their childhood, a happy smile of connection.

After watching Herta feed her chickens for a bit, she made her way downstairs to find a bit of breakfast and discovered that her hostess had already made it and her plate, with a glass cover, was sitting on the table. These country dwellers were early risers….. More eggs, with mushrooms this time, and parsley fried potatoes and a pot of tea --- she could get used to this…..

When she had eaten, she went outside for a bit of air --- and to see the chickens and Herta. She found Herta in the garden, weeding her patch of vegetables, for the weeds were already coming in. Herta told her that she always started with the vegetables --- that way, if she became too tired, the flowers could take care of themselves….. After all, she needed the vegetables more in this economy --- to eat…..

It was a nice garden, orderly and well-tended, in spite of what Herta had said about the weeding. It was just the right size for a single person, of a certain age, to manage without over-tiring. She motioned Liz to one of the chairs and she sat there, looking up into the sky through the open, but leafy, branches of a well-pruned tree. With a full stomach and such a beautiful sight, one could become very drowsy…..

"Better not fall asleep," Herta called to her, "Professor Weber will be coming soon."

"Oh, I thought we were to go to him."

"No," Herta said, "His walls may have ears, but mine do not --- and, besides, he usually buys some of my vegetables!" She smiled at the last, knowing that Liz would find it amusing, as well….. Then, she continued, "I will make soup, dumplings, sauerkraut, and a roast chicken with savory dressing, some pickled beets, and strawberry dumplings for dessert. Ach, the time flies --- I had better begin."

And, begin she did. Liz watched her, for she had never seen fruit dumplings made and wanted to know how it was done --- especially the strawberry variety.

They bantered back and forth, the two ladies, as Herta worked and Liz watched, helping find a bowl or utensil from time to time, and washing the ones Herta was done with as they came available. Liz was amazed at how organized Herta was --- she couldn't imagine herself being able to accomplish so much, so fast, and in such an orderly fashion.....

By 1 o'clock, all was in readiness --- with the hen cooling on the counter to allow the juices to settle so they wouldn't run out when she cut into it. At that moment, there was the sound of a car in the yard and, in a few moments, a rap on the front door. Herta, took off her apron, patted her hair, and went to open it.

"Guten tag, Herr Professor!," Liz heard her say, then she switched to English. "She is in the kitchen helping me. Come, come..... You may see where I do my cooking."

As she walked into the kitchen bringing her guest to Liz, she smiled at her --- and winked.

Professor Weber, upon seeing Liz, said, "Ach, you didn't tell me you were entertaining a movie star" as he smiled broadly at her. "And which films have you starred in, my dear?"

Herta chuckled and said, "Oh, Alfred, you never change. Always the teasing..... She will think you are crazy....."

He made a face of wide-eyed, indignant shock, saying, "Oh dear, you don't think I'm crazy, do you?"

Now, he had Liz laughing, as well, and she responded, "No more than Frick and Frack."

At this, he burst out laughing and said, aside, to Herta, "This is a rare one! She'll outdo us both."

So began their visit and it proceeded in that vein the whole afternoon. After a number of hours, he said, "I suppose that we need to talk about your husband, now."

"Oh, yes, please," Liz answered. She had enjoyed the banter and amusing conversation as much as they, but she did need to ask her questions and know their answers. After a moment's thought, she began with, "Did you meet my husband in 1939?"

"Yes," answered the Professor, "Yes, I did. I was not at the university, then, because of the Nazis, but he wanted to see it, so we met here at Herta's cottage. He was young and very enthusiastic about the ideas he had. They were good ideas --- prosperity does stop wars, for there is no need to grasp, when one already has. We spoke at great length, your husband and I. He is intelligent and creative. If he has survived the war, he could be a statesman, but I fear he prefers his engineering and science."

Liz smiled at the praise of her Franz. It was the way she felt about him, too, but it was always nice to hear someone else validate that opinion.

"Do you know if he left for Frankfurt?" she asked.

"Yes, he did. He rang me from the station and, also, sent a note to my home from Luxembourg."

Good! the news she was awaiting --- he had made it to Luxembourg! "So, he must have gotten as far as Luxembourg, then?" she interjected.

"Apparently, though a note is not the same as someone seeing him there. Anyone can carry a letter to a post office. It need not be the writer..... It need not be written by the person whose name is signed....."

"I understand. I must still go on to Frankfurt to ask if he arrived there --- before I go to Luxembourg."

"Yes, I believe it is so," the Professor answered.

"Can you tell me what the note said?" she asked.

"Not exactly, and I have been unable to locate it. He was thanking me for seeing him..... and I remember thinking that it was I who should be thanking him --- for sharing his youthful perspective and energy with me."

"Was the note handwritten or typed?"

"By hand..... yes, by hand."

"I hope that you will continue searching for it," she interjected, "This may be very important. If it is not his writing or if he said something unusual which would be a clue, if may lead to our finding him."

The professor noted the intensity with which she was searching for Franz outlined in her face and audible in the intonation and cadence of her words. He promised her that he would look through his papers more carefully and notify her immediately of anything he might find. He felt sadness for her in her difficult search, which might reveal tragedy at its end, and took her small hands and enfolded them in his large ones, saying, "We will keep our spirits high and hope for the best outcome."

Liz nodded, already thinking of her next lead --- Frankfurt.....

Though the atmosphere had been dampened by this exchange, Herta was able to bring the flow of conversation back to some of the carefree banter with the mention of tea and cookies. Professor Weber had never turned down a cookie in her house.....   .....or any other house, for that matter..... She brewed the tea, a tisane, actually, for it was from her own garden's herbs. Ginger root and fennel made a spicy licorice tasting tea and went well with the blander almond crescent cookies she had baked a few days earlier and rolled in powdered sugar. The serenity of taking tea together pervaded the conversation and relegated Liz' search to the background of their minds. The attention has changed its focus and Herta's garden was the spotlighted item, now; providing less stress.

The professor asked how she managed to grow so many luscious vegetables on a small piece of land and she pointed out that she had chickens to help by eating the bugs and providing nutrition for the plants with their droppings.

"Ah, yes," he said, "Everything has a use....."

Herta laughed, and said, "Naturlich! Und warum nicht?"

Liz could not help but smile at their easy conversation. These two must have known each other for a long time, she felt.

They visited until it was beginning to be twilight. The professor noted the waning light and said, "I believe it is time for me to go or I shall lose myself on these country roads before I come to my house. Herta, do you have some vegetables I might buy?"

"Of course," came the quick reply, "They are waiting for you in the cellar. I will bring them."

As she watched Herta opening the cellar door, Liz had a vision of Franz being taken into a room in a cellar by a man in a uniform. It left as suddenly as it came, leaving her startled at what she had seen and wondering if she were going mad. She didn't say anything to either of her companions, though, for fear of diluting their interest in helping her in her quest.

Herta bustled back out of the cellar with a bundle of vegetables, as well as a cloth bag of potatoes, which the professor gladly carried to the car. After putting them in the trunk, he gave Herta some money in payment, which her body language said she wanted to decline, but he put both his hands around hers and nodded his head --- looking intently into her eyes. He knew that this was her current means of support for anything she needed above and beyond what she could produce to eat. He was compassionate and caring; a man with a great heart.

In leaving, he said good-byes all around. He bent to kiss the hand of each of them, making them giggle like schoolgirls and adding a gleam to his eyes. They waved at the car as he turned it around and headed back in the direction he had come from, then, Herta turned and went into the garden in back to put the chickens in their coop for the night and Liz followed behind her to watch --- until they both went inside to clear the table before eating a light supper.

The day had been very satisfying and left them mellow and somewhat quiet --- each thinking her own thoughts and only occasionally venturing to speak. The evening passed, thus, and, after cleaning up the few supper dishes, each made her way to bed, saying good night and basking in the glow of the afternoon's conversation.

Liz, too mellow to move, lay there thinking about the vision she had seen. Is was as though she were in a meditative state, where time seems to be altered and one is living slower that events are happening. In that detached mode, she drifted into sleep; hoping for dreams to bring her understanding.

❧Chapter 24 – Heidelberg, Sunday☙

Liz awoke early….. very early, and lay there in the semi-dark; calm, quiet, and half asleep, holding the threads of a dream in place as she tried to understand it. She had been watching Franz, in the midst of a battle, injured and bleeding, trying to get out of the line of fire. It still felt so real, as if she were still dreaming --- or experiencing it.

Bit by bit, the more tenuous threads faded, but the feeling that she was seeing more than a dream persisted as she came into more awareness of her surroundings and began to feel truly awake. She stretched and took a deep breath and released it, then, another deeper one, held it, then released it, too. Her body was tingling from the stretching and she felt vibrantly alive.

So, now, what was this about the dream? Was she connecting with Franz, his memories, his dreams, or what? Her mind toyed with a number of possibilities and categorized them: impossible, possible, probable, improbable, and ridiculous. She found herself being of at least two minds and not being able to make a decision as to what she saw actually was. Finally, like Scarlet O'Hara, she decided to 'think about it tomorrow' and, since the sun was coming in through her bedroom window, she slid out of bed and dressed for breakfast.

Downstairs, she found Herta busy in the kitchen with breakfast --- small, thin pancakes with jam and butter and foamy cocoa to drink.

She put the plates and silverware on the table, poured the cocoa, and slipped into her place to wait for Herta to finish making the pancakes. It didn't take long for her to have a platter full to set next to the plates and, when they were both seated, breakfast began.

Liz asked if she had slept well and Herta answered that she had, asking, "And you?"

"Yes, but I had a strange dream."

"About what?"

"Just strange. I saw my husband on a battlefield, wounded and bleeding, but alive."

"Not so strange in wartime, but perhaps it was made by your fears for him."

"Maybe. I don't know….. I don't know what to think of it….. or how to feel about it."

"Perhaps if you let it go --- don't think about it --- an answer will come."

Liz felt better for having said something to Herta and she tried to let it go, but she knew that it was there in the back of her mind, waiting to be foremost in her thoughts again.

She could feel it there, hiding, and waiting. It didn't make her anxious, but it did make her curious. And, for Liz, unrequited curiosity was indeed a heavy burden to bear.

It was a relaxing day. In the morning they did light work in the garden and, after lunch, Herta took her in the car, through Heidelberg, past the University and pointing out points of interest, such as, the hospital Patton had died in.

Liz found it fascinating and told her as much. Herta volunteered that Patton had been taken to Luxembourg for burial, so Liz could see his grave as well. Liz was not particularly fond of cemeteries, but said that she would visit it --- and knew that it would please her parents and Franz', in any case, though merely the fact of her being in Luxembourg where their parents had been born, would thrill them. She knew that she must also go to Heffingen, a tiny farming community, where some had been born.

Herta stopped the car from time to time, when she wanted to point out more than one landmark, and they spent a pleasant afternoon talking about the history of Heidelberg with "visual aids". It was a bit like taking a tour bus, but being the only rider.

As the day began to wane, Herta turned the car toward home and, like any good horse, it seemed to find its way there without much guidance. She drove it into the barn and Liz helped her close the doors before they put the chickens in their coop and went inside.

Supper was leftover chicken with tiny German-style dumplings, and a salad of fresh garden greens slightly wilted

by hot bacon drippings, but neither minded the leftovers ---
Herta's cooking was good. So was the dessert --- more of
the cookies from the day before, with a cup of the
ginger/fennel tea.

After dinner, Herta asked Liz if she played rummy. Liz'
parents had taught her how to play and she often played with
them and Franz' parents, as well, which surprised and
pleased Herta. "So!" she said, "We will have a little game."

They played for hours and, though Liz played well, Herta
managed to finish ahead each game, but one. Their easy
camaraderie as they played reminded Liz of Ana and Frieda.
She was so happy that she had met new friends on her
journey, for she needed their help greatly if she was to find
her Franz.

Finally, Herta said, "I could go on playing all night, but
eventually we must sleep and you do have a train to meet
tomorrow."

"You're right," agreed Liz, "I should rest well. It will be a
long day and I'll have much to do in Frankfurt, with little
time to sleep, since I'll have only the one night there --- and
then an early train to Luxembourg and a far longer journey.
Shall we wash the dishes we left to soak?"

"Oh, I will do it, myself --- you go to bed," Herta offered,
with a wave of her hand, but Liz insisted on helping and they
were done in a few minutes.

"Good night, then, my dear," Herta said.

"And to you, too," Liz answered, as she went up the stairs to her room, thinking of how much fun they'd had.

In her room, Liz readied herself for bed, planning to pack the next morning, since her train didn't leave until 1 o'clock. She knew that going to bed at this time, she'd be up plenty early enough. In short order, she had washed up in the bowl on the washstand with spring water from the pitcher, brushed her teeth, as well as her hair, and changed into her nightgown. In only a few minutes, she was in bed, under the down covers, and thinking of Franz. She tried to think of one of the times they had made love, but all that would come to mind was the view of him on that battlefield --- and bloody.

Then, she tried to go to sleep and finally, fitfully, she was able to let go of enough of the memory to fall under the spell of Morpheus.

❧Chapter 25 – Heidelberg to Frankfurt❧

In her dreams, she found no true solace, for she dreamed of Franz again. This time, she saw him in a hospital bed with bandages wound around his head and his hands. She didn't feel afraid, so she surmised that he had survived whatever this was --- if it was a true vision of what had come to pass.

She woke up once, with a start, but went back to sleep quickly and had another dream (or vision) of Franz. This time he was walking down a corridor, in a hospital, with only a few bandages on his head. His mouth wasn't moving, but she could hear him calling to her and speaking French.

When the first rays of light began to find their way through the window, she woke again. It was as it had been the morning before --- she was mellow and able to stay in that half-asleep state in order to better remember the dreams she had experienced. So, Franz had been in a hospital, she felt --- and wounded….. Was he speaking in French, because he was in France? Belgium?

She thought about the upcoming trip to Frankfurt, hoping that she would learn more, and glad that she would be heading for Luxembourg the next day. For some reason, this was her focus. Of course, she realized, it would be, since she was hoping to find relatives there, but it seemed as though there was more….. Always these presentiments!

Then, chiding herself, she remembered that they were all she had to go on --- hunches.....

At this point, she decided not to linger a moment longer in the luxury of the feather bed and its down comforters. Flinging them away, she got out of the bed, drew off her nightgown, and dressed in a simple frock until time to go to the train station.

Before going downstairs, she packed her bags so that she could have a good morning with Herta --- free from thinking about whether she had remembered everything. Strangely, one's memory always seems to be less accurate at the last minute......

Herta was in the kitchen making breakfast --- this time mushroom quiche, almost the twin of Ana's. Liz was tempted to ask if they had learned together.....

The breakfast was excellent, as always, and they conversed about the tour Herta had given her the day before. Liz told her how much she had enjoyed it --- seeing the buildings, but also hearing what she had to say about them. It was better than having a tour guide, because she could sense Herta's genuine feeling for the city.

Lingering, they spoke more of personal things, such as Liz' love for her husband and she asked Herta if she had been married. "No, sadly not," she said.

"But, did you have a suitor, perhaps?" Liz asked, with the forthrightness of youth.

"Yes, there was a man..... a good man..... he died in the first war," she replied.

"I'm so sorry, Herta," Liz said, wishing she had bitten her tongue, "I didn't mean to make you sad."

"Oh, I am only a little sad --- it was too long ago --- almost 30 years," Herta said, looking wistful in spite of her bravado.

Liz went and put her arms around Herta's shoulders as she sat there in her chair. The older lady patted Liz' hands where they met on her right shoulder and thought of the many years since then. They had not been lonely, for she had much to occupy her, and she knew many people --- good people, like Alfred. But, sometimes, she wondered how life would have been different if her Gerhardt hadn't taken a bullet on the Italian Front. She could have had children.....

Finally, she said, "It was a very long time ago, my dear --- now it is time for us to wash the dishes and point you in the direction of your man. We will pray for his safety and for your reuniting."

The dishes were quickly finished and put away. As it was past 11 o'clock, Herta told Liz to assemble her things by the front door, so that they would be sure to have everything ready to go. Liz obliged her and by 11:30 all was as it should be. Liz had changed into her traveling suit and coat and put the frock back into her luggage, Herta had fed the chickens and packed a lunch for Liz, and Liz was standing by the front door.

"I think it is time for us to go," said Herta, putting her hat on and buttoning her coat.

So, after loading the luggage, they got into the car and Herta eased it up the drive and onto the road. In less than 45 minutes, they were at the station.

Herta parked in front of the porter stand and one immediately came forward to carry Liz' luggage to the baggage check office for her. As Liz said good-bye to Herta, she pressed some money into her hand and said, "This is for helping me, dearest friend. I would never have found out so much without you. Consider it advance payment on some vegetables for next time I visit." They hugged, and Herta felt as though this was the daughter she had never had. It stirred up the old sadness a bit, but it was far too old to rise very much. Looking on the bright side, her cure for sadness, she thought how nice it was to have young friends --- or, for that matter, any friends..... as she thought of Alfred.

A car behind hers honked for her to move, so she said her good-byes and got into her car. Liz stood and waved until her car had disappeared into the distance, then she turned and went inside. They had already purchased her ticket the day they came to Heidelberg, so she needed only to go to the baggage check office with the porter. In a matter of minutes, she was seated and waiting for her train to arrive. It was on time, and, as she watched the passengers who had left the train walking to the baggage claim, a voice came on the loudspeaker telling ticket holders, for the run to Frankfurt, to board immediately.

She walked out onto the platform and then up a few stairs into the train and found her seat. She placed her lunch on the seat beside her, observing that the car wasn't full, and pulled out a travel brochure to read: Frankfurt Am Main.

As the train left the station, she mentally said another good-bye to Herta and one to the Professor, then looked at the scenery passing by for awhile. After about 20 minutes or so, she began to read her brochure and learn more about the city ahead of her. The Blue Note was certain to be well-known to the taxi driver, for it was listed right there in the brochure. The train made many stops --- a local --- but she didn't mind, for she had no appointments until the evening. Eventually, she put the brochure in her purse and began to look into the bag of lunch.

Herta had packed her a lunch fit for a king --- strawberries, cheese sandwiches, boiled eggs, and the tasty crescent cookies, as well as other cookies made with rye flour. There was even a small jar filled with spring water and a handkerchief to wipe her hands.

She ate the sandwiches and the strawberries, judging them to be the most perishable, then, just as she was closing the bag, snagged one of each cookie variety --- for a taste --- but, saved the eggs, and the rest of the cookies, for her trip to Luxembourg the next day, since she might arrive in the evening.

The afternoon wore on as the train made its stops at every little town --- another local. But, then, she saw more of the country this way, because it didn't fly by so fast. This time, no one sat by her, so she pulled the brochure out, now and again, to read a bit more about the city. She was almost there --- and earlier than she had anticipated --- given the number of stops they'd made.

When the train arrived, she claimed her luggage and proceeded to the taxi stand with her porter following closely. In a matter of minutes, she was on her way to the room she was using, for the night, in a private home. She asked the taxi driver to carry her luggage up and then take her to The Blue Note, exactly as she had been instructed. Mr. Henri had been right --- the taxi driver knew exactly where it was.....

❧Chapter 26 – Frankfurt Am Main, The Blue Note❧

She had felt that her traveling suit would be adequate even if The Blue Note was a full on nightclub, but she was surprised to see the au courant look of the dresses when she walked through the doors. Paris must already be in overdrive.....

She asked the headwaiter to bring her to Mr. Froehlich's table and he took her instead to the manager's office, where the man she expected to meet was waiting.

"Good evening, Miss Hart, or should I say Frau Tischler?" Mr. Froehlich said, "Would you like some beverage? We have mixed drinks, wine, soda waters, juices, or even coffee."

"Oh, coffee, please," Liz said, "And please have them bring cream, not milk, and some sugar."

Froehlich nodded to the waiter, who went for the request.

"So, you search for you husband?" he asked, stroking his chin.

"Yes, I am," she answered, "He disappeared during the war."

"Yes, yes, I know all about it," came the impatient reply.

"What do you know? Do you know where he is? Have you seen him?"

"Slow down, lady --- you're going too fast. No, I don't know where he is. Yes, I saw him in 1939. I also saw him in 1940 --- in Köln. He had escaped from the Nazis, he said, and asked for help. I did what I dared do in those times --- got him false papers, some money, and a ticket for Amsterdam via Brussels."

Liz sat there with her mouth open. Franz alive in 1940! This was indeed news!

"You should close your mouth before a fly goes in," Froehlich said, "Wouldn't want that to happen....."

He had the desired effect --- Liz laughed and closed her mouth.

"After I helped him, I didn't see him again --- or hear from him, which would have been nice once the war was over....."

"So, you didn't meet him here?" she asked.

"Oh, yes, in '39. Then, in '40, in Köln when he said he'd been kidnapped by Hitler's crew --- something about working on their submarine hydraulics....."

"Yes, yes, he's an engineer. Did he say where he had been held?"

"Yes --- in a cellar in Bonn, not very far from here. Apparently, they took him off at Trier, before reaching the border of Luxembourg, where he was ticketed to, and brought him to Bonn. He didn't say much about who helped him escape from them, after so many months, but I am of the opinion that it was a Frenchman. He should have made it to Brussels and then to Amsterdam, though --- I don't understand what happened to prevent him --- the papers I gave him were real ones, from a man who died."

"No matter," Liz interjected, "The important thing, now, is that he was held in a cellar and he escaped them, as he showed me. Also, that he may have gotten as far as Brussels --- or been injured on the way. Perhaps a train crash or a bombing..... When, in 1940, did you see him?"

"Just before the Battle of France --- early May. Why?"

"Because, if he was involved in that battle, somehow, he might have been injured.....," she said.

"So, you think that is why he has never contacted you --- he was killed there? Then, how could he have shown you something?"

"It could be, but I believe that he is still alive somewhere, that he was injured --- probably in the battle --- and that he either has no memory or is being held against his will --- perhaps in a hospital."

"Amazing. You are absolutely amazing. How can you be so sure?"

"I'm not certain, I just feel something that tells me he's alive --- and I've been having these strange dreams."

"So, now you are for Luxembourg? Why do you go there if he never made it?"

"Because, we both may still have family in Luxembourg and I promised I would visit them --- even if he never made it that far."

"Ah, I see. You are fulfilling an obligation."

"Yes, that's it," she said.

"I think, Miss Hart, it is time for you to eat. Surely, you've had nothing since lunch --- and neither have I. What would you like?"

"What's on the menu," she asked.

"Almost anything you want, but we specialize in southern USA cooking. It goes with the blues theme and it sells a lot of food --- they all want to act like movie stars and eat American food. I can recommend the gumbo."

"Then, I'll have the gumbo with French bread," she said, "And what are you having?"

"Oh, for me, it's the southern fried chicken with biscuits and honey. I've always been partial to sweets --- both in food and women." With this pronouncement, he pushed a button under the desk and a waiter appeared almost immediately. He took the order and was back in under 5 minutes with a tray of steaming food for them.

"Service is good when you're the boss," Froehlich said, wiggling his eyebrows up and down in an imitation of Groucho Marx.

Liz smiled at his antics; he was right. She sampled the gumbo and found it to be excellent --- judging by the gusto with which 'the boss' was eating, his meal was a gastronomic delight as well. He offered her one of his biscuits and honey and she selected one from the plateful. Biting into it, she could smell the rich honey as a bit dripped onto her fingers. The taste was, indeed, something to write home about, she decided. It was not quite the proper complement for gumbo, but it was certainly worth trying again --- perhaps with the chicken…...

She wasn't quite sure what Froehlich was, beyond his role in life as an owner of nightclubs and cafes, and she was certain he was more --- a lot more --- but, he was a good conversationalist and dinner companion. Of that, she was certain.

As they talked --- mostly about the war and the economy (both global and local), the occupation, the arrests and trials --- she drew him out and found him to be very pragmatic. He seemed to take life as he saw it and fit it into his own plan, rather than wringing his hands about the difficulties. In short, he was like her: proactive.

Eventually, they finished their meal and he sent for dessert: deep dish apple pie. It came, in one deep pie pan for them to serve themselves from --- steaming, still, and scenting the room with apple fragrance.

Liz didn't eat as much of the treat as he did, but she put away a good share of the pie.

With full stomachs, they looked at each other, and both began to speak at once, then he deferred to Liz, who began, "I just wanted to say that I should go back to my room and get some sleep --- I have an early train for Luxembourg."

"Funny, that's what I was going to say --- that you should get some sleep, because you will have a long day, and I imagine today has been one, as well." He pressed the hidden button and a waiter arrived. "Are there any taxis outside?" he asked.

"Always."

"Then escort my guest to the best of them and tell the driver to collect from me."

Liz smiled, and thanked him. Then, as she turned to go, she heard him say, "If you don't find your husband, please let me know." Without turning, she nodded and followed the waiter's lead.

As they walked through the 'café', she could see that this was a very successful venture. People were trying to erase the war years from their memories and step into the future, a brighter future with hope.

The ride to her room on Schifferstrasse was relatively short and she thanked the driver, then sought the comfort of her room and its large bed. This was a featherbed, since she was staying in a private home --- turned into a bed and breakfast. She hoped that in Luxembourg it would be the same rather than the firm horsehair mattresses so prevalent in European hotels. Leaving the curtains open to allow the morning sunshine to enter and wake her, since she had no alarm clock, she climbed into the bed. The comforter was warm and the bed held her body heat, as well. As she lay there, with many thoughts whirling through her mind, she thought of what Franz might be experiencing. The more she focused on him, the more other thoughts --- thoughts of their courtship and of their married life --- came into her head.... She remembered the day they spent at an unfrequented spot when they stopped on the English coast on their honeymoon.....

The blue roadster sped along the country road between the hedgerows. Franz and Liz could smell the sea, though they still had a bit further to go. Liz breathed the brisk smell in deeply, savoring each breath of the salt and seaweed tang. Franz watched her out of the corner of his eye, keeping track of the rise and fall of her bosom with each intake of air and noting the fluttering edge of her skirt hem as the breeze caught it from time to time.

It seemed to take forever, but in truth they drove out onto the headland less than thirty minutes later. Their view was breath-taking --- the day was amazingly clear and they could see far out to sea. Though the sun shone, it was not overly hot or humid.

They had brought their painting tools and planned to paint later in the day when the shadows would make interesting plays of light on the cliffs and waves, but first they would head down the track to this remote beach and enjoy a very private swim and sunbath. To this end, Franz began unloading their baskets, then, covered the roadster with a tarp in the event that a summer shower should come up.

So it was, that carrying their equipment, and bantering back and forth, they began the descent to the deserted beach below. Liz led the way into the pristine cove, with Franz happily bringing up the rear so that he could watch the naughty breeze playing with her hemline.

She laughed as she walked, singing snatches of popular tunes, and giggling at the lyrics. Franz loved watching her enjoying life. It made him feel connected with her, somehow, and more alive than when he was alone.

Finally, they reached the beach and found a smooth, wave-worn rock to lean against as they sunbathed after their swim. A dry cave, worn into the cliff nearby, provided a dressing room for Liz to change into a bathing costume, while Franz slipped behind the rock. In no time, both were ready to enjoy the water.

Liz came out timidly, so Franz confidently extended his hand to her and led her to the sea. It was not frigid, but far from warm and inviting, so they played and splashed in the shallows, sometimes touching hands or a bit of skin as they laughed and splashed in games of chase.

Eventually, the light breeze was chilling them and they turned to the blanket laid in front of the warm rock and sat in the sun, absorbing the warmth of the sand in the shelter of the rock, while enjoying a luncheon feast of meat pasties, fruit, and little tarts washed down with spring water provided by the landlord of the inn where they were staying.

Their bathing suits were dry by this time and, as they lay conversing on the blanket in the sun, they moved closer and closer, until they were finally in distinct danger of becoming entwined. Franz took Liz' small hand in his and began caressing it with his fingers, stroking it gently as one would a baby's face. The slower he stroked, the more erotic it seemed and the more aroused he became. Liz was stimulated by the slowness and deliberateness, as well, and her breathing began to have little rough edges to it, with a shudder from time to time.

Franz rolled on his side to face her and, using his other hand, began tracing the outline of her lips with a fingertip. Again, slowly, ever so slowly, allowing each cell he touched to register that it had been touched, awakening in Liz a hunger for more….. …..and more…..

Her breathing was far beyond rough edges by this time and she used the hand he was not stroking to reach up and touch his face, then rolled to her side, facing him with eyes heavy-lidded with mounting passion as her body arched toward him, presenting itself, like an opening flower, to he who was the sun of her life.

His hand left her lips and, trailing his fingertips over her shoulder and down her arm to her breast, he first cupped it, then gently squeezed it and felt his own back arching toward her. The languor of the moment was far beyond sensuous. Without being undressed, they were writhing as though they were in the final throes of passion.

Liz broke the contact of her hand and began lightly stroking Franz' face with both her hands, allowing them to trail down his neck to his chest and under the shirt of his bathing costume, where her tiny fingers danced across his skin.

Franz, not to be outdone, began running his hands up and down her back, no longer erotically light, he was kneading the flesh of her buttocks and pulling her to him. She could feel the proof of his arousal as he ground his hips into hers and a veritable log pressed against her belly. He pulled at her clothing, opening fasteners and bringing her to a state of near nudity, kissing her and stroking her as he worked.

She lay, passive, back arched and breasts pointing to the sky, allowing him to be in charge..... .....for the moment. When she was nearly naked, she began to undress him. Franz helped. In no time he was also nude, his proud staff pointing upward as well --- at least until he rolled over on top of Liz, spreading her thighs, and entering her dripping cleft in one gentle, sliding movement. He stayed in that position for a moment, savoring the feeling of being inside of her with every fragment of his being, and preparing for his onslaught.

Now, his manhood was pointed at a downward angle, sliding in and out of the cleft he was so enjoying breeching with a rhythm born of their mutual passion. Liz met his every thrust with equal vigor, matching his passion and his arousal with her own. They no longer heard the cries of sea birds, nor the waves upon the beach. Their ears were tuned to a different sound, the sound of their love-making, the sound of their breathing, and the sound of their bodies slapping together.

Faster and faster they moved as their impending orgasms neared. Then, suddenly, it was upon them, as they vocalized their passion and their release. Liz' legs wound tightly around Franz as he lay upon her, fully spent. She savored his weight, the pressing down upon her like the hand of a giant, but finally he lifted himself groggily from her and rolled over to her side, an arm draped lazily across her as though too fatigued to grasp tightly.

The lovers remained entwined this way for some time, then began to realize that the shade and protection of the cave might be a better place to rest. Together, they took the baskets and blanket, as well as their discarded clothing, to the cave and snuggled together, as naked as baby birds, for a nap with a second blanket over them added to the one beneath.

Time had flown. Liz awoke to the sound of water close-by and lay there trying to get her bearings. Where were they? The air had become cooler and the light dimmer. Oh, yes, the cave….. But, what was the sound of water? She sat up to have a better vantage point of the beach and saw that the water had moved closer. Alarmed, she stood up and walked to the opening, where her eyes met a sorry sight --- the tide had come in and the downward track from the cliff now led directly into the water.

She returned immediately to Franz and began to whisper his name as she kissed him. He awoke, but thought she was ready for another round and began groping for her soft body in the dim light of the cave. "Fraaaaannnnnnzzzz," she wailed, "We're stranded….."

Now completely awake, Franz asked her what she was talking about. Liz quickly gave him the lay of the land, a story which he jumped up to verify for himself, then sat back down to think about. "Hmmm," he began, "Looks like we're in here until the tide turns. Well, it could be worse --- we have plenty of provisions, two thick blankets, and our lanterns."

"But, what if the water comes in here?" she asked.

Franz took another look out of the cave opening and said, "It doesn't look like it'll rise that high, but we'd best move to higher ground in the back, in any case." With this, he lit both lanterns, put his bathing suit back on for warmth, and set out with one of the lanterns for the back of the cave, looking for higher ground.

The cave wasn't a huge cavern, but rose consistently toward the back with the sand eventually giving way to the same limestone as the walls. He left the lantern there and walked back toward the other light. Now he and Liz, who had put her own bathing suit back on, brought the baskets, their clothing, the blankets, and the other lantern to the back of the cave. Together, they spread out the blankets on the last of the sand and placed the provisions, their clothing, and one lantern higher still on a broad limestone ledge about 4 feet higher than their bed. That lantern had been turned off, but they kept the other beside them, which they left burning with a very low light.

As they ate a bit of their provisions, they talked of many things: the sketches they had not been able to paint, the tide cycles --- or at least as much as they knew of them --- and how cozy this cave really was. Those topics exhausted, they spoke of other things: their dreams and hopes, politics, religion, and their beliefs. Being in the middle of nowhere seems to bring these things out of people in the same manner as a long journey by train --- even people who have known each other since childhood.....

As they snuggled close for warmth, between the blankets, like the filling in a sandwich, the familiar arousal eventually began to assail them. The feeling of flesh upon flesh was far too much for them to resist. Franz began stroking Liz again and, for her part, she was busy, too. Soon, their clothing was once more shed and they were busily exploring each other's bodies.

Their earlier passion somewhat slaked, they proceeded more slowly. Liz, under the cover, began to kiss Franz' chest, then his stomach. Franz, for his part, squeezed and kneaded her breasts, when he could reach them, and anything else he could lay his hands on in between.

Liz finally reached his member, which had been as firmly hard as a walking stick from the moment they began. She ran her fingers lightly across it and Franz groaned, thrusting his pelvis forward. She cupped his sack in her hands and he moaned with need. In the dim light of the lantern, he couldn't see the light in her eyes as she had an idea, but he felt it when she put her thoughts into effect. She leaned over and began to lick his shaft up and down, loving the salt taste on her tongue. Hearing his groan as he pushed toward her, she knew what she must do, and do it she did, as she took him into her mouth. The feeling of his swollen member in her mouth delighted her as she sucked on it, nibbling here and there, running her tongue under the edge of its mushroom-like cap all the way around, and pulsing it with the back of her tongue. He began to groan more steadily, gently thrusting and retreating as she sucked.

Then, suddenly, as though awaking from a trance, he said, "I have to be inside of you, feeling you," and with a single graceful movement was above Liz, sliding, once again, into her wet, juicy cleft and making her buck, like an untamed horse. He rode her as she bucked beneath him, not trying to unseat him, but seeking that closeness, that connection, as well. It was longer this time. The climax didn't come as soon and they stopped to rest, then began again, time after time, the sensations rising and falling with their efforts. Finally, they could feel the end nearing and, as they came together, with a number of tense jerks, each reached that peak they had sought, then, collapsed into the other's arms and slumber.

Their exercise had warmed them sufficiently that the blankets were adequate to the task of keeping them warm until the morning. Throughout the night, they held each other, basking in the warmth of that nearness of their beloved as they slept.

In the faint light of the dawn, Franz woke with a stiff member. He looked at Liz lying half-asleep next to him and began to rub her breasts, then, tweak her nipples between his fingertips. She stirred, but continued to doze, as people often do in the open air. His hands began to explore and soon he had two fingers inside of her still-wet opening. He slid them in and out and she began to move her hips back and forth. Scooting under the cover, he began to do for her what she had done for him the night before. He licked and sucked at her cleft, all the while moving those two fingers in and out.

By this time, Liz was wide awake and making little noises of her own, a song of arousal and impending satiation as his fingers slid in and out, in and out of her. She reached for his organ and began squeezing it with her hand, which made his ministrations all the faster and more intense. It was not long before he moved into a position straddling her with his north to her south and his member above her face, so she took it into her mouth to savor as he was suckling at her much smaller version, that tiny button at the apex of her cleft.

When their orgasms were finally upon them, the strength of the contractions was greater than they had ever experienced. It was as though they were transported to another place entirely, with the waves of ecstasy rolling through their bodies.

This time, hunger wouldn't allow them to sleep. Naked, they began rummaging through the provisions seeking a suitable breakfast. Hard-boiled eggs, bread, and ham slices came out and they feasted in the salt air. Liz made a quick trip to the cave's mouth and saw that the tide had retreated greatly, but it looked to be a bit before they could leave. She put her clothes from the day before back on, then, huddled between the blankets and Franz did the same. Sated in both hungers, they lay and talked, a hair's breadth apart, in each other's arms, snuggled under the blankets, waiting for the tide to retreat. Eventually, as all tides everywhere do, it receded and they made the upward trip, with all of the things that seemed so light going down, now, so heavy on the ascent. "Pity we didn't have a chance to paint," Franz said as he held the door open and handed Liz into the roadster, once the tarp had been removed and the baskets and blankets had been stowed.

As he bent to plant a kiss on her lips, before taking his own seat and sending the roadster rocketing down the shepherd's track away from their beach, she answered, "There'll be another time, love."

The Liz of 1946 lay there, in the featherbed, remembering each word and each feeling, aroused to the point that a spontaneous orgasm began almost the moment her hand touched the little button hidden between her thighs. Her body rocked with it, the waves flowing down her vagina again and again, and, jerking her almost upright as each reached her labia. Afterward, she slept.

❧Chapter 27 – Frankfurt to Luxembourg, Henri❧

Looking at the clock on the dresser, Liz realized that she needed to get moving --- time was essential at this point and she had more information and a lot of hope..... Now, the dream or vision, whatever it had been, of Franz being wounded in a battle and bleeding, made sense. Now, Liz could search with some focus and more knowledge. As she put the few items she had removed from her luggage back in their places, thoughts surfaced about the huge task before her in Luxembourg. Now, she might not need Mr. Henri or, perhaps, it was time for her to direct him in the search.

Liz ate the 'continental breakfast' offered by the bed and breakfast --- fresh bakery and coffee. It was very good, but all starch and sugar --- no protein to keep the body going. She asked if they had anything else --- like eggs or meat --- and was told that she could buy some fried sausages if she wished. She wished --- and put 4 large sausages, wrapped in waxed paper and a white paper bag, into her purse for later, on the train. Then, she asked the desk clerk to get her a taxi.

Within half an hour, the taxi driver had come and taken her luggage downstairs to the car and, seeing that she was comfortably seated, made for the train station. Once there, he found her a porter and put her luggage onto the man's cart. True to her generous nature, she tipped the taxi driver well and he smiled, saying, "Come visit us again."

The porter, seeing this, made sure to give her good service with her baggage when she proceeded to the baggage check office and he received his reward as well. He, too, smiled and bowed, saying, "Thank you gnaedige Fraulein."

Liz smiled at his words, but thinking of her Franz, and found a seat in the waiting room until the time her train would arrive. She thumbed through a newspaper she had bought for awhile, but, eventually, the fumes from the fresh newsprint began to burn her eyes and she set it aside for the moment. It was then that, looking maybe 10 feet away to her right, in the rows of facing bench seating, she saw him --- Mr. Henri. He, like her, was reading a newspaper and appeared not to see her --- or, perhaps, was purposely ignoring her?

She sat there, wondering if he would come and sit by her or drop off a note, but nothing happened. Perhaps, she thought, he was planning to take the train to Luxembourg, too. Or, was he just verifying that she was on the train? More questions --- just when Mr. Froehlich had answered some of her questions about Franz!

She read her paper again for a bit and, when she looked up from it, Mr. Henri was gone --- the place he had been occupying was empty. So, she thought, he must have been making sure I was here on time. Oh, all these questions and mysteries!

It was not long before her train arrived and the rasping voice on the loudspeaker announced in three languages that her train was available for boarding. She gathered up her purse, newspaper, and the bag containing her leftovers from the day before and her sausages, as well as a number of pieces of bakery from the bed and breakfast. At least, she would not arrive in Luxembourg, in the evening, hungry. Holding her coat over her arm and carrying the rest, she went out onto the platform and boarded the train.

Once inside, she could see that this car was fuller than the one yesterday, though it still had plenty of seats. She found one which a family of 4 had just vacated and, sitting down, placed her bag on the seat next to her. Only one other person came aboard the car after her, a young woman, well dressed and with a pleasant expression on her face. Seeing someone close to her own age, she asked if the seats across from Liz were taken, and hearing that they were not, she sat down in the window seat directly across from Liz.

"Is this your first time traveling?" she asked, in German.

"Oh, no," answered Liz in German, as well, "Is it yours?"

"Yes, and I find it so exciting --- but a little frightening," the girl revealed. "Where have you traveled to?"

"Oh, I have traveled quite extensively in Europe and the United States," Liz said.

The young woman's eyes grew larger, then she asked, "What is it like --- the United States? Do you know any film stars? Clark Gable? Vivian Leigh? Leslie Howard? Olivia de Havilland?"

"Actually, yes, I did see them. I went to the premiere of 'Gone With The Wind' in Atlanta, Georgia," answered Liz.

The woman --- actually, girl would be more accurate --- for she could not have been more than 19, rolled her eyes ecstatically, and asked, "What was it like? What did they wear? Was she as beautiful in person?" in rapid succession.

Liz, chuckling, said, "You will have to let me tell you a little at a time. It's too big a story for 5 minutes," and knew that she had found a travel companion who would keep her busy and entertained all the way to Luxembourg --- if the girl was going that far..... In a matter of moments she had ascertained that, indeed, that was the girl's destination. She was taking a trip there to visit her grandmother and perhaps, if they suited each other, she would stay with her and care for her in her declining years.

As their time together passed and they conversed about the girl's grandmother, she (Emmalina) said that her elderly grandmother had other children and grandchildren living in Luxembourg. They were all very busy with work and school, so they had invited her to come and live there to care for the grandmother. It sounded to Liz as though maybe this was an exploitation of Emmalina, but, perhaps, the girl would find a suitor there and all would be well in the end.....

It seemed that Liz was destined to travel via locals, and never the express trains, here, in Europe. It gave her a lot of time to visit with Emmalina, though, and they talked and laughed their way through much of Germany. It was fortunate that Liz spoke German, for Emmalina spoke no

English and only a bit of Luxembourgish and a little French from school.

Glad of her rations, Liz had shared all day with Emmalina and she had shared hers with Liz, as well --- for all the world like two elementary school girls with their best friend, Liz thought. It was a nice feeling, the camaraderie, and Liz relaxed into it, giving it full rein. She gave Emmalina her address in Illinois and also the name of the pension she would stay at in Luxembourg --- and Emmalina reciprocated with her grandmother's address. Interesting, Liz thought while looking at it; Heffingen, the origin of her mother's family.

Although the train traveled reasonably fast, it was the stops in so many little towns that slowed the whole business down. It must slow, then stop, allow time for passengers to board or depart, and, then, ease away from the platform and begin to pick up speed again --- at the least, a 15-minute procedure for each stop. Add to that the border stop for identification and stamping of passports, to say nothing of searches for former Nazis attempting to escape justice…..

Thus, it was, that they arrived in Luxembourg at almost 11 p.m. They, picked up their purses, coats and bags, and, finally, when they stepped down onto the platform in the nearly empty station, Liz remembered that someone was to meet her here --- a taxi driver. No one was there to pick up Emmalina, however, so after rousing the baggage claim clerk and claiming their belongings, they piled her things into the taxi with Liz' and took off for the Pension Moselle.

When Liz' things were unloaded and carried inside, Liz spoke to the driver and gave him the address he was to take Emmalina to, along with a generous tip for his trouble and instructions to return to the pension at 10 o'clock the next morning for her.

Then, giving Emmalina a hug and waving to her as the car disappeared into the night, she went back indoors and followed the sleepy clerk carrying her baggage up the stairs to her room. It was on the second floor and expensive by Luxembourg standards due to being more easily accessible. Narrow 4 or 5 storey houses were the norm in Luxembourg City --- nestled close to each other, like joined row houses in the U.S., to retain their warmth in winter.

The room was large and there were only 2 to a floor in this house --- one facing the street and the other facing the back, a garden behind the row of buildings. Liz' room faced the street. She was hungry, though she had eaten during the day --- probably her breakfast hunger, as her mother used to say….. It didn't matter, though, for she opened her bag and ate a leftover piece of sausage, an egg, and some cookies, then washed them down with the last swig of spring water and went to refill the jar from the bathroom tap….. She felt better and knew that she would sleep better, as well. Fatigued, she climbed into the bed and did just that.

ℒChapter 28 –Luxembourg, Heffingen, Anna℘

Morning came with the sun streaming through the window --- too early her body screamed! She had forgotten to pull the drapes together after she looked at the lights of the city the night before. She got up and closed them, then climbed back under the covers to see if sleep would claim her again, but her mind was her enemy this morning and no matter how she tried, sleep evaded her as that mind attempted to begin plaguing her with its questions and its logic.

She lay there for the better part of an hour before giving in to her brain. Once she did, the thoughts came like a flock of birds, one after another..... She hardly had time to acknowledge one, before a different one was there taking its place and demanding her attention. Most of the thoughts were of Franz, but others were of Mr. Henri and how he fit in --- also, Emmalina and her situation. Was she a relative, Liz wondered? Time would tell, for she would visit Heffingen, and soon. This was Wednesday, and she wanted first to visit Patton's grave --- after breakfast, of course.

She found, on descending, that the pension did not offer even as much as the bed and breakfast in Frankfurt had --- in the lobby there was a tray of bakery and some cups for coffee or tea. She supposed that one took it back to their room but, rather than walk back up the stairs, she sat in one of the 4 straight-backed chairs and breakfasted there. After Patton, she would find a café and have a more proper breakfast!

True to his word, the taxi driver pulled up in front at 10 a.m. sharp. She went down to meet him and saved him a trip up the stairs. He opened her door and after she had been comfortably seated, got back in and asked where she would like to go. He was not surprised when she told him. Many visitors, Americans and otherwise, were visiting Patton --- crediting him with single-handedly winning the war..... She was younger than most, though, it seemed.

She walked across the broad expanse of grass to the General's grave and sat down beside it --- to have a chat with the General. Whether he was in some other realm or his spirit no longer existed, she wanted something universal and eternal to know how she felt and how she respected this harsh man who had played a major role in stopping such an evil as had occurred in Europe these 10 years and more. After awhile, she took a picture of the marker, for her parents and Franz', and then walked back to the taxi after saying a prayer of homage and thanks to the American soldiers buried there.

When the driver asked her where she wanted to go next, she asked if he would like to have lunch with her. Surprised, he took her to a small café he knew of --- nothing fancy, but good food. They ate fried fish, potatoes mashed together with carrots, and beets which had been grated and fried with butter, salt and pepper. Dessert was fruit tarts with coffee, rich and creamy. They talked. He was surprised to discover that she spoke his three languages and English, besides, but when she mentioned her ancestry, he understood.

They lingered for a few hours and then she asked him to take her to Heffingen. "Are you going to visit the girl?" he queried.

"Not this time," she answered, "You see, I have relatives there, as well."

So, they began the 45 minute drive and, by a little after 2 o'clock, they were in the tiny village. After installing the driver under a large, spreading tree, for a nap in his taxi, she looked around and decided how to proceed. Since she didn't know the address of her relatives, she knocked on a likely door and asked the man who came to it if he knew Anna Kayser. He said that he did and pointed to a house down the road, saying, "Over there," before closing the door and retreating to his house. She had asked him in Luxembourgish, so he had no undue curiosity.

Walking down the street to the house he had indicated, she wondered how she would find her great-aunt. She knocked on the door and waited. After awhile, the door opened and an elderly lady peered out into the sunlight, eyes squinting at the brightness. "Who is it?" she asked.

"It's Lisbet, your grand-niece," Liz answered, again in Luxembourgish, "From America."

"From America?" the old lady questioned, bemused.

"Yes," Liz answered.

"But, how did you get here?" her great-aunt asked, seemingly unaware of the obvious.

"On a boat and a train," Liz offered.

"Oh, come in, come in." Grosstante Anna said, realizing how foolish it seemed to be standing there at the door, "Where are your bags? Are your parents with you?"

"No, Tante, I am staying at a pension in Luxembourg, because I have business there, but I wanted to come and talk to you, as well." Thus began a conversation lasting hours and covering family, education, the war, and, finally, Franz, his disappearance, and supposed defection.

Her aunt was shocked at the news, saying that politics are always bad, and governments almost as bad, but she wondered why they couldn't get their stories together and figure out that he was no defector.

Liz told her about the dreams, then, and the information about his escape from the Nazis, she had gleaned from Mr. Froehlich.

"Ah," said Tante Anna, "You have the gift --- or perhaps the curse, depending on how you feel about it. With this, you will find him. Believe it!"

At this point, Liz remembered her poor driver, sitting in his car under the tree, and told her great-aunt that she must go, but that she would return for another visit before she left for America. The old lady's heart was filled with joy to hear that for, in that short time that they visited, she had come to life, again, thanks to Liz. In all her life she had never bonded so quickly with a person.

"You promise that you will come again?"

"Yes, Tante Anna, I will come again," Liz answered, bending to hug the old lady and kiss her forehead. "Be good until I return."

"Oh, I'm too old to be bad," Tante Anna answered, with a giggle.....

Liz let herself out the door and went back to the taxi. The driver was leaning against the car waiting for her and asked if she was ready to go. She nodded, opened the door, and slid onto the seat.

On the way back, they talked a bit, but Liz felt strangely quiet. At first, she couldn't put her finger on it, but then she realized that she was feeling sad for Tante Anna, because she was getting so old and had no man to love her. As they came into the city, she asked the driver which restaurant he would recommend for dinner near her pension. He said that there was one only a block away that was good and she asked him to take her there. True to his word, there was a restaurant close to the pension and he stopped in front. Liz had no inclination for night life and planned an early evening, so she paid him handsomely for the day's work and asked if he could do the same the following day.

"Yes, I can. Do you want me to come at the same time?" he inquired.

"That would be good," she answered, "And we can get a lot done. If you would like, we can have breakfast earlier, though," she said with a grin.....

He smiled back and touched his cap in a small salute, before driving away.

Liz ate well and took her dessert back to the pension with her for later. She had had a full day --- so many experiences to think about and process..... What would she have done without her driver, she wondered as she hung her coat in the armoir. It was then that she noticed a small piece of paper on the floor near the door of her room, as though it had been shoved under it. She walked over and picked it up, then opened it to see what it said.

You are doing well. Continue to follow your own intuition. Stay in Lux. as long as necessary. I will be aware. The driver is to be trusted with anything. Contact will be made when needed. H.

ᏭChapter 29 – Luxembourg, ThursdayᏮ

Liz woke up the next morning with the note still held tightly in her palm --- like a talisman. When she had slipped into bed, she had lain there thinking about all that had transpired since her journey began --- or, at least, from the moment she saw Gibraltar. She had met so many wonderful, caring people and she wondered how such a terrible war could have been allowed when so many people were good. It was a mystery, indeed, but she suspected that fear was the answer and that when good people are afraid --- or even indifferent --- they don't acknowledge the signs of impending disaster. These thoughts filled her mind, again, in those early morning hours --- the ones when we are still and open --- and she felt that, in that short time, she had become more than she had been. It is an oddity of human growth, that we have spurts, stops and starts, as well as, 'aha moments', and this was one such for Liz.

Today, I will see Paul Tischler, she decided, and, after that, I will be able to focus on Franz entirely.

Her taxi was waiting in front of the pension at 10 o'clock, when she descended the stairs. Trustworthy, she thought, just like the note said, as he opened the door and saw her into the car. "The same café?" he asked.

"Oh, yes," she answered. "I hope that the breakfast is as good as yesterday's lunch was."

"It is," he said, "And cheaper, too," which brought a chuckle out of Liz that she tried, unsuccessfully, to stifle with a smile.

The café was emptying of its breakfast customers and Liz had many tables to choose from. She liked a table at the window, where they could look at the quaint architecture and see people coming and going as they ran their errands, and they sat down. Their breakfast was, indeed, wonderful --- omelet soufflés with kirsch, potato dumplings topped with breadcrumbs browned in butter, sausages, and hot, rich coffee with cream and sugar.

They talked as they watched the people pass by. Sometimes, he gave a running commentary on the buildings or the people they saw --- sometimes, she asked questions of him. All in all, it was a good morning and, when they left the café, she saw that he had been right --- it was cheaper than lunch.

Now, she would have to find Paul Tischler, if he was still alive --- and living in Luxembourg. They tried the telephone company, with no luck. Then, her driver suggested that she ask at the electric power company, since more had electricity than telephones. In this, they were lucky; finding a Paul Tischler living in Luxembourg City.

They proceeded immediately to the address they were given by a helpful clerk. It was one of the tall, thin houses stuck together like the brownstones of the eastern states, only these were much higher, maximizing the smaller land area of Luxembourg, a country lacking hundreds of thousands of square miles to spread out in…..

It was a well-kept building, as all here seemed to be in spite of the war. When her driver had parked, Liz walked up the steps to the door and pulled the bell chain. After a few minutes, she could hear heavy footsteps inside and the door opened. A large-framed older man, with hair so blonde it was almost white and ice blue eyes, stood in the doorway. "Ja?" he queried.

After asking his name, Liz began, in Luxembourgish, to explain who she was, where she had come from and why she was there. Listening closely, as soon as he realized that this was a potential relative from America, he asked her to come in and have tea.

The parlor and kitchen were on the same floor, not truly the first, for there was a basement, but the floor that the front door opened to. He showed her into the parlor and soon brought hot water in a teapot and cups, creamer and sugar bowl on a tray to serve from. He poured both cups ¾ full, leaving plenty of room for cream and sugar, then began to ask questions.

"What is the name of your husband's grandfather, his wife, their children? And your family?" came fast --- all rattled off like machine-gun fire.

Slowly and calmly, Liz told him that they had all originated in Heffingen and began giving him the names and ages. She had been told that almost all of Franz' family and extended family had immigrated to the U.S. within a few years of each other, so Paul might well be the only one left. Within her own family and their friends, some, like her great-aunt, stayed in the old country. Often, they were the oldest son and his family --- the inheritors of the family farm. The younger sons went to the new country to make their way and hopefully, their fortune.....

As he took in her words, he began to glow..... This was the wife of his cousin's son..... There were still Tischlers in the world! He had a wife, but they were both old, and their sons had died in the war --- one of wounds, the other of influenza. None of their other babies had lived past infancy. When his sons died, he and his wife had moved out of the vicinity of Heffingen, with no one to help with the land, and used the money from the farm's sale to buy the house in Luxembourg City, closer to the services they would need in their old age. He had been trained, as had all of his family, in joinery --- finish carpentry, also called woodworking. Their family name reflected this --- Tischler is German for carpenter.

When Liz had finished, he told his story. She was touched by his earnestness and the sadness of losing his sons. When his tears fell, hers fell with them in a coming together, not just of relations, but, of friends. They had forgotten the tea, but now both sipped, not noticing that it was no longer hot, just lukewarm. Each of them was reviewing, in their mind, all that had been said and all that they remembered of the people named. It was a time for quiet and reflection, an honoring of those who had passed, as well as those who were still alive. Family.

Finally, Liz broke the silence saying, "Anna Kayser still lives in Heffingen."

"Old Anna?" he asked, then continued, "I thought she would have been gone many years now. How does she look?"

"Pretty good for her age, I would say," Liz answered. "It would be a good thing if you visited her from time to time. Your wife would like it, I'm sure, and Anna seems lonely."

"Yes, why not?" he said. "And your husband? What of him?"

Then, Liz told him why she was traveling and asked, if he should hear from Franz, to contact her immediately at the Pension Moselle.

He was startled. Perhaps the Battle of France had claimed another Tischler..... He promised to contact her immediately if he heard anything --- and to visit Anna.

It was at this point that sounds came from the hallway and he jumped to his feet to help his wife bring in her purchases. Telling her they had a guest and to go into the parlor, he made for the kitchen with the bags.

Liz waited and, in a few minutes, a woman a little older than her mother came into the room. Patting her hair into place, she looked careworn and a little flustered. Liz rose to greet her and tell her who she was.

When they were both seated, the lady told Liz that her name was Maria and that her grandmother had also been a Kayser, so they were related, too, by blood. Thus it is in small towns

--- and small countries, as well….. They spoke for a few more minutes, before Paul returned with another cup for Marie, and then sat for awhile going over other family stories, much as people do at reunions.

Finally, Liz asked them to allow her to take them to dinner at the restaurant where she had enjoyed her meal the night before. After much discussion, they agreed, and the taxi was summoned. This time, the driver was included and all four of them partook in the lively conversation this addition brought about. They spent many hours eating --- trying new dishes, and sampling the fine liquors of Luxembourg. Liz had to be firm about paying their minimal tab, but Paul finally capitulated, allowing her to do it.

When it was time to leave, she paid and tipped her driver, then, asked him to drop the Tischlers off at their home and be back at the pension, in the morning, at the usual time.

Nodding, he gathered the Tischlers, like a sheepdog herding sheep, and moved them toward his taxi. As he opened the door, they began waving to Liz, but he finally managed to get them inside and on their way home.

Liz strolled the block to the pension deep in thought. Now, she had fulfilled her family obligations and it was time to get to work. She would meditate this evening to see if she could feel where Franz might be, then pray to have dreams of him when she slept, as well.

ೕ Chapter 30 –Luxembourg, Friday ೞ

Liz awoke to raindrops falling against the windows of her
room --- not hard, but loud enough to be heard. She lay
there, feeling mellow, and remembering the dinner party the
night before --- as well as her meditation afterward.

She had seated herself in the chair after pulling a small table
in front of it and placing one of the candelabra in the room
on the table. After turning off the electric lights, she lit only
one of the candles and sat comfortably, staring at it and
allowing herself to be still and quiet within. Then, she asked
a silent question, "In which direction do I need to go in order
to find Franz?"

She had thought of him, his energy, and their connection ---
remembering their love and more..... At first, she had no
response, but then, she began to feel, as she turned her head
from side to side, a stronger pull to the right, which was
northward-oriented. When she stood up and turned to face
that direction, she felt that, as the crow flies (or, in this case,
as the energy flows), she was facing him. So, this is it, she
decided, I must go north.

Now, in the morning, with rain on the window, she
wondered whether that was feasible, but getting out, from
under the cozy covers and, going to the windows, she saw

that this was only a light spring shower and the sun would be drying it up very soon.

She pulled out a map of Luxembourg from her purse --- one she had picked up in the lobby --- and looked it over carefully. Today, they would travel north, toward Lorenztweiler, and she would "feel" if he was still north of her location when they arrived. Perhaps they would continue further north --- but first, the café!

With that thought, she bathed and dressed, then almost skipped down the stairs to the lobby and down to the waiting taxi. Her driver was ready and he asked if they would go to the café again. She answered in the affirmative and in less than 15 minutes they were being seated.

They had quiche and sausages this morning with the steaming coffee, cream and sugar like the day before. This time they took sweet rolls, but had them boxed for the trip and asked for extra sausages and bottles of water as well. Who knew what they might or might not find in the way of cafés in small towns and villages?

The rain had stopped almost completely when Liz left the pension and by the time they left the café no trace could be seen --- not a cloud in the sky. There was still the smell of rain, but only on the breeze.

They traveled north toward Lorentzweiler, a journey of only 7 or 8 miles, but it was slow going with the occasional farming vehicles on the road. In a little over half an hour, they had arrived. This was no big city, merely a village, as were most places in farming regions. They stopped, got out of the car, and Liz thought about Franz and let the energy surround her. She could still feel the connection, but it seemed to be more to the southwest of her, now.

They sat and visited, then she tried it again. Definitely, it was to the west and southward. They got back into the taxi and drove back on another route which was fairly parallel to the first, but ¾ of a mile to the west. About 3 ½ miles down the road, they stopped and Liz tried to make the connection again. This time she felt it was due west. This time, they ate the sausages and some of the small sweet rolls. The driver asked her about what she was doing and she told him that she could feel Franz' energy and was trying to pinpoint it. He looked surprised, but said no more.

The midday meal eaten, they headed south once again and, this time, Liz tried feeling the energy as they were traveling. It wasn't the same as when she stood still and did it --- the twists and turns of the road made her feel a little dizzy when she tried to feel the connection…..

Finally, they stopped, again, about a mile north of Luxembourg City and, at that point, Liz felt that the connection was definitely to the northwest. This helped to pinpoint it, but she wanted to go back to the pension and think about what she had felt, just to get the lay of the land a little better. She had made notes to remind her where on the map she had felt the direction shift and hoped that she could discover from that which specific town or village his energy was coming from.

The driver left her at the restaurant near the pension, again, at her request, promising to return to her pension in the morning.   She was no adventurer --- having found a restaurant which served lunches and dinners and had variety, she preferred to stay with it than to search out another.   She ate the pike with green sauce, boiled potatoes, and a plate of spring greens with lemon juice over it.   She became daring with dessert and ordered the cheesecake with a brandy sauce topping.   She enjoyed the rich coffee that they brought her with it, then, completely satisfied, she returned to the pension.

When she was in her room, once again, she used the candle to help her sink into the deep meditative state she had experienced the evening before.   When she tried to connect with Franz' energy, it still seemed that it came from due north.   This contradiction confused her and she stopped the meditation and began pacing, eventually walking to the windows As she looked out onto the street, suddenly she realized that her room faced east, not southeast, because she could not see any of the sunset.   This would cant the energy source to the west somewhat, so her perceptions on the road had been correct, after all.

Looking at the map, she saw that there were three communes to the west of the place where it had seemed that the energy changed direction.   One was Kehlen, another Kopstal, and the closest was Bidden.   On Saturday, they would have to go to these three so that she could feel how they related to the energy she was sensing.

At that point, she decided to get some rest and, hopefully, dream of Franz or feel the connection more intensely.   She crawled under the covers and lay there waiting for sleep to come, but it was elusive until she decided to go back into that meditative state she had accessed earlier. As she lay there, letting the meditation flow, feeling the nothingness and floating on a current, she drifted easily into slumber --- perchance to dream.

℘Chapter 31 – Luxembourg, The Search Narrows℘

Liz awoke from sleep the next morning as gently as she had drifted into it the night before. There was no alarm clock, no sunbeams --- she had remembered to draw the drapes --- and no noises from outside to wake her roughly, so, she was able to remember what she had been dreaming. It was, of course, a dream about Franz. He was walking through what appeared to be a hospital corridor, wearing an orderly's uniform. Then, he was shown working as a farm laborer. He kept calling, "Lisbet, où êtes-tu ?"

As she lay there, without moving, and letting the impressions come without forcing them, she felt that he was giving her a history, or timeline, of his experiences, which became closer to the current date each time it came into her consciousness.

At some point, she had the insight that, perhaps, if he had moved, or was moving, from place to place, her impression of where the energy was originating might shift with time and, to be accurate, she would need to check it often.

As she continued to lay abed, she still felt strongly that he was alive and that this was not a spirit or ghost's energy that she was perceiving. It did not have the feeling of being an echo; rather the feeling that this person was still alive and well --- and longing with their entire heart and being --- as was she.

"So," she asked herself aloud, "What is the strategy?" From somewhere deep inside came the answer --- that she must be driven to many parts of Luxembourg to sense the energetic connection's strength and direction in those areas. She desperately hoped that her driver would understand and not think she was crazy.....

From her bed, Liz could see the wall clock --- 9:45 a.m. Time to get out of bed, she thought, and let her action follow that thought. In a few minutes, she was dressed and ready for the day. Wearing a frock and a sweater, she walked down the front steps to where her taxi was awaiting her.

They breakfasted at the usual place, talking of their travels the day before. Liz told him about her thoughts --- as well as her directional error with the windows (he smiled) --- and proposed that they work on the western part of Luxembourg, to begin with, especially the towns of Bissen and Kehlen, and the commune of Kopstal. He was happy to drive her anywhere she wanted --- she was an easy fare and, besides, she bought him breakfast and sometimes lunch or dinner..... This was, after all, postwar Europe, even though the rich farmland of Luxembourg brought forth many crops and the Nazi occupation had precluded the kind of damage that beset many areas of Germany.

He drove her first to Kopstal, where she got out and sat for awhile under the shade of a tree, and he napped in the car. Her verdict was 'north', so, north they went.

The next stop was Tuntange, near the Belgian border on the northwest portion of Luxembourg. She sat in the shade, again, while he napped and, when she was ready, they left. This time, she had felt the energy to the south.

On the way back to Luxembourg city, they stopped in Kehlen, a commune of Luxembourg. This time the energy was difficult for Liz to discern --- or, at least, decide in which direction it was coming from. Perhaps she was tired --- the ride had been longer than the day before --- and slow-going in the hilly terrain….. She made the decision to call it a day, return to Luxembourg, buy some dinner and return to the pension after she'd eaten.

The following day would be Sunday and she planned to give her driver a day off and stroll through the city sightseeing.

When he dropped her off at the restaurant near her pension, he asked if she would need him the next day and she answered, "No, I thought I would give you a vacation day and I would walk around the city looking at buildings and things."

He thought for a moment, then asked her, "Would you like to go to a party? My wife's mother is celebrating her 75th birthday and we will make a party at her house."

Liz thanked him and said that she would like to have a rest day, then, as he walked back to his taxi, she called to him, "At what time?"

He came back to her, smiling, and said they were planning to begin at 5 o'clock in the evening, because some of the family worked on Sundays. Taxi drivers and a nurse. He added that he could pick her up at 4:30 if she would like to join in the celebration.

"Yes, that sounds good --- I would like it very much.," she answered. "What gift would make her happy?"

"Oh, whatever ladies like --- flowers, cologne....."

"Thank you for inviting me," she said, echoing his smile.

He grinned and turned to leave, when he heard Liz say, "You've never told me your name, you know."

Turning back, he answered, "Nick, ...Nicolas Evon."

"Thank you, Nick, I look forward to the party," she said, pushing the restaurant door open as he turned, again, to the car.

Inside the restaurant, she was seated immediately --- there was plenty of space, since she was an early diner. She ordered the roast duck and potato dumplings with sauerkraut, enjoying some of the same dishes that her mother and grandmothers cooked.

While she ate, she thought about the afternoon's trip and the results. She wondered if she was just spinning her wheels with this energy connection. Was he there, but moving around? What was happening?

Pondering this phenomenon, she played with her dessert, a piece of apple cake, smelling of cinnamon and other good things. Without resolving her questions, she finished her coffee and dessert and made her way back to the pension and sleep.

As she lay in bed thinking of Franz and how much she longed to find him and how confusing it was that the direction of their connection seemed to move, she began to think about their honeymoon again and another experience they'd had while staying at the country estate of an English friend, who had loaned it to them while he was away on holiday in the south of France.

Franz held the door open for Liz as she stepped out of the roadster after the short ride to the estate's small lake, her skirt blowing up above her knees in the summer breeze. A quick hand covered the forbidden flesh with her skirt, returning it to its sanctuary.

"What a delightful place," she cooed, as she surveyed the lakeshore and the waterfowl floating further out.

Franz reached for the picnic baskets and the tarpaulin they would sit on as they ate and sketched, then led her to a grassy knoll overlooking the scene. He laid the tarp, preparing the table and, quickly, the baskets had disgorged their contents: watercolors, brushes, pencils and paper from one, and sandwiches, potato salad, fruit and homemade cider from the other.

He offered his hand to Liz and soon she was seated with him, drawing and laughing as they nibbled their sandwiches. He felt so good in her presence. He couldn't have explained it if he had been asked, he just felt at peace.

Occasionally, as they worked, their fingertips chanced to touch and each seemed to experience a catch in their breath for a moment, before that touch broke away. It began to build a tension between them, not a tenseness, rather a being aware of an undercurrent, a surge of energy, that connected them.

They drew and painted for many hours, laughing as they chatted, teasing, smiling, as the drawings and watercolors came into being: ducks diving, dappled water, green trees reflecting in the mirror of the lake.....

As the day waned, the touches became longer, the contact more electric and connective, and the glances into each other's eyes full of hidden meaning.

At last, Franz stood up to stretch and, reaching for Liz' hands, pulled her up to stretch as well. His hands didn't release hers, though, and he pulled her into his arms. He looked her straight in the eyes, then leaned forward to touch his lips to hers, taking her lips prisoner with the sweetness of that contact.

They stood there, arms wrapped around each other, every nerve coming alive, tingling with a fire they could hardly contain.

Finally, they sank onto the stiff canvas and at first sat, then lay, kissing each other deeply and stroking each other as much as they dared. Franz ran his hand along Liz' left leg from ankle to knee and, then, upward very slowly under the cover of her skirt. She shuddered involuntarily, a shiver of anticipation, not at all due to the twilight breeze. As he stroked her leg, higher and then higher, she began to shake with the force of her arousal. She wanted him, she needed him, her body was arching with its longing for him, and while he was endeavoring to hold himself in check, he was reacting to her arousal in a way, and with a force, he had not known before.

As he kissed her, he stroked her breasts, as well as her back and her bottom, then finally lifted her skirt and slid her silk underpants right off over her garter-belt and stockings. Thus, he could use his fingers to great advantage and slide them gently into the slippery juices dripping from Liz' nether recess. He found the copious secretions arousing and gently moved his middle finger from one end to the other of the groove between her legs and back, sliding in the slick mucous as easily as if it were warm butter.

Liz began to moan, muscles tensing and relaxing alternately, wriggling as she lay there; the object of his ministrations. Her breathing was becoming ragged and labored as his fingers brought her close to a climax, then, it was upon them. She rocked back and forth, moaning louder and more insistently, shuddering with the waves of sensation coursing through her body, then tensing one final time which seemed to last forever.

Franz held her in his arms, kissing her, stroking her, and waiting for her orgasm to abate before he began it all again. Then, slowly, he began to stroke her, lightly this time, fingertips tantalizing her nerve endings, his tongue trailing down her neck and lightly stimulating her earlobes. She began to shudder again from time to time and, as he brought her to another full arousal, she began to explore with her own hands.

He had undone his belt at some point with his left hand and unbuttoned his trousers to release his erect member, which had swollen into a strong firm shaft as he stroked her to that first orgy of sensation. Now, it was demanding release and he could not keep it penned any longer. His Liz found that shaft, moved the underclothing aside, and began to touch it, stroke it, and squeeze it.

Franz' ability to hold himself in abeyance was being sorely tested. He wanted her to be beyond ready and far on her way to a second or perhaps even a third orgasm before he entered her, but he was struggling to achieve this. Each wriggle of her body brought about an equal reaction within his. Even the slightest touch of her hand on his shaft brought him almost to the brink of the roller coaster ride into supreme ecstasy.

Liz, for her part, was so beside herself with pleasure and sensation, that she had little notion of the difficulties Franz was experiencing. Her heart was pounding and her body seemed to have a life of its own, set completely apart from her mind. She wanted the sensations to go on forever. They felt so GOOD. This man knew how to play her body like a violin, an artiste giving her the greatest concert of her life.

He rolled his fingers around the little button at the top of her secret recess and brought more moans of purest pleasure from her lips. He bared her breasts and suckled at the nipples, sending waves of sensation across her body, then, finally, he entered her.

She almost screamed with the pleasure of his entry as she threw her head back, arching her back and driving her body against his. He had thought he would release all as soon as he entered her, but to his surprise --- and delight --- he still had work to do. His hips swaying from back to front, he slipped in and out, like a hummingbird's tongue drinking the nectar of the flower. The rhythm was ancient, and the ritual of love in many ways the same as it always is, yet for them it was new, fresh, a magical physical meeting full of sparklers and fireworks.

Franz could feel his own impending orgasm growing nearer. Muscles tensing and only partially relaxing, a moan escaped his throat as he exploded into his release. Liz' hips pumped with as much force as his own, and shaft and scabbard met each other with a fierce seating until the lovers collapsed into each other's arms, spent and longing for sleep as the twilight grew dimmer and night was at the point of falling.

Crickets and other night noise-makers began a serenade to the two entwined lovers as they lay there, too languid to move more than a fraction. Even the tiniest stroke of a cheek was beyond either one of them for the moment. Breathing evenly and normally at this point, the torpor seemed like sleep, yet wasn't. Their arms and legs seemed too heavy to move, so they didn't even try.....

Finally, Franz, loosely draped about her person, managed, "Are you warm enough?"

Liz mumbled something unintelligible and he pulled away and asked his question once more, to which she answered, "Not so warm as I was a short time ago....."

He put his arms back around her and drew her close again. The warmth of their combined body heat was a comfort in the breeze of the waning evening, but soon they would have to rise, put their clothing to rights, pick up the remains of the picnic, and return to the roadster.

Liz of 1946 lay there remembering the love and the passion they shared. As she remembered, it took only a small effort for her little fingers to work their magic between her legs.

Already, they were slipping and sliding, ever so lightly, on the wetness within those lower lips as she built the passion to its highest point. Her hips could not stay still --- they gyrated from front to back, then in circles, as her heat and her passion rose. It was as though he were inside of her even then, sliding in and out and fulfilling her body's every need with the magic of his rigid saber. Her fingers slid faster, though just as lightly, and her head arched backward into the pillow as she moaned in her ecstasy.

Oh, now, here it comes, she thought, as the wave overcame her throbbing body immersing her in its power. She lay there, holding her furry mound and trying to breathe normally again, and finally, gratefully, allowed sleep to overtake her.

ᦸ Chapter 32 – Luxembourg, Sunday, The Party ᦹ

Liz woke up with her hand still between her legs. Squeezing the furry mound there, she remembered, with a decided glow, the evening before. She lay there basking in the morning light and thinking --- pondering the connection between Franz and herself. Finally, remembering that she had no 10 o'clock appointment that morning, she decided to think about it another day and drifted back to sleep.

When, at last, she awoke again, she came slowly out of a dream --- once again of Franz --- and remembered a great deal of it. He was driving an old army ambulance, transferring patients from a field hospital to a sanitarium sort of setting, then, going back for more. In the blink of an eye the scene changed and he was working in fields cutting something with a scythe, wearing farmer's clothing with a hat, and having sunburn. Again, he was driving the ambulance --- this time to a battlefield --- and then working in the fields, where he was planting seed.

As she came into full consciousness, she took this sequencing of scenes to mean that they were consecutive --- a timeline. So, putting it all together, she reasoned the sequence --- first, she had seen him being taken to the cellar, though that was explained. Then, she saw him wounded and he was in a hospital though, later, he worked in the hospital as an orderly who might have only transferred patients. Next, he was harvesting and it must have been late summer --- perhaps at a lull in the battles. And, finally, he was going to the battlefield to collect the wounded and, afterward, working in the fields planting, which might be spring. 1941. Perhaps...... But, then, what was he doing all of the time up until 1946?

And, of course, the one really big question she had was whether she was feeling the energy of the timeline or of his current energy --- or of both..... She could tell that it was going to be quite a can of worms to untangle.....

Being awake enough to realize the conundrum she was dealing with meant that she was awake enough to go sightseeing, so she pulled herself languidly out of bed and made ready to see the city on foot. She had saved part of her apple cake from the night before and nibbled on it as she dressed --- not really satisfying hunger, rather building the desire to eat a hearty breakfast. But where? She enquired at the desk downstairs, but found that there were few, if any, restaurants open on Sunday in this predominantly Catholic country. So, she asked the clerk if the pension had any food she could buy to keep her strength up until she found a restaurant --- or until dinner. He said that they did and brought out a selection of sweet rolls, strawberries and apples. She selected 2 sweet rolls, a bowl of strawberries and an apple, giving the clerk a tip for his help. She sat in the small lobby eating them from a dish and looking through the brochures for something she hadn't already read. No, nothing new, but the strawberries were certainly choice, fragrant and sweet.

When she had finished them, she went out onto the street looking for things to see and a place to eat one of her sweet rolls. So many old buildings..... It didn't seem necessary to know their individual history --- just to look at them, admiring the craftsmanship, was adequate. As she walked, taking in the vista of churches, public buildings, even the private homes, she gained an appreciation for the character of the lives of the Luxembourgers. There was a neatness, a tidiness, to the whole. Of course, their tiny country had been occupied and, thus, escaped most of the bombings and artillery shellings that many others had experienced. They had been a site of hospitals and sanitariums for recovering soldiers.

The day stretched out before her and, in her wanderings, she found a souvenir shop, situated not far from the Notre Dame Cathedral of Luxembourg, which was open. It carried quite a variety of items, from rosaries and bibles, to handkerchiefs hand-embroidered with the likeness of the cathedral, as well as ones with other landmark buildings, and, of course, The Bock, that fortress of renown.

Finally, though, she settled on a small bottle of perfume --- lilies of the valley, with a stem of the flowers inside 'pickled', so to speak, in the alcohol. It was so pretty that she couldn't\ pass it up. Adding a handkerchief embroidered with 'the praying hands', she completed her gift to Nick's mother-in-law, and asked the clerk to wrap them. The lady found a white box which would contain them both and wrapped it up with a gay flowered paper and a blue ribbon.

"Your mother will like this, madam," she said.

Liz didn't correct her, feeling it would be rude to do so. She paid the bill, thanked her for her help, and exited onto the street to look at more.

She found one of the many city parks and ate a sweet roll and her apple there, feeding the crumbs to the songbirds. Unlike Hansel and Gretel, whose crumbs the birds ate, she had a good map and could easily find her way back to the pension. At 4 o'clock she returned and changed her ensemble to clothing more befitting a party --- a pretty light blue dress, rather than the drab clothing she had worn for her walk.

When she opened the door of the pension, Nick was just arriving. He got out and opened the taxi door for her, saying, "My family is excited to meet you."

"And I am looking forward to meeting them, too," she answered.

This time, they went southeast from the city, as they headed for Hesperange the largest town in the commune of the same name. Smaller than Luxembourg city, by far, it still boasted a decent population count.

As they drove the few miles to their destination, Nick pointed out the sites of cultural importance, even the ruins of the Hesperange Castle, a building dating to the 13th century..

Liz was interested, just not as avid as she would have been over seeing them before her day of sightseeing..... She didn't say that to Nick --- he was much too excited about showing her something new to tell him that she was tired of seeing the sights

Fortunately, the drive was short and, soon, he was pulling up to his mother-in-laws' house. Liz was escorted indoors with the feeling that she was some sort of a prize. And, indeed, she was, for his mother-in-law had never met an American.

Everyone was there when she made her entrance, and, suddenly, she knew how they felt at the Academy Awards when they stepped out of their limousines to the waiting fans.....

She was introduced to everyone --- the birthday lady first, then, Nick's wife, Marie, and finally everyone else..... Liz knew that she would never remember all of their names or faces, to say nothing of their relationship to Nick.....

In a house so full, even a large one, she was constantly inundated with conversation. It was good that she had spent her day in the serenity of walking and sightseeing, for she would not have the ability to be around so many people otherwise.

The hum of conversation became very intense --- actually, she didn't know whether anyone could hear themselves, much less someone else --- though, they nodded vigorously.....

The dinner was all finger food from a buffet, for there would not have been room for them all to be seated at one table --- foods, such as Liz had never seen, nor imagined, as well as those with which she was familiar --- Swedish-style meatballs and fruit tarts. Everyone ate heartily as they talked, even Liz.

Later, when it came time to open her gifts, Elena, Nick's mother-in-law, opened Liz' box first, to honor her guest. She was surprised and happy to receive both the perfume and the handkerchief and praised Liz for her gift selection..... Then, she proceeded on to the rest: a new teapot, a dress, a head scarf, a piece of sheet music (she played the piano), 2 records and much more..... She sat in the midst of her family's bounty looking like some empress of old receiving tribute.

They sang songs to her, when she had finished opening the gifts, and everyone clapped after each new song. It was obvious that she was filled with joy to have such a large family. Liz felt good being a part of a family gathering of Luxembourgers other than her own --- and Franz'. He would have loved this, she thought.

Out in the street, a young man in laborer's clothing stopped to listen to the merriment. Two cousins, out in garden for some cool evening air, and a cigarette, asked him to come in and join the party, but he refused them politely, saying that he had errands to run. The cousins watched as he ambled away, then one said, "He didn't seem to be in any hurry to get to his 'errands'. Maybe a nagging wife, eh?"

The other man laughed, saying, "As always, you've got it right, Jacques."

Inside, Liz was beginning to get a little tired and, after another hour, she asked Nick if he would mind driving her back to the pension. He agreed and told his wife that he would be back in half an hour, then took Liz to the taxi. On the way to the pension, they saw a man laying on a park

J. Matheny

bench and Liz asked Nick about it. He answered that there were still some displaced soldiers wandering around --- some being men who had lost their faculties or who had no home, or perhaps, sadly, no family to return to. He told her that sometimes the police would pick them up, but they were breaking no law other than not having a place to go, so the police would simply give them a meal and send them on their way.

These were different times than before the war. This sparked a lively discussion on the new United Nations group, which lasted until he dropped her off at the pension.

As they drove up, she asked, "Can you make it noon tomorrow? I don't know how long it will take for all this wine to wear off."

Nick smiled to himself, chuckled and, remembering some of his boyhood hangovers, said, "I understand, and yes, I will see you again at noon."

When he had stopped the car, he walked her up to the door, to make certain that she had no missteps on the cement stairs, and then returned to the party.

Liz, back upstairs in her room, took off her clothes, climbed beneath the covers, and fell into a very deep sleep. Libation often has prodigious powers to soothe the troubled mind.....

ᔕ Chapter 33 - Luxembourg, After the Ball ᔦ

Liz' head was fuzzy the next morning --- due to a few too many glasses of excellent Luxembourg wine, she was sure. It seemed as though, every few minutes, someone had toasted something the night before: the hostess' 75th birthday, her children, Patton, the Allies, Eisenhower, Roosevelt, Churchill, and, of course, Luxembourg, itself..... .....and the glasses rose in the air, then descended to their mouths over and over. They could have gone on all night --- and, at the time, she thought, a few might do so. Liz, however, knew the limits of her body and that she planned to search further for Franz the following day.....

As she lay there in the bed, squinting at the late morning sunlight illuminating her room, she had vague memories of something, some feeling, no, she thought, some sense of having been near Franz last night. Was it in a dream, she wondered, or was it a connection? She was trying hard to sort it all out. Was the connection telling her to search in the south, now? This was confusing and, with her wine-thick head, she was having no luck at all in sorting it out. Better get Dad's old remedy.....

She lurched out of bed to the water pitcher on the dresser and poured herself a glass of water, drank it, then poured another. Once she had finished drinking two glasses, she felt considerably more capable of facing the day and, after a quick shower, she dressed, brushed her hair and was ready for the road.

Nick was waiting for her in the taxi and asked if she had eaten, but, looking in the rearview mirror, he knew the answer before she said a word. She asked if they could go to the same place as usual and he turned in that direction.

Later, with a light breakfast and a bit of coffee inside of her, Liz was more certain that she would make it through the day and, beginning to feel more lucid, she said, "Let's go to the South today, Nick. I have a feeling."

He was surprised, but obliged her, and the taxi headed back in the direction of the previous evening's frivolity.

As the countryside passed by, Nick told her that the party had, indeed, gone on until after midnight for some --- not him, but the older people reminiscing about their youth and talking about the wars, the occupations, and the hope for the future. So much hope.....

They knew that there would always be a call for the wares of the steel industry areas of the south and for the produce of the rich farmlands in the 'Gutland', but they also spoke of their hope for more tourists, Nick told her, who would come to visit Patton's grave, as well as those of the many other soldiers buried in Luxembourg's cemeteries --- tourists who would spend their money on souvenirs, lodgings and meals; a softer industry..... And, one which didn't require so much effort to prevent polluting of air or water.

Liz thought about this and knew that she hoped they would see it come to pass, then, she told Nick to just drive around the cities of the south and in each, she asked him to stop and let her feel the energy.

He headed first toward Hesperange, where the party had taken place. Liz felt it was very strong there, but had no sense of its direction, for it seemed to be all around her. Nick continued, at her request, further south, easing westerly toward Bettembourg and Dudelange, stopping each time near points of interest, such as the Mt. St. Johns ruins or churches to allow her a view of her heritage.

After Dudelange, the taxi veered due west toward Budersburg, Schifflange, Esch-sur-Alzette, and Differdange, homes to steelworks and a well-known music school. Finally, he turned north to Petange, then northeast to Bascharage, and Dippach.

With each stop she stood silently, seeming to him to be meditating or praying, but she was, in reality, sensing the strength of the energy she felt, the connection that was so strong, and from which direction it seemed to feel stronger.....

In spite of her condition when they first began that day, she was feeling a stronger connection than before. As they stopped at each location she marked, on the map of Luxembourg she had been given at the pension, an arrow pointing in the direction she felt had the strongest pull on her. Soon, it was obvious that Hesperange, or perhaps a little north in Luxembourg City, itself, lay the epicenter of the connection. She smiled wryly with amusement when she saw that, thinking, what if it was only a power plant that she was tracking with her energy sensing.

When they reached Luxembourg City, it was evening already and Nick asked, "Would you like to try a different restaurant tonight?"

Liz answered, "Yes, I think so, but would you eat with me? I don't want to eat alone tonight --- do you think Marie would mind?"

"I'm certain she would not," he answered, "She attends a class, after work, to learn how to mark with typewriter machines --- on some weeknights."

Liz gratefully accepted his company after the long day of riding and stopping.

He drove her to a restaurant in another quarter of the city --- closer to the monuments and city center, an area more visited by tourists. The food was good; more French style, than Luxembourgish, though. Lots of sauces.....

They talked. Nick asked about her feeling of the connection that day and she answered, "It seems that the arrows all point toward an area between Hesperange and Luxembourg City --- that's not as large an area as I was feeling, before. Perhaps, tomorrow, we could concentrate on this area. Maybe we can visit the hospitals? There are hospitals here, aren't there?"

"Oh, yes, there are hospitals. Where there are graves and wars, there are always hospitals and sanitariums," he answered.

For a moment, Liz felt foolish for asking such a silly question, but then, by the look on his face, she realized that he was not mocking her. "Have you lost someone?" she asked, suddenly somber.

He nodded. "Yes, I have. Some were friends or neighbors; a few were relatives. I miss them all. Some people think it is easy being occupied, but it is not. Our friends who were Jews are all gone --- some to another country, many to the Nazi camps."

Liz didn't know what to say. Part of her wanted to comfort him, but she didn't know how. Another part wanted to ask him to talk about it, to help lift some of his burden, but she felt an ambiguity as to which approach, if either, was correct. In the end, she did nothing but nod --- as he had.

When dessert came, he became lighter-hearted --- chocolate truly is a cure-all --- and Liz had ordered chocolate cake topped with chocolate mousse for both of them.....

Over dessert and coffee, they planned the following day. They would meet again at 10 o'clock and he would drive her to every health facility in a radius of 3 miles. If they couldn't finish in one day, they would continue the next. "I suppose you should drive me back to the pension, now," Liz said, when their plan had been made.

"Yes, it's time. Marie will be happy that you didn't eat alone. She is very touched by your search --- and Elena, too. They are praying for your success," Nick replied. Liz, in her turn, was touched that someone so recently met would pray for her and for Franz.

That night, when she returned to the pension, she lay in bed only a few moments before allowing the residual taste of chocolate in her mouth to pull her into a dream of Franz --- his seventh birthday party. It was only family, but it was one of her favorite days. They were young, yet, they already were so close. One of his presents was a big box of chocolates and he shared it with her. His mother had to put the box on a high shelf, before they could eat enough to make themselves sick, and Liz always thought of him after that --- whenever she smelled or tasted chocolate. It was a soothing feeling, remembering that party and the chocolate. She slept well.

❧Chapter 34 – Luxembourg, Hospitals☙

When the sunrays made morning patterns on the floor of her room, Liz stirred, remembered her dreams of chocolate and the ones that came after, the ones of her honeymoon. It was early, too early for Nick to pick her up, and her fingers began to explore her body as she thought of the dreams. The one she was having as she drifted out of slumber was the first day of the week they had spent at a villa in France --- one with a pool. They swam and made love in the water and out of it, but in the water was even more fun.

She lay near the edge, sunbathing with the top of her suit undone in back and, suddenly, Franz pulled her into the pool and slid the bottom off of her. She reached to even the score, but found that he had already removed his swimsuit and she grabbed something much more interesting.

Franz returned the favor and soon they were frolicking in the water like a pair of fish --- mating fish.

When she grabbed the side to pull herself out, Franz took her ankles and, holding her legs apart, brought himself high between her thighs. Letting go of her ankles, he took her waist with one hand and his steel-like saber with the other and began to rub it against her secret opening. Liz' juices began to flow and soon he was inside of her, moving his hips effortlessly back and forth in the water and into the waiting, throbbing, place between her legs.

Liz was twisting and turning, meeting each forward thrust of his hips with a push of her arms against the pool rim, seating the connection securely. Over and over he entered and she pushed against him, then away. Faster and faster became the pace. They could not have stopped if they wanted to, for the pace was so intense. Two bodies in perfect unison, dancing a dance as old as time, seething with heat and passion, building to a finale and culminating in a shuddering, wild orgasm, while they were as naked as nature had made them.

Franz held on to her until they stopped shaking, then, finally turned her around and began kissing her. Liz arched her back and wrapped her legs around him, rubbing her secret place against his now flaccid member to thank it for the sensual game they had played.

They stayed there kissing and touching like the newlyweds that they were for quite some time and, to her surprise, and possibly his, the part which had recently pleasured her began to rise again. He squeezed her breasts, pinching her nipples gently between his knuckles until she moaned with need and began to rotate and rock her hips against him. The water made them feel as buoyant and slick as a pair of dolphins and their hands slid over and into each part of the other's body and their own. This was such a clean feeling, touching each other and making love in the water......

They walked to the shallow end, by the steps, and Franz sat on a step at the waterline. Liz knelt in front of him, and began to lick and suck on his stiffening manhood as her hips rotated around and around. Suddenly, Franz said, "I need to be inside of you," and, quickly moving to a lower step, turned her around so that he could hold her breasts or her waist from behind as she sat on his lap and his saber entered its appointed scabbard.

She loved the sensation of feeling him inside of her --- that fullness, combined with the need to slide up and down on him, and the friction bringing them both to a fever pitch. In the heat of their passion, Franz held her by the waist, lifting her up and down on his lap at an ever increasing pace, until he heard a sound in her throat like a keening, a sound of passion requited, a sound of need fulfilled, then, without missing a beat, his orgasm began and, after only a few more strokes, he held her tight to him as he finished, shuddering repeatedly as the last drops entered her.

The Liz of 1946 shuddered as well, as her fingers lightly caressed her little button and moved upward to pinch her nipples until she moaned. Then, leaving the left to continue pinching, she teased the button with the slippery sliding until her entire body was writhing and, finally, she shuddered her release.

In a moment, head clear as a bell, she drew a deep breath and sat up. Lots to do today, she thought. She pinched her nipples once more for good measure, then washed up in the water basin on the dresser, paying special attention to the tender little button and savoring it's lingering tenderness.

"That's all for this morning," she scolded it aloud, then pulled a pair of underwear out of the drawer, as if to underscore her resolve.

Shortly, dressed for the day, she left the pension and got into Nick's taxi. They ate breakfast at the same little café and made a plan of action over the omelets and sausages, then wrote it down as they drank their coffee. Being a taxi driver has its advantages --- Nick knew all of the hospitals and care centers of any kind in the extended Luxembourg City area and, methodically, they began to work their way through them. With photos that Liz had brought with her, they asked every staff person, in each facility they came to, if they had seen Franz. It was tedious work and by 4 o'clock they were feeling the effort, but then realized that they should go back for the evening shift as well. After one day of this, they wondered how they could make it easier.

It was 7 o'clock and Nick said, "Marie asked me invite you for dinner this evening. Would you like this?"

Liz began, "Oh, I don't want to be a bother...," but Nick quickly cut her off, reassuring her that Marie would love to have her be their guest..... That settled, they drove up to Nick's house in a very short time and found that Marie's culinary masterpiece was almost complete.

Marie enjoyed cooking very much and had made rabbit paprikash with potato dumplings for the entrée. Her side dishes were creamed spinach and a variety of homemade pickled vegetables. Liz was delighted, as were the host and hostess. They ate with the easy conversation of long-time friends. It helped, of course, that Liz spoke the three languages they were fluent in --- especially Luxembourgish.

When Liz began to tell Marie, over dessert, how their day had gone and how many places they had been to show the photos, without results, Marie thought for a minute and said, "My mother had a negative made from an old photo so that she could make copies for all of her children. It was not too expensive, but it was not cheap, either. If you did this, you could leave a photo at each place you visited and save some time. Even the patients could see it."

Liz was stunned. Why had she not thought of this? She took both of Marie's hands and said thank you, over and over..... Marie beamed and Nick, looking at her through loving eyes, beamed as well.

Refining on the plan, Liz asked for the name of the photographer who could do this and wrote his name and direction down for the next day. Then, Marie offered the information that he was not far away and worked late. In a matter of moments, Liz had hugged Marie, thanked her for the photo idea, and was whisked off to the photographer's shop by Nick.

The photographer usually worked into the night, processing prints and special orders, things that were difficult to do in daylight --- while customers were interrupting --- and he was still working with a number of hours to go. When he heard Liz' story, he agreed immediately to help and also said that he could have her order ready by 9:30 the next morning.

Bemused, as though she couldn't believe her luck, she sat silently during the short trip back to the pension. When Nick handed her out of the car, she said, "Tell Marie that I am so very, very grateful, Nick. This will speed things up tremendously --- and I'm glad that he's able to make us 300 copies overnight....."

Saying this, it really began to sink in that she could make the effort more comprehensive by far.

She walked up the steps to the pension's door feeling that she was floating on the hope that Marie had engendered in her. In her room, she wanted to go to sleep, but found herself reading through the brochures on Luxembourg's cities and their attractions over and over --- each time feeling as though it was the first. It was as though she was being driven --- could there be something that she wasn't seeing?

She washed herself with cold water in the basin on the dresser and, finally, she began to settle down and feel like she wanted to get under the covers. Her mind was too busy with thoughts of the search to entertain thoughts of their honeymoon, but even that settled down under the warm covers and she floated, at last, on the seas of forgetfulness.

❧Chapter 35 – Luxembourg, More Hospitals☙

It was morning, she knew, by the sunlight streaming through the windows when she opened her eyes a crack. Looked to be about 9 or so, she thought….. Better get up and be ready to work hard……

By the time it was 10 o'clock, she was already in the taxi with 300 pictures in a box on her lap --- Nick had picked the order up on his way to the pension. As she surveyed the quantity, she was a bit cowed by the task ahead.

Nick broke into her reverie with, "He even added your pension contact name to the bottom of the photo where the studio name is listed. They will like the free advertisement." She opened the box, took one out, and was impressed by the accuracy of the man's work. Surely, this would get some action going.

They stopped for breakfast, but ate even faster than they had the previous morning, opting for sausages and hot cereal with strawberries. After hearing their mission, the restaurant owner gave them a thermos of coffee and two cups on the verbal promise that they'd return the next morning.

And, then, the day began. By about 1 o'clock, they had visited every building from the day before and had begun to visit new ones. This went considerably faster, because they could leave the photo and wait for a response. Even the photographer would benefit --- advertising his business without having to pay for an advertisement in the paper or even postage for a flyer.

When it was nearly 5 o'clock, they had already dispersed over 60 photos to places where Franz might be or might have been. They had stopped at restaurants, pensions and hotels, at Nick's suggestion, as well as the medical facilities already on their list..... He might be working in one or staying in one if he earned any money.....

They were tired, but on a roll, and decided to continue a little longer, widening the circle and hoping that even if he were living on the streets, perhaps, someone who saw the photo might recognize him.....

Twenty more photos were distributed before they stopped for dinner. Nick knew a good restaurant, in the quarter they were delivering photos to, and they stopped for dinner, this being one of Marie's school nights. After their long day, they feasted on a sampling of fresh sausages with fried boiled potatoes and cabbage salad. Liz asked Nick if he minded smelling pickled herring when she saw it on the menu and he countered with, "Not if I can have some of it!" They laughed at his joke.

When they left, it was for Nick's house, and they brought a supper for Marie and dessert for them all so that they could eat it together.....

Listening to their description of their travails, when she came home, Marie readily became excited, saying, "This is what I had hoped for! So many people will hear of him and know that he is missing. You may not have to go to all of the outlying communes, since a visit to the city of each canton will alert the populace that there is a missing person who may have been injured or not know who they are --- someone who may have been living among them for as long as six years….. This is the important. I think that it is also important to let them know that he once spoke our three languages and English, as well."

Liz and Nick were quick to agree: the more that was known about him, the more likely that he would be found.

Marie also suggested that her teacher might be willing to make an assignment for the typists to type up quarter-page sheets of information to go with the photos and said that she'd go to the school the next day and ask….. "Now, did one of you say that there was a dinner for me?" she asked.

Nick laughed, saying, "That's my Marie!" and pointed her to the containers.

"Oh, and there's dessert here, too," she said, "Enough for all of us! I'll make coffee."

With a lopsided smile, Nick winked at Liz and said, "There's only one like her….."

Liz enjoyed being with them, she realized. They were comfortable --- actually, even more comfortable than her parents or Franz'. She asked Marie, "May I help you?"

"No, I've already done it and we'll all serve ourselves. I have some tarts and cookies if this cheesecake is too rich….."

Nick snorted, then said, "Too rich? When Christmas comes in June!"

They bantered this way throughout the balance of the evening, sharing family stories and becoming fast friends, as well as a team on a mission.

It was almost 9 p.m. when Nick delivered Liz to the pension and they agreed to meet the next morning as usual.

Liz, light with the feeling of hope and a joy in having these new friends to help her, felt that a big part of her burden had been rolled away. Now, she seemed happier and more confident that they would find him --- some way, somehow.

She fell asleep easily and slept soundly, not even hearing a knock on her door at a little after 8 a.m. until it became quite loud.

Throwing her robe across her shoulders, she went to the door and found the desk clerk waiting in the hall. "Yes?" she asked.

"Madam, there is a man to see you and he is waiting downstairs," he said. "Will you please come downstairs at your earliest convenience?" Liz dressed and was descending the stairs within 20 minutes.

In the lobby, a man was sitting on one of the hard chairs, holding his cap in his hands. When he saw Liz, he stood up, saying, "Good morning, madam, I may have some information for you. Is there a reward?"

Liz smiled at him and answered, "Perhaps, if the information proves to be valid."

The man continued, "It's like this: there's this man that I see sometimes. He comes and goes --- I think he works near my shop, maybe, but only occasionally. I haven't seen him in about 2 weeks, though. He speaks French with me if he buys something."

Liz asked, "What kind of shop do you have?"

"Oh, tabak-traffik, madam, things like cigarettes, cigars, paper goods, pencils, candy, newspapers....."

"And where are you located?"

"On the Avenue de la Liberte, near the Pont Adolphe," he answered.

"Yes, we left photos in that area," she said. "Thank you for coming directly to me," then, taking a piece of paper and a pen from the lobby desk, she asked him to write down what he had just told her and sign and date it, then give it to her.

He did as she asked, and when she was having the desk clerk witness it, she saw his name and said, "Thank-you Mr. Kayser, for bringing this to my attention. I have had you and the clerk sign this paper so that you have proof that I was told your information. I am not paying now, but when I find my husband, or even proof that he no longer lives, I will reward those who have helped me in my search. The clerk, who had been happy to oblige, heard this and hoped it meant him, as well, while Liz folded the document, then, put it in the care of the clerk.

Back in her room, she paced, wondering how soon others would come forward to give information. This reminded her --- she hadn't written to their parents in two weeks and the last telegram had been over ten days ago. She must tell them that Tante Anna Kayser was still alive and, also, about the photos and the first response, as well as her friends, Nick and Marie.

In this frame of mind, she saw that the clock was now showing 9:45 and went downstairs to wait outside for Nick. Fortuitously, he was just pulling up when she opened the door and they were off to the café that had such wonderful breakfasts. They brought the thermos and cups in with them and, after seating them with menus, the proprietor went and refilled the thermos and brought them clean cups. They were not quite so hurried this morning, having refined their plans already and, after a breakfast of quiche and strawberries, they set out to continue the work they had begun the day before.

More photos, more businesses and medical facilities.....

Little did they know that quite a bit of interest was accruing at Pension Moselle. Six people had already come to give information and had been told to return the following morning at 8 a.m. If any more showed up, the clerk swore that he would begin setting appointments and asking Liz for a salary.

By 5:30, they had left another 100 or so, of the photos, and were planning to ask the photographer for another batch, but when they went to Nick's house for dinner, they found that Maria had already ordered another 300 and had been able to convince the teacher to assign her morning class to type the information sheets to hand out with the photos. She was so pleased with her progress, as well as theirs, that she threw her arms around Liz and hugged her.....

She had bought a chicken to roast and by 7 o'clock they were dining on a savory bird with spring greens, pan dressing, bread dumplings and gravy. Liz vowed that this was the best meal she had eaten in Luxembourg and Marie glowed like the sun. Triumphantly, she brought the dessert out after they allowed their meal to settle --- prune tarts, much like the kolaches of the Czechs. Paired with coffee --- manna from Heaven.....

When she returned to the pension, Liz found that a note had been pushed under the door. Apparently, the poor desk clerk had been inundated with people bringing information and had begun to set up appointments for them so that the tiny lobby wouldn't overflow at any time. He requested that she pay a small salary, since this was outside of the scope of his normal services. Gladly, she thought, tucking the note into her purse and getting ready for bed.

She had earned her rest that day and, knowing that she would have appointments to keep on the morrow and that she and Nick would go further afield in an ever-widening circle with the photos, she crawled under the covers and slipped into the beautiful land of pleasant dreams.....

Chapter 36 – Luxembourg, Appointments

Thanks to going to bed as soon as she returned to her room, Liz was up by 7:30 in the morning and getting dressed. She went down to the lobby before anyone had arrived and asked the desk clerk to bring her some coffee in a mug with plenty of cream, if she was to interview all of the people he had made appointments for. In minutes he returned bearing her mug.

Minutes later, the first appointment arrived. After visiting with him for about 5 minutes, she could tell that the individual this man was talking about could not be Franz and she told him to leave his name and address with the clerk in case they had no better leads. This happened with the next 5 people. Then, the seventh, eighth, and ninth, were gold mines. Liz made them longer appointments for Saturday morning and Sunday afternoon, when she anticipated having the time to listen more closely and for a longer period. She asked them to give their names and addresses to the clerk, so that, should Franz be found before then, she could notify them and cancel the appointments.

By 10 o'clock, when Nick arrived, she had weeded through the people with appointments, discussed a generous salary with the clerk, and given her eager employee guidelines for setting the appointments.

Sailing out the door and down the steps, she felt like an executive --- or perhaps, the thought came, like a police detective with staff.....

On their way to the café, she regaled Nick with the first round of appointments. He was amazed at the response in such a short time, but agreed with Liz' assessment that many, in this postwar period, might be enticed by the hope of a reward for any information they knew, whether true, false, imagination, or factual. Some, though, like the old lady who swore she saw him, might just be motivated by romantic hearts..... She had won a Saturday appointment with Liz, though.

As they ate breakfast, they talked about the route for the day's distribution and decided that they would begin going further out from Luxembourg City and its suburbs to the towns, like Hesperange, and the ones they had traveled to on Monday, visiting in each a few hospitals, along with some shops, restaurants, and lodging houses. Before long they were on the road and leaving photos.

Again, it was past 5 when they returned to Luxembourg City, tired, hoarse, and ready for the weekend. Liz would be interviewing the people who had appointments and getting the statements of those who seemed to have potentially helpful information to share. She suggested that they go to the restaurant near the pension so that he wouldn't have to do as much driving afterward and he agreed without discussion.

They ordered the restaurant's forte: fish. She had the pike with green sauce and he opted for the brook fish, but they shared. It was a very quiet dinner due to their fatigue and, afterward, he made certain she took the leftover sweet rolls from breakfast with her and left the empty coffee thermos in the car for Monday.

Liz found another note under her door from the clerk --- this one a good note. He listed all of the weekend appointments by name and address and had given them 25 minute appointments with 5 minutes between for her to summarize, rest, or drink a cup of coffee. Good man, she thought, as she looked at her bed and felt it calling. He broke the weekday appointments, for the following week, into two categories: new and returning. The new were 10 minute appointments and the returning were like the weekend's 30 minute allotments.

But, she had work to do, if she was to be ready for her weekend appointments, and she dutifully sat down at the small writing desk and outlined her weekend. Franz, who had often called her disorganized, would have sung a different tune and been proud.

Next, she wrote to his parents and hers, as well. Letters of hope and reassurance, telling them of her experiences and her progress.....

Then, entirely fatigued, she turned to the bed and, with barely enough motivation to hang her clothes, she slipped under the covers and, after thinking of Franz for a moment, dreamt of him the entire night. In some of the dreams, he was in the hospital and in others he was working as a laborer, a field hand --- as before. This time, she could see that he had some scars she was not familiar with. In the last dream about him, he was riding in a truck with a load of produce --- just riding, not driving.....

Finally, only moments before sunrise, she had another dream --- this time not about Franz. There was a man named Joel, after the biblical prophet, he said. She couldn't see him clearly and, then, he told her that she would find Franz and that it was he who would bring her to her husband.

❧Chapter 37 – Luxembourg, Joel Desautels❧

Liz awoke to her wake-up call --- a knock on the door at 7:30. She knew that she dared not lay there and go back to sleep, so she got out of bed and put on her robe, then sat for a few minutes in the easy chair. She wondered for a bit what that last dream was all about.

With the impending interviews ahead of her, she hurried into a pair of slacks and a shirt, brushed her hair, grabbed a sweet roll, and headed down the stairs to the lobby. The clerk had a mug of coffee, with cream, waiting for her --- this man knew his business!

The first appointment was on time, as were the rest, each arriving and giving their information thoroughly, signing their statement and having it witnessed by the clerk, who then collected them for Liz.

Liz felt that they all had good information, even the elderly lady, but none was definitive until the last --- a man named Joel Desautels, who professed himself to be a medium. He told Liz that she would find Franz soon, that he would tell her that he had worked in a hospital to pay for his medical care and also in the fields as a laborer, that he had been wounded in Belgium in 1940, in The Battle Of France, and eventually ended up in Luxembourg by making his way through the Oesling portion of the country in the north ---

which, mountainous and richly forested, forms part of the Ardennes forest.

She asked Mr. Desautels to return for another appointment on Tuesday at 10 o'clock and reminded herself to remember to add it to the clerk's list of appointments.

She had taken longer with Mr. Desautels than the others, and it was almost 11:30 by the time they finished. Feeling a readiness for lunch, she went upstairs to fetch her purse and soon she was headed for the little restaurant near her pension with Nick, who had been waiting in his taxi for her. Due to the early hour, they were the only lunch customers and discussed the plans for the day over their meal. Liz touched on the information from Desautels with Nick and saw his face change, becoming very serious. "Yes, he is a well-known medium," Nick said, with a furrowed brow "However, there are many who fear people with these gifts --- especially in very religious countries. I would not speak of his involvement here, in Luxembourg."

As Liz listened to Nick, she felt that it was time to return to visit Tante Anna Kayser and perhaps take her for a ride in the taxi as they distributed pictures in that area, so she said, "I will take your advice, Nick --- now, let's go and visit my Tante in Heffingen. Would Marie like to come, too?"

For his part, Nick was pleased to take her wherever his car could go and felt that distributing in one place was as good as another. He was certain that Marie would love to come with them and he was entirely correct. So, they set out --- Marie sitting with Liz in the back seat and chatting about all of the sights.

It was only about 45 minutes later when they arrived at Anna Kayser's house in Heffingen and, going to the door, Liz had no answer to her knock, but, rounding the corner of the house to follow the sounds she could hear, she found Tante Anna sitting in a chair in the garden, shelling fresh peas and tossing the pods to her chickens, while telling them what beautiful eggs they laid. She smiled, then stepped around in front her before saying, "Hello, Tante Anna, it's Lisbet from America."

The older woman beamed up at her as though a bright light had been turned on inside of her and asked if she was well and whether she had found Franz.

"No, Tante, not yet, but I have been searching and I have many possible leads --- even from a medium," Liz answered.

Her great-aunt became very serious and asked, "Which medium?"

"Joel Desautels," Liz offered.

Sighing her relief, she said, "Yes, he will know. He is very gifted and you should trust what he says," the old lady averred.

"He will return to see me on Tuesday."

"Good….. good. He will find the boy --- his powers are strong and he is accurate."

"Now, Tante, would you like to go for a ride in the car with us while we pass out photographs of Franz?" Liz asked.

She might as well have asked if the old lady would like to meet General Patton, the response was so strong, "Yes! oh yes, of course. I will tell you where to go." Thus it was, that for the next 3 hours they traveled, from town to town in the eastern region, leaving photos with all the cafes, shop-keepers, and medical facilities. Sometimes, Tante Anna would stop them to greet some acquaintance of hers, but mostly only directed Nick to the towns. It reminded Liz of farming and other rural communities, where the town was a meeting place, a hub, for those who worked or lived on the land. The tiny towns even had meeting halls, much like the granges of the United States, or used the churches for meetings, since life revolved heavily around that base.

As it grew closer to the dinner hour they headed towards Mersch, which was close --- Nick had planned this --- and went to a tiny restaurant for dinner. Tante Anna was thrilled to be in a restaurant and, coming from a tiny town of farmers, her excitement was easily understandable.

The proprietor came to their table and sat to visit with them while his wife and daughter prepared their meal. There was no great variety in such tiny establishments. They usually offered only one --- or at the most, two --- choices. When the meal came, they were surprised by the quality of the offering, but should not have been, for, this was the country --- where food is always freshest. Tante Anna's smacking lips said it all --- this was a good meal, and one she didn't have to grow or cook for herself!

Afterward, they drove Tante Anna back to Heffingen and helped her to shoo the chickens into their enclosure for the night, then, said their good-byes and drove back to the city.

Nick and Marie dropped Liz off at the pension at nearly 9 o'clock and, as she slowly walked up the steps after watching the taxi's taillights fade into the night and then turn a corner and disappear altogether, she assessed how much she had experienced and grown since she left for Europe. She was not the same little bride, caught in the time warp of war, waiting for her husband to come home. She realized that, if she found Franz, it would be wonderful, but that even if she didn't, she had found so many special people that her life would still be fuller than it had been before her search, and she could still be whole.

Upstairs, in her bed, she thought of the latest note from her employee, the clerk. Twenty-two more people had come forward with information in the afternoon and now had appointments. Ah, the power of advertising! Her father had always said it.....

She thought of her family and Franz' and hoped that her letters would reach them soon, then, as she tried to figure out when they should be received, the arms of sleep stealthily and efficiently claimed her.....

❦Chapter 38 – The Search Continues❧

Liz lay in bed, after waking late, lazily watching the sunlight make patterns on the carpet and walls. This was one of those lovely morning times, when everything seems mellow and we sometimes think deep thoughts and ponder the meaning of life --- or remember what we've dreamed.

On this morning, Liz was thinking some deep thoughts, as well as, remembering her dreams. One had been of Franz --- not of him calling to her, but of him looking at her and nodding. Another had been of Tante Anna, living all by herself, so alone and no one left to care for her in her old age.

The second one seemed more pressing and, as she lay there, she thought of Marie's mother, Elena, another older woman living alone..... What would it be like if they could live together and go back and forth from city to country as they pleased? Oh, stop that Liz, she heard her mind admonishing. Take care of your search before you find another project!

She listened to herself and went back to the dream about Franz nodding. Was he telling her that he was pleased with the direction she was going in? Or, perhaps, that he wanted her to consult further with Desautels? This one would take a bit more intuition.....

Meanwhile, the need to relieve herself was overcoming the sensuality of the warm bed and she decided to capitulate.

Once she was dressed, she realized that she had no interviews until 1 o'clock and it was only noon. So, she curled up with a book, a sweet roll and an apple in the easy chair by the window.

When she finally went downstairs at 12:55, the first informant, a Georg Lang, had already arrived. He was a laborer and told her that, a few years earlier, he had worked in the fields and lived in the same dormitory with a man who strongly resembled Franz, but more than the resemblance, he said that the man had spoken American English --- or perhaps Canadian --- in his sleep, but seemed to have no knowledge of it when he was awake. Liz asked many questions, but he had no idea of the man's current whereabouts, so she took his information and his statement, asking the housekeeper, who was washing the stairs, to witness his signature in the clerk's absence.

The rest of the afternoon produced precious little, though she interviewed 7 more people.

Then, after she fetched her purse and crossed the lobby to go out in search of dinner, Mr. Desautels opened the pension door and stepped inside.

Seeing her, he asked if he might speak with her for a moment and she told him that she was just going out in search of a meal. "May I accompany you," he asked, politely.

Liz thought for an instant, then, impulsively agreed, saying that there was a restaurant about a block away.

"Yes, I saw it --- is it good?" Desautels inquired.

"I thought you were a medium," she replied.

" Touché," he said, and she laughed.

In a mere fifteen minutes, they were comfortably seated across from each other looking at the menu, when Liz remarked, "The pike in green sauce is quite good and so is the duck --- I've had both."

"At the same time?" he asked, with a twinkle in his eyes.

Liz chuckled and smiled, then answered, "Of course not….. but you already know that, don't you?" then continued, "What else do you know, Mr. Desautels?"

"Please. Call me Joel," he was quick to reply. "I know many things, madam. They are not always things I want to know or to see. In your case, I do not have a sense of this being a person who has passed over and must, therefore, conclude that he still lives. How he lives, or whether his brain and body functions are totally as they should be." He stopped for a few moments, then began again, "I cannot say for certain at this point whether they are, since I have been shown his flight from a train in southeastern Belgium, in May of 1940. He crosses into Luxembourg after being wounded by the battle being fought at that time. I feel in my own body a wounding here (pointing to a point over his left ear) and here (putting a hand on his right thigh), however, I am still able to walk and, knowing approximately where I am, I feel myself flee toward the country where I have family --- quickly, like a racing pigeon."

Then, as she sat there, mesmerized by his words, he continued, "I am absolutely certain that he is within 40 kilometers of us at this moment and his energy feels close, very intense and close. I am not certain whether I am feeling his feelings for you in this respect, or if I am feeling his actual physical presence so very close, but I believe that it is the latter and, also, that he is, in fact, less than 20 kilometers distant."

"Can you feel the direction of his energy?" Liz interjected, when he didn't continue quickly enough.

"Me, oui, of course!" was the reply. "He is to the south --- almost directly south at this moment."

South, she thought, frowning in concentration, then said, "That would be on the roads to Bettembourg or Frisange."

"Oui. madam, c'est vrai. Cherchez-le là. Look for him there," Desautels agreed.

At that moment, the proprietor asked if they had decided on their order and, for the moment, they were distracted. Liz ordered the duck with orange sauce and spring vegetables with potato dumplings, but Desautels opted for the pike, saying, "We shall see how good your recommendation is, Madam Tischler," with a wry grin and a definite twinkle in his eyes.

Liz laughed and retorted, "At least they cooked it well for me!"

Desautels enjoyed the repartee with her. She was intelligent and, he felt, quite intuitive. Perhaps a future student, he mused….. then, said, "You have been feeling his presence, too, have you not?"

Liz' face became serious, then, she took a deep breath and began to speak, "Yes, I sense his energy. At times it seems to come from the west or even northwest, but at others from the south. It confuses me that I feel it differently on different days. Sometimes I dream of him and he is doing different things, like a timeline."

At this point, Desautels interrupted with a wave of his hand, saying, "And, do you stay in one place all of the time or think the same thoughts all of the time? Does he not sleep and dream at night like you?"

Startled into silence by his observations, she tilted her head to one side in thought for a moment, then, to the other side as she answered, "You're right, he may be working in a different place than he lives or, maybe his job takes him to different places….. And, of course, I can understand that he may be dreaming at the same time I am, but probably of his experiences during the war. I just didn't think of it that way, I suppose. How foolish that I thought of him as stationary, like some kind of tree. It must have been that I assumed, if he was able to move, he would find his way home to me." Rubbing her temples, she continued, "What a child I've been, making so many assumptions and having so many preconceived ideas….."

Taking pity on her, Desautels interjected, "No, my dear, merely in love."

At that point, their dinners arrived, forestalling any tears on her part and bringing a smile to the medium's face when he saw the magnificent portion of pike with green sauce --- this was indeed a treat, his expression clearly said.

Over dinner, they allowed the conversation to be about the meal. Liz passed a slice of duck for him to sample on her bread plate and he made a face of enjoyment, which had her giggling like a girl again. Ah, she thought, these Frenchmen….. But, on its heels, she found herself wondering if he were French, Luxembourgian, or Belgian and, since the young (especially Americans) often do not observe the niceties, she spoke her mind and asked him.

"Now, that is a conundrum," he answered, "My father's family is of French origin, but he was born in Luxembourg. My mother's family was of English origin, but had moved to Luxembourg while her mother was expecting her, so she was born here. They met onboard an ocean liner, when their families went to see the 1893 World's Columbian Exposition in Chicago, Illinois, avid to see the fair and to hear the premiere of Dvorak's New World Symphony, so we are a multi-national family --- or at least I am, for they have already passed."

Thinking for a moment, Liz said, "I suppose that Franz and I are the same --- our grandparents were all from Luxembourg and they immigrated and began a business in America, then our parents were born there. Later, we were born there, too, and married each other. Oh, not that fast, of course," she said, with a grin.

Desautels laughed. Oh, if he were only 20 years younger! He was half French, after all.....

Then, he became suddenly very serious and said, "I am told that he is in a building, a ruin, that is old. When he comes to this area, he stays there."

Trusting him, now, Liz asked, " Will he stay there long?"

The medium closed his eyes and, after a moment, he said, "He has work nearby for 3 more days, but then he will depart for another area where there is more forest. He feels safer among the trees."

So, there were three days in which to find him, Liz noted.

They stayed and talked for a long time, stretching the dinner into dessert and coffee, then, continuing until they were the only diners left. The proprietor came and sat with them at the end of the evening, bringing a complimentary bottle of wine to share and visiting over it with them, like old friends, while his family cleaned the kitchen and prepared for the next day's meals.

Finally, they left for the pension, where Desautels walked Liz up the steps and bent to kiss the back of her hand before leaving. As he descended the stairs, he turned to say, "I will be in contact with you if I hear anything."

Liz went inside and up to her room, then sat in the easy chair for awhile thinking and planning. The next day, they would go south and begin a more detailed search. Franz must be found before he left the area or they would have to begin all over again. She felt the urgency of the mission intensely and was glad she had shared the wine --- it calmed her considerably, allowing her to slip under the covers of her bed, at last, and into the arms of the night.

❧Chapter 39 – Luxembourg, Three Days❧

Liz slept very well, but she had appointments to keep and the clerk tapped on her door at 7:30 to warn her of the time. After one good stretch, she looked at the clock and fairly leaped from her bed.

As she dressed, she remembered that she had two half-hour interviews and six of the shorter ones before Nick was due and she could eat breakfast, so she grabbed her last sweet roll and headed down to the lobby, where the clerk, knowing her preferences, had a mug of coffee and cream waiting. The look of gratitude she gave him made him smile and nod at her. Somehow, it reminded her of Franz and the dream......

After a good-sized bite of the sweet roll and a few sips of the coffee to wash down with, the first information bearer arrived. Thankfully, she saw on her schedule that the clerk had arranged the longer interviews first and the later ones for the following hour --- this would give her a few minutes between them to catch her breath and finish her roll and coffee.

Each of the two longer interviews had the possibility of some sightings, and she asked them to write out the information, and then take it to the desk clerk for witnessing as they signed and dated it. He kept them for her.

The next hour was not very helpful --- only one that might have a sighting and she asked him to do as the others had done.

Finally, she thought, breakfast! Looking outside, she saw the taxi and hurried upstairs for her purse. As she passed him, on the way out, the clerk handed her a handful of letters she had received in the morning post.

Once inside the taxi, she began looking at them on the way to breakfast. One from Ana, in Switzerland, which she would save for later, and 5 from people who said they had seen Franz in various parts of Luxembourg in the last 6 years. Some leads were better than others, but she put them all in her purse.

When they arrived at the café, Nick asked how her interviews had gone and she apprised him of the results. Then, she spoke to him of Desautels and his information. Nick sucked in his breath and said, "Then we are close. How shall we proceed now?"

"First," she said, with a smile, "I think we must order breakfast....."

Nick grinned back and said, "Marie was right."

"About what?" came the quick retort.

"She said that you are fun."

Liz grinned back at him and said, "You bet!" then ordered crepes filled with ham and topped with cheese sauce and, on another plate, rye toast with unsalted butter.

Nick, liking the sound of her selection, asked for the same.

Taking out her map, Liz planned their attack….. Beginning at the pension, they would make their way slowly southward, toward Hesperange, stopping anywhere they saw a building or people working in the open --- also, at any ruins they might see.

They ate with little to say, staring at the map….. …..and thinking. Liz spoke first, saying, "I think he will be working at something where it doesn't matter if he's been sleeping in the open."

"That's probably true," Nick agreed, "So, shall we go until it gets late and then return the next day at that point?"

"Yes," she answered, "I think that's all that we can do."

By 11:15, they were on the road with a refilled thermos of coffee and 2 fresh cups, as well as sweet rolls, thick ham sandwiches and fruit to stave off any hunger.

Liz sat in the back seat, letting her mind and heart be open, and trying to feel the energy of Franz as they stopped every quarter mile or so for her to look around and see if there were any ruins. This was a tedious process, but when they came close to Hesperange and the Castle ruins above the city, she could feel it much stronger. These ruins were a national monument, but were privately held --- at some point at least seven plots including ruins had been sold and private residences built on them. Finally, walking among the stones, she could feel his energy and knew that he had been there, had walked where she walked and touched these stones as she did.

She went back to the taxi to talk with Nick, but saw that he was off walking the area. So, she sat there trying to be quiet, to just allow the energy to come in and tell her where Franz was. It was very difficult to be in that serene frame of mind, because there was some construction being done on one of the houses and she could hear the workers talking, as well as the disruptive noise of their work. The intensity of her own inner feeling of urgency kept her too alert, as well. It was frustrating.

Finally, she got up and went toward the workers to see what they were talking about. As she stood there, distracted by their conversation, and not trying so hard to go within, she suddenly felt something from Franz, a feeling, rather, a knowing, that he was no longer at this place, but had gone further south to the site of another ruin.

Seeing Nick a ways away talking to a man, she walked toward him. Observing her, the man pointed toward her as though asking Nick something and he nodded. A few seconds later, she reached them and found that this was the foreman of the work crew and Nick had asked him if he had seen Franz, showing him the picture.

He told Liz that he had spoken with a man a couple of days before who looked quite a bit like the picture of Franz. The man had spent the night sheltering against one of the castle ruins' partial walls and he had told him that this was not allowed on private property when he saw him there in the

morning. He asked him if he needed work, since he could use an extra hand, but was told that the man had work lined up further south, that he was traveling to --- and the foreman saw him heading toward the road, which led south to Bettembourg and Dudelange, a short time later.

"Did he look exactly like the picture?" Liz asked.

"Not exactly," replied the foreman, "His hair was not so tidy, and longer. He had a few scars," the man said, indicating the placement with gestures to his own body, "One above his left ear that made his hair stand up a bit, another on his left cheekbone, one thin one splitting his left eyebrow neatly in half, and a scar on his lip, as if it had been split at one time." The man continued, "His hands don't show in your picture, but they were like the hands of my men; rough and calloused. He had a moustache, too, but from my point of view, blondes shouldn't bother to grow one --- they're usually thin and sissy-looking." He showed her his own hands, to illustrate his comment about being calloused, and then said, "He seemed a little bit vague, like his mind was somewhere else --- reminded me of some of our boys who were too close to the shelling up in Belgium in May of '40."

Liz thanked him for his help and asked for his address so that she could let him know if she found Franz, intending to send him a reward if the vagrant he had seen turned out to be her husband.

She was very excited at this news and could barely contain herself, almost dancing as she walked, in her eagerness to get back on the road. This was a bit of good news --- a hot trail.

When she and Nick returned to the taxi, she got into the front seat with him and seemed to fuel the car with her own energy --- she was that excited. This was Franz, of that she was certain.

As they passed through the countryside, slowly, scrutinizing every dwelling they passed and every person they saw, they seemed to be almost holding their breath. All systems on high alert, they missed nothing, scanning each bit of data as a possible lead to Franz.

They traveled through Bivange and Berchem with Liz keenly aware of the energy trail --- could it be possible that they had only traveled a few miles? It seemed like a dozen, at least.

In Livange, they paused to eat some of their sandwiches and renew themselves with a cup of coffee. Only about a mile and a half to Bettembourg, Liz saw, as she scanned the map. Getting close, she thought.....

Another 4 miles or so, of the tedious inching toward their goal, passed, with Liz on the edge of her seat the entire time, projecting her energy, her consciousness, forward toward that ultimate goal of finding Franz, willing him with every fiber of her being to be there in her mind, to connect with her, and to help her feel in which direction to go in at each of the crossroads.

Finally, they came into the furthest outskirts of Dudelange, a major industrial city of Luxembourg, located in the heart of the steel production belt in the southern part of the country. Passing a street named Rue de Ribeschpont, as they made to

go further into the city, Nick commented, "Sometimes, on St. John's Eve, we go to Mont St. Jean to the stations of the cross in Budersberg, down that road," pointing off to the west, then continuing, "There's a very ancient ruined castle there. Not much left of it --- just a few foundations --- I think the villagers used it as a free quarry to build their homes."

Liz sat as still as a mouse for a moment, then said, "Okay, we'll go there first --- please turn around and take that road."

Nick complied and, within moments, they were on their way to Budersberg and the castle ruins. A mile further down the road and they were in the tiny dorf, of only a few streets, nestled at the foot of the Mont. They stopped there for a few minutes, to see if Liz could sense Franz and for Nick to see if he could find anyone who had seen him or knew of any work being done by a laborer. At the third house he tried, an elderly man came to the door, obviously too old to work. He told Nick that there was repair going on at a house on the next street, because he had heard the sounds for the last two days --- and it was getting on his nerves.

Returning to Liz, Nick shared what he had heard and brought the car around to go in the direction that the man had indicated. Soon, they could hear the sound of construction --- or, perhaps, it was deconstruction. When they seemed as close as they could get, Nick parked the car and went in search of the source of the sounds while Liz sat in the car --- as nervous as a bride.

Following the sounds of tools on masonry and a trail of bits of fresh mud --- probably fallen from someone's boots --- he came to the retaining wall of a garden with a wrought iron fence embedded at the top, beginning at the height of his waist. This allowed him to see quite a distance, toward the house, where he could discern men walking back and forth pushing wheelbarrows, as well as, a few carrying large stones and pipes, through the stems of tall, fragrant lilac bushes planted against the fence. Then, calling to them, he managed to get their foreman to come through the gate to talk with him.

He showed him the picture of Franz and the man nodded his head immediately. He had taken the foreman's truck into Dudelange about twenty minutes earlier in search of parts for the new plumbing system they were installing along with the renovation to this house. He would be back in an hour or so if he found the parts easily, the foreman assured Nick.

Nick asked if he looked different from the photograph and the fellow reiterated the description given by the foreman in Hesperange. Nick thanked him and returned to the car to tell Liz what he had heard.

Sitting there on pins and needles, she could barely be still as she watched him walk toward her. Had he found anyone? Had he found Franz? Her heart was beating intensely and her stomach was churning at the ham sandwich she'd eaten like a milkshake machine. She held her hands out and saw that they were shaking, as well. As soon as Nick opened the door she asked, "Well?"

"This foreman says that he's gone into Dudelange to see if he can find plumbing parts and should return in an hour or so."

"Can't we go and look for him?" she asked.

"I don't know all the places he would have gone and the foreman may not, either. It seems better to wait here until he returns and we can meet with him when he's finished his work for the day. I know how anxious you are, but you wouldn't want to work a hardship on the foreman, would you?" Nick answered.

He watched her as she sat there thinking, so different from how she had been a few moments earlier --- all nerves and excitement.

"Yes, you're right," she said. "I have to wait --- and I can wait, now, knowing that he is so near."

Nick breathed a sigh of relief. He'd been afraid for a moment that she would be too keyed up to be able to switch into a calmer mode, but she had come through, with flying colors, and stepped back a few paces to the serenity that she usually displayed. Now, they would wait.

Distracting her with friendly banter, he asked her which was her favorite band in the U.S. She took that lead and ran with it, talking about all the big names and her favorite songs, letting the energy of anticipation leech out of her through her words. Her favorite war era tune was Boogie Woogie Bugle Boy with it's bouncy rhythm and she loved the smooth voices of the Andrews Sisters when they sang it. She and Franz had danced to all of the Big Bands: both of the Dorseys (but they felt that Tommy would be the more successful), Bennie Goodman, Glenn Miller, and, of course, Ellington and The Count. It had been a good ploy on Nick's part and, in remembering and recounting her experiences, she regained the serenity he knew that she was capable of.

J. Matheny

They continued to talk about music --- a safe topic and one that could draw her out and keep her stress level low. It was as though even the memory of the music could lull her into serenity…..

As they waited, the sun sank lower and lower. Finally, at nearly 6, the truck pulled up near the garden gate and a man got out. Liz sucked in her breath and Nick got out of the taxi to go and talk with him. Then, the man went into the garden and Nick returned to the car.

Before Liz could ask, Nick said, "I believe it's him. I told him that when he was done with his work today, we would like to talk with him about another job. So, we'll wait here. He'll only work a short while before they'll all be looking for dinner. And, in any case, he said that it would go fast now that he has the proper fittings."

They sat and waited in silence, each thinking their own thoughts. Liz was not up to being distracted by the bands anymore and Nick was thinking of the drive back to Luxembourg City. It seemed that an eternity had passed when they finally saw the man open the garden gate and, swinging his rucksack on his back, head for the taxi. In the twilight, Liz sat there knowing that he wouldn't know it was her until he was at the car, where she waited, wondering, what his reaction would be.

As he approached, she finally couldn't contain herself anymore and she slipped out of the car as he walked the last few steps and stood before her. He asked, in French, "Are you the person who needs some work done?"

"Yes, if you are my husband," She answered, in English, certain that this man was Franz.

He shuddered slightly, as if he had a sudden chill, then repeated his question in Luxembourgish, seeming to think she spoke no French.

Seeing that he would not answer her in English, she asked him to get into the taxi and help them to find a restaurant in the vicinity so that they could sit down and discuss the work she required.

She sat in the back so that he could direct Nick --- and so that she could listen to his voice and watch their interaction. She knew without a doubt that this was Franz --- or his identical twin --- but the fact that he had not immediately recognized her was troubling. She wondered if his head injury had caused a memory lapse and he truly seemed to not understand English.

He directed Nick to a modest restaurant in Dudelange which he said had excellent food and asked if he might take the time to wash his hands before they ordered. It was not long before he had returned with clean hands, as well as fresh clothing from his rucksack, and sat down with them to order. Nick asked him what their best dish was and he said that the roast pork with potato dumplings was excellent, so they all followed his suggestion and ordered it when the waiter came to their table.

As they waited for dinner, they began to ask about his skills and where he worked; seeming for all the world like a couple looking to hire someone for a legitimate construction job.

Seated across from Liz and Nick, Franz began to stare at Liz longer and longer --- as though she were someone he had met before, but just couldn't place.

He tilted his head to the side a bit, and seemed to be listening to the sound of her voice, trying to place it, too, making a great effort to remember where he had heard it before.

As Nick spoke to him, Liz noticed the so familiar landmarks on the visible parts of his body --- the small mole below his right ear, the tiny scar on the tip of his chin where he fell on a manhole cover as a little boy, and the inadvertent homemade tattoo she had given him at age eight, when she poked the back of his hand with the nib of her pen. There was no doubt whatsoever that this man was Franz and she didn't know how she would be able to contain herself, then thought of his obvious memory loss, realizing that it would be abusive for her to hurry him.

She suddenly realized that both men were looking at her and said, "I'm sorry, I was just thinking. What was the question?"

Franz asked, "When would you want this work done?"

Liz bunted, saying, "How soon would you be available?" just as their dinners arrived at the table. Whew, she thought, that was a close one.

The three of them chatted easily while they ate, avoiding the subject of the war and only commenting on the rebuilding going on in so many countries. "So it is: tear down, then build up," Franz said. "This is why I like the ruins so much. You see the progress of history as you study them."

It was all Liz could do to keep from crying when he said that, for it was a statement he had often made on their honeymoon as they looked at old buildings and ruins.....

As she listened to the men talk, her mind was a whirl of thoughts, so, she pretended to be vitally interested in her dinner. She didn't want to leave Franz, now that she had found him, but how could she ask him to come with her? And, what's more, where could they go? Back to the pension? What if he needed to be back at this job in the morning? How could she convince him if he didn't remember her? And, shockingly, he didn't seem to remember English, either!

At that point she remembered the man she had spoken to the day she met Desautels --- the laborer who had known a man who spoke English in his sleep. Georg, she mused..... Georg Lang! Oh, how she hoped that she could easily find him again. Maybe seeing him would help Franz to remember. Oh, and Desautels, himself --- perhaps he could direct her how to proceed.....

She made a mental note to herself to try to contact them first thing in the morning. This might be a task for the clerk.

It was then that she realized Nick was asking her a question and she turned to listen as he said, "I've asked Franz to come and spend the night in the spare bedroom at my house tonight, Liz, so that we can talk longer and he can give me more of an idea of his experience for our project. I'll take him to work in the morning and pick him up afterward. He thinks, now that he has the proper fittings, he can be done with his part of that project by noon and I can linger over breakfast and a newspaper in Dudelange, then bring him back to Luxembourg City. Does that sound good to you?"

"Oh, yes, that would work perfectly," she quickly agreed. "We don't want to clutter his mind with our project until he's finished with the other."

Meanwhile, she was wondering how fast she could get Desautels to call at the pension the next morning, while thinking of the interviews she still had to conduct..... Hopefully, Nick could keep Franz busy until she was able to consult Desautels and Georg.....

On the way back to Luxembourg, they rode as before: the two men sitting in the front seat and talking, while Liz sat in the back, listening. The few times that she entered into the conversation, she could see her voice was having more and more of an effect on Franz and remembered the times she'd tried to remember where she had met someone or how she knew them --- a frustrating effort at best.

Nick saw her to the door, reminded her that he would return with Franz sometime after 12:30 the next day, then returned to the taxi and waved, as did Franz, when he pulled away.

Tomorrow, she thought, tomorrow.....

Strange as it might seem, when she finally lay in her bed and thought of Franz, the real Franz, as he was now, she didn't

feel the same heat as she had, remembering their passionate honeymoon. This Franz didn't have the fire of youth that the other one had possessed, but seeing Franz not quite the same had also interfered with her ability to selectively remember that passion of his being. And, of course, this Franz hadn't touched her body, yet --- not even so much as a handshake.

Her mind was far too full to allow her the luxury of touching her own body this night as he had touched it. It was as though a weight lay on her heart; a weight like a stone. She knew that there were interviews at 8 o'clock, so she lay there dutifully trying to sleep, then remembered that she had purchased a small, soft pillow filled with lavender flowers in one of the stores they took a photo to. Getting up again, she located it in a drawer and placed it under her head to let the fragrance lull her mind so that she could allow sleep to overtake her.

Deeper and deeper she drifted into sleep until she was dreaming of two children playing on a summer day.....

❧Chapter 40 – Luxembourg, FRANZ❧

The usual early rap at the door awakened her. Part of her felt like rolling over and going back to sleep, perchance to dream again, but another part of her knew that she must get up, dress, and see the people who were trying to help her. It was the courteous thing to do and she had been well brought up.

Soon, she was walking down the stairs and saw the usual mug of coffee awaiting her on the corner table. She smiled, coffee was an ordinary thing, but such a comfort..... She saw by the clock that she was earlier than usual and stopped to talk to the clerk. He was surprised that their effort had been so immediately successful and empathized with her over the state of her husband's mind. He had hoped that the little extra income would continue, but was pragmatic over losing it and had the good sense to realize that he had learned a valuable lesson in the successful use of advertising.

Just before she spoke with the first person bringing information, she remembered to ask the clerk to contact Desautels and ask him to meet her for breakfast, at 10 o'clock, at the restaurant a block away if he was available. Thinking for a moment, she asked if he could find the paperwork for Georg Lang, as well.

Liz conducted each interview after telling the informant that she had now found Franz, but was looking for more information to understand what had happened to him since 1939. They remained sympathetic and all gave bits of information that might be of use --- just nothing earth-shaking.

This time, there was one longer interview at 9:30 and all the rest were of the 10-minute variety. The clerk took all of their information after they had spoken with Liz and kept it for her.

At 9:55, she asked him to refer any important callers, other than those merely seeking a first contact offering her information, to the restaurant down the block. He smiled and agreed --- perhaps he was still on the payroll.....

Mere minutes later, she arrived at the restaurant and saw Desautels already awaiting her. She asked if the clerk had contacted him and he said, "No, I've been out all morning and I just felt that I needed to be here today."

Surprised, she began to tell him all that had transpired the day before, including each detail and her feelings, as well, then sat back and waited to hear what he had to say.

"Hmmmm," he said, "This is an interesting case. Something has made him forget some things, but not all. He cannot consciously recall English, but does he recall German?"

Liz offered, "I don't believe so. Nick said something to him in German, but he didn't seem to understand the words that were not the same as Luxembourgish."

"Perhaps he has built blocks to the languages he has fear of speaking or, in the case of the German, fear of pain associated with it. Does that sound reasonable?"

In point of fact, it did, she had to agree, since she had every reason to think that he was not treated gently by his kidnappers. Whether or not it would prove to be the case was another story, but she was grasping at straws and this one seemed like it might be a whole raft, paddle and all.

They ordered and their food was brought quickly --- the wonderful hot coffee with cream and brioches --- and spinach quiche..... They continued their conversation as they ate.....

Desautels asked if he could meet Franz and Liz immediately agreed, having hoped that he would be willing. "I would appreciate any help you could give me, Joel. Nick should be bringing him here by about 12:30 or so. Perhaps we could linger over our coffee and visit," she suggested.

By this time it was already close to noon and the minutes had flown by. They were two people very suited to discussion.....

Desautels asked Liz what she knew about hypnosis and she answered, "Do you mean like Svengali?"

"No, dear lady, I meant like Freud or Hull, researchers in the medical profession. The capability of hypnosis to assist in healing the mind has only been touched on, not fully explored. I suspect that your husband may benefit from its use as a method of treatment."

Liz became excited and asked, "Do you know anyone who can do this? Can you?"

"Yes, in point of fact, I can, but the patient must consent and I must conduct preliminary interviews with the patient. I know others, more proficient than myself in this technique, who might also be brought in."

At this point, Liz could see the taxi stopping up the street at the pension and Nick, after going into the lobby, looking in the direction of the restaurant and then driving toward her. She said to Desautels, "They're coming now. Let's discuss something else." Desautels promptly began an oration on the history of Luxembourg, which Liz found interesting enough that she wished it could continue.

Nick and Franz walked into the restaurant and saw Liz with Desautels at the table by the window, then made their way to them. Liz waved at the open chairs, saying, "Come and sit. Have you eaten today?"

"Only breakfast," Nick answered, and within moments Liz had caught the proprietor's eye and he was taking the lunch order for the new arrivals.

Liz asked that he bring more of the delicious coffee and a variety of desserts for herself and Desautels to choose from, as well as for Nick and Franz when they had finished eating.

The coffee was brought immediately for all four of them, as well as the dessert tray, and it was only a few more minutes before the newcomers were enjoying lunch. Liz presided with all the dignity of a monarch, Desautels noted, mentally tipping his hat to her upbringing.

Desautels and Liz held up the bulk of the conversation as the other two enjoyed their lunch --- both had opted for the pike with green sauce as entrée. When they had finished, though, the desserts became fair game and, in a short time, the proprietor needed to refill the tray and bring more coffee.

Desautels asked Franz, "What is it that you do for a living?"

Deferentially, Franz answered, "I work with construction mostly --- mainly with plumbing --- however, I have an understanding of motors and of electricity, as well."

Desautels asked, "What training do you have in these areas? Did you go to school or apprentice?"

For a moment, Franz looked a little bewildered, then hesitatingly said, "It seems... as though I know these things... without training. The doctor, where they took me when I was wounded (touching his left ear), said that I must have been trained... but I can't seem to remember it. I just do what I need to do automatically as if someone is guiding my hands." He looked troubled at his inability to remember how he knew what he knew.

Desautels, seeing his discomfort, quickly changed the focus of the conversation to a more general topic --- the desserts --- saying, "Now, then, which of these jewels did you find the most enchanting?"

Franz quickly said, with a smile, "All of them," earning a round of applause from his three companions.

The proprietor, overhearing his answer to the question Desautels had posed, interjected, "Then, you must have more, my friends!" and, within moments, their tray had been replenished, with fresh bakery, by his youngest daughter.

Their conversation continued and they talked of many other topics. It was important to Desautels that he gauge the parameters of the memory loss, for he knew that he might see Franz soon, to assess whether he could help him in any way to become more the person he had been before, and he thought of a researcher he knew, in France, who had been studying cases somewhat like this before the war.....

Meanwhile, Liz sat there, enjoying the conversation about mainly male topics and also the company of three men. As the afternoon shadows grew longer, Nick suggested that they adjourn to his home where Marie had insisted they gather to sample her cooking. Desautels declined, having accepted a prior invitation, though his wink at Liz told her he was evening up the numbers, by bowing out. She smiled at him and nodded her understanding, mouthing the words 'thank you' silently.

After going upstairs to her room at the pension for a coat, she returned to the restaurant, where the men were waiting and, dropping Desautels off at his home, they made for Nick's place.

Marie was cooking when they arrived and Liz offered to help, but Marie had other plans and asked Nick to help her. This left Franz and Liz in the sitting room together without much conversation at first.

Liz felt like a schoolgirl on her first date and then the absurdity of it hit her and she began to laugh. At first it was a snicker, then a giggle, and, before long, she was laughing out loud.

Marie and Nick, in the kitchen, were looking at each other and smiling, thinking that all was going well, but Franz was looking at Liz and wondering, without a clue, what was so very funny.   Finally, Liz stopped laughing long enough to tell him and he began to laugh, too, confiding that he had felt the same way.   And, that was how the evening progressed --- every time they looked at each other, one or the other would begin to snicker and before long all four of them --- Nick and Marie as well --- were as merry as if they had been tippling for hours.....

That night, both Nick and Franz went home with Liz --- Nick driving the taxi and Franz, sitting in the back with his arm around her, to walk her up the steps and, shyly, kiss her goodnight.   As the two men drove into the night waving at her, her heart sang with joy and she fairly floated up the stairs to her room.

Once inside, she changed into her nightgown, brushed her hair and then sat in the comfortable easy chair looking out the window at the billions of stars overhead and whispered to the sky, "It's as though I'm being courted all over again."

In another quarter of Luxembourg City, Franz lay on the comfortable bed in Nick and Marie's spare bedroom unable to sleep. He felt like a schoolboy suddenly, filled with joy and energy, unable to think of anything but her laughter, how it tinkled like bells to his ears, how her smile looked, and how she made him feel. What was happening to him, he wondered, that made his heart want to leap out of his chest and made his body want to make love to her. It frightened him a little, yet it felt right, somehow, as though they had done it all before --- in a dream.

Finally, Franz fell asleep in the bedroom and he did dream --
- many dreams of Liz.….

❧Chapter 41 – Luxembourg, Courting❧

Waking early the next morning, Liz penned letters to their parents to let them know that he was alive and reasonably well --- at least physically. She asked them to be patient while she worked with him on remembering and on coming back to being the Franz that they all knew and promised that she would take good care of him. Then, when the usual rap came at her door, she was already dressed and ready to go downstairs with her envelopes.

Opening the door, she startled the clerk, who then nodded, noting the letters and, handing them to him, she asked him to post them.

Downstairs, she waited while he brought her coffee and asked him to sit down with her since it was more than 30 minutes before the first information bearer would arrive. He obliged her and she told him more of the state of affairs with Franz. A romantic at heart, he was touched --- this was exactly like his beloved operas --- and he hung on her every word until the door of the pension opened and the first interview of the day began.

At 10 o'clock, Nick brought Franz to the pension and all three rode in the taxi together to the other café Liz liked, which was a little further away from her pension, for breakfast. Liz and Franz shone with a light, a kind of radiance, that sure sign of lovers, and Nick beamed, as well, feeling he'd had a hand in it --- in any case, it kept him from feeling like an extra wheel.

They ate omelets and sausages, but Liz and Franz could have been eating sawdust and would never have known it, because each one's attention was so riveted by the object of their affection.   In the midst of her glow, Liz happened to think about the fact that they'd told Franz that they needed to hire someone for some construction work. Her light didn't wink out, but suddenly she realized that there would be an accounting, a time when he would ask what the work was and whether the job was his..... Her mind frantically sought a plausible project and, suddenly, she thought of Grosstante Anna in Heffingen.   There were many projects she could find for him there --- cleaning the chicken coop and repairing so many other things..... They could go together for a few days --- maybe even a week or longer.....

She lifted her cup and took a sip of coffee, then added more cream, sipped again, and said, "Well, Nick, I think we should show Franz our project in Heffingen."

After being there twice already, and knowing that the old lady was alone, he quickly picked up the thought that Liz was toying with and said, "Yes, I think we should see if he's interested in it."

So, it was, that they left the café and headed northward to Heffingen. Franz sat in the back seat with Liz, again, his arm nonchalantly draped on the back of the seat and his thigh touching hers. Liz could positively feel fires burning in her loins and, truth be told, Franz' loins were seething, as well, though neither knew of the other's rising passion.

The 45 minute ride to the tiny village little more than 5 miles from the German border was an eternity for Liz and Franz --- they were young enough that their hormones were in high gear. Simply put, these two had chemistry.

When Tante Anna opened the door and saw Liz' face she was thrilled, saying, "So soon, you come again!"

"Yes, Tante, I've brought someone for you to meet."

Tante Anna squinted through her glasses at Franz and said, "He looks just like your Franz, only he has more hair."

Franz looked a little bemused, but shook her hand and said, "Thank you, Frau Kay......," stopping in the middle after beginning to say a name that had not been mentioned, yet.

Liz, on high alert, noticed that he had started to say Anna's last name, then faltered. Sooo, she thought, the memories were closer to the surface than she had realized. She and Nick looked at each other in that moment, each aware of what had occurred. This would be more to discuss with Desautels.....

Liz explained to Tante Anna that she felt some updating and renovation was needed in her not-so-tiny house, to which, Anna said, "But, I have no one to do it and little money."

Liz calmed her fears with, "My family has money Grosstante. You are part of our family and we want you to be happy and safe. We could bring you to America, but I think you like it here, so we want to make this a better place for you. Nick's family would like to come and visit you from time to time when I'm back in America and we must make your bedrooms pretty for guests and build you a better water-closet --- one inside the house --- as well as a bathing room."

Tante Anna's eyes grew big at these plans and she said that she would very much like to have company. At that moment, Liz remembered Emmalina, the girl from the train and asked, "Grosstante, is there a girl in the village who came from Germany to care for her grandmother about the time I did?"

"Ohhhh, yes! that old Frau Dachdecker! I've seen the girl only once, but she seems pleasant enough. She's plain, though, and I think they wanted her out of the city where the husbands are looking for prettier girls," she said, rolling her eyes, "They probably feared she would be an old maid and never leave home. Here, the men look for hard workers and good hearts," she said, shaking her finger in the air to punctuate her statement.

Liz, heard this pronouncement with a ball of amusement rising in her throat and threatening to escape in laughter. Nick, seeing it coming, asked, "And is old Frau Dachdecker a tyrant?" with a smile.

Tante Anna, charmed by his manner, said, "Oh, yes, that girl has her work cut out for her," with a serious nod and a roll of her eyes.

At this point, Liz could no longer hold in the laughter and let it burst forth as a fountain of sound, echoing through the house and bringing forth peals of mirth from the others, as well. It was a long while before any of them could keep a straight face.

Franz kept a safe distance from Liz while they were there, wanting to preserve a good impression on Liz' relative, so, Liz said, "Why don't we go down to Mertz to the restaurant we visited before," winking at Nick, who quickly picked up his cue.

"Tante Anna, would you like to ride in the front seat with me? That's where the best view is for a petite lady, such as yourself."

Tante Anna, positively radiant under the spell of his flattery, raised up to her full 4'10" and said, "I understand that Queen Victoria was petite, also, ...and liked a good view."

What a character, Liz thought, grinning from ear to ear with the others, and men certainly seemed to bring it out.....

Within a few minutes, they had put the chickens in their coop and were on the road to Mersch, laughing as though they'd already downed a bottle of good wine.....

Franz, in the backseat with Liz, casually draped his arm over the back of the seat and allowed his thigh to touch hers once again. Before they arrived at the restaurant, he put his hand on his knee, then, finally on hers, fingers upward, inviting her hand to join it. She put her hand into his and he enveloped it with all of the passion the rest of his body was feeling. She could feel his pulse beating strongly in his muscular fingers, a sensuous rhythm, which spoke to her body in its most private recesses.

Dinner was good. The owner had roasted a spring lamb and served lamb with roasted potatoes and rutabagas --- and with fresh greens and pickled beets on another plate. The fare was excellent, as was the wine. Even Tante Anna had two glasses with her meal, but she asked for schnapps with her pastry, while the others drank coffee.

She sat in the front seat again with Nick on the way home, liking his easy laughter and charming ways --- Liz could see that visits by him and Marie, as well as her mother, Elena, would bring welcome company to her Tante, and she smiled to herself in the dark of the backseat, where Franz had just put his hand on her knee again, but not with its fingers upward this time --- rather, with them wrapped around it.

The muscles of her groin were doing some serious calisthenics with his hand there on her right knee and, finally, she leaned her head back on the top of the seat and drew a deep breath. Franz began to massage her knee with his fingers and she thought she was going to have an orgasm right there --- in the car with her great-aunt only a few feet in front of them. In a way, having to keep silent and maintain composure made the arousal all the more intense, and her vaginal muscles began to pulse and feel thicker --- and heavy with passion held in reserve.

Franz was tightening and relaxing his thigh muscles to keep himself under control as his body began to want to move in the rocking motion of love-making. This seemed so natural, his passion for Liz, and so familiar, as though he had known her all of his life. She hadn't moved his hand and he could feel the heat radiating from her knee and her body like a furnace. Her heat ignited his and it was all he could do to keep from making love to her right there and then, in the backseat, as they wound through the hilly terrain.

When they arrived at Tante Anna's house, they escorted her indoors and Liz helped her slip into her nightgown and slide into her featherbed and under the down comforter, then kissed her forehead. Tiny tears formed in Tante Anna's eyes and rolled down her cheeks.

"What is this, Tante Anna?" Liz asked.

"No one has tucked me into bed and kissed my head in more than 70 years," Tante Anna said,

Then, it was Liz' turn to be tearful as she imagined a little girl wanting her mother to tuck her in and kiss her forehead, but mother thought she was too old for that.

She said to her aunt, "Many will do that for you, now," and kissed her forehead again, and gave her a hug as best she could with all of the covers between them.

"Shall I leave a candle for you?" she asked.

"Oh, no, I know my own house in the light or the dark. Please, come again --- soon."

"Goodnight, then, Tante."

"Goodnight, Lisbet."

On the drive back to Luxembourg City, Liz and Franz sat in the backseat, again. He held her knee lightly, at first, and then allowed his fingers to slip just under the hem of her skirt so that he was touching flesh rather than her skirt. She leaned her head back again and opened her legs a little bit. Seeing this move as encouragement, Franz allowed his fingers to slide upwards as much as he dared --- slowly, to avoid offending.

Liz wanted to grab his hand and plant it on her furry mound, but she allowed the teasing and tantalizing to continue --- a second courtship of her body, which might at any time remind Franz of who he was.

Forty-five minutes through a darkened countryside is a long time and the two of them put it to good use: Franz turning toward Liz and using both hands on her body and she, touching his as well. Their lips met and surrendered to each other again, but more passionately and deeply than on the steps of the pension.

Franz lifted her skirt and, feeling that she wore no underclothing, finally touched her mound and then ventured to slide a finger through the wetness he found there. She jerked as he touched the button at its apex, then pushed herself toward him, inviting him to do more.

It's a good thing taxis are built to carry luggage in the backseat, as well as passengers, she thought, as he knelt before her, kissing her and squeezing one breast, while sliding his finger into the opening of her private recess. Then, he lay her down on the seat and began to kiss everything that was bare and, finally, enfolded that button, which had made her jerk, with his lips and began to gently suck it, as she lifted her hips to his face like a gymnast and rocked forward and back as he suckled. But, the milk of this nursing was not flowing from the nipple, rather from the recess and, after feeling it with his fingers, he wanted to feel it with his manhood. He waited until Liz was making little moaning sounds in her throat, for all the world like a cat in heat, and he opened his fly to release his shaft from its imprisonment and give it the freedom to amplify the pleasure of them both. Nick found a place to park off the road at this point and went to relieve himself a hundred feet up the road to let them be more private.

All alone, in the dark, Franz entered Liz as she sat on the edge of the seat with her knees spread wide apart. He felt her surge toward him to swallow him with her secret cave, and caress his manhood with its walls, until its spurting juices flowed into her and his surging hips brought her to the completion that his fingers and lips had begun. They stayed there, locked into each other's body, like a statue forged by some erotic artist, and experiencing tiny, involuntary thrusts forward as her muscles tightened and his responded. He found her mouth again and kissed her, passionately, all the while squeezing both breasts and pinching the nipples between thumbs and forefingers, for she wore no brassiere.

She slid her hands down his back over his shirt and below his belt to his buttocks, then squeezed them. He rewarded her with a forward thrust, which brought another moan of pleasure from her throat, but when they heard purposely loud footsteps approaching, they quickly put themselves to rights and sat beside each other as before.

Nick opened the driver's door, got in and said, "The wine went through me. Everybody having fun?"

They quickly answered at the same time, "Yes! The dinner was excellent."

Nick continued driving toward Luxembourg City and Liz' pension, as the two in the backseat sat there in each other's arms, kissing.

When they arrived, Liz suggested that Franz might like to come upstairs with her. He asked, "Are you certain?"

She answered, "Yes, Franzl, I am."

Nick heard the exchange and waved them up the steps, then turned the taxi around and held up 10 fingers. Liz held up only 2. He got the message --- 2 o'clock --- and smiled.....

Inside the pension, Liz penned a note to the clerk, asking him to do the interviews, because they were all the 10 minute ones, and asking that he not disturb her .....and her husband.....

Then, she led Franz up the stairs after her, opened the door to her room, and led him to the bed, where she unbuckled his trousers, then unbuttoned them, letting them slide to the floor. Taking them to the chair, she bent over to lay them neatly over the back of it, then s-l-o-w-l-y lifted her hem to tease him with the sight of her thighs, and took off her skirt over her head and, bending over the chair to let him see her buttocks in an inviting position, placed the skirt over his trousers. Then, walking back to him, she waited for him to remove his shirt and then her top. She walked to the chair again and bent over, laying them across it as well. When she returned to him, they stood there both naked in the lamplight, each touching and caressing the other's body, lightly, then firmly, then lightly, teasingly, again. Liz stroked his stomach and felt the muscles tighten, then Franz did the same to her and she felt hers tighten. Finally, he took her in his arms and, putting his hands on her buttocks, squeezed them, lifting her to the bed in one move. She rolled aside, pulled back the covers, and rolled over, then under them.

Franz had other ideas --- he pulled the covers back, exposing her to the light, and, kneeling between her legs, took her by the ankles and lifted them in the air toward her head, then entered the slit between her thighs with his now-stiffened saber, completely filling that tightness with himself and feeling, again, the oneness he had craved since they met.......

He didn't know what or why it was --- or how it came about --- but, for him, she was not like other women. She was different, ...special, ...unique. He felt certain that they had known each other since forever and knew that they belonged together now --- and always.

Liz had already known that, because she had never forgotten it, and she opened and flowered to the passion that he took her with, giving with the same intensity as Franz. When he ultimately collapsed upon her in the last passionate throes of his orgasm, she held him to her as though she would make them one flesh rather than two parts of a whole --- her being filled with love for him and her body rocking with her own fulfillment.

At last, after many minutes, he found himself able to roll off of the support of his forearms and lay beside her, his hand nestled atop her furry mound --- as though to proclaim his possession of it, and her.....

✌Chapter 42 – Some Remembering✍

Liz lay there watching the morning sunlight make glowing patches on the floor and walls. Franz was still asleep and she didn't want to wake him, preferring to see him there, warm and safe in the arms of sleep in her bed, when unexpectedly, he began to fret and talk in his sleep, saying, in English, "No, I can't help you. I won't help you. I am only an American building business ties for my company, nothing more." He was silent for awhile, then began again, repeating himself, and adding with agitation, "No! No! Don't hurt her!" With this, he startled himself awake and looked around dazedly, shaking his head as though to clear it and rid himself of cobwebs. He stared at her incredulously, as if he'd seen a ghost, then began to weep.

Liz didn't understand, but she carefully put her arms around him and comforted him. Finally, when he was ready, he began to speak, slowly, hesitatingly, and, at times, with choking sobs, in Luxembourgish, their private language since childhood. "If you're here….. then you're not dead, but I saw them torture you….. and kill you. How can you be here?"

Not knowing what to say, at first, Liz said nothing, then, after a time, started with, "Franz, I was at home during the whole war. I was not in Germany. They must have used

294

someone who looked like me to fool you. I hope that she was only acting and didn't die," and continued, after a few minutes, "Then, you must have refused to help them if they pretended to kill her. I know that you must have felt you betrayed me, but it's what I would have wanted --- for you to remain loyal to what we believe in: freedom and right action. Many men died to protect that dream and, if you had helped the Nazis, many, many more would have died --- good, honest men with homes and families, too. You saved them --- you!"

By this time, she was crying, too, and they held onto and rocked each other as they allowed her words to sink in and cleanse them. She didn't know where they came from, just that they had come out of her mouth and they were helping her to heal her beloved Franzl.

It seemed like a few minutes, but hours had passed since his dream and they were still holding each other there on the bed and rocking gently, from time to time. Finally, Liz sat up and asked, "Shall we dress?"

Franz, unable to meet her eyes, yet, after the secret of his betrayal coming to light, took her hand and kissed the palm then, saying, "You are too good for me, Lisbet."

Liz pulled him upright and, taking his hand, said, "No, Franz, you protected our country while I sat at home doing little for it. It is you, who are too good for me," then continued, "but, I hope that you will consider staying with me and loving me as you once did."

"Of course, I love you!" he all but shouted, "You are my soul, my heart, my reason for being. How could I not love you? How could I not stay with you?"

They held each other and rocked for awhile longer as they sat there, then Liz reminded Franz that it was time to dress and seek nourishment.

He hadn't been thinking about food, but suddenly felt ravenous, and said, "Yes, if we don't find something to eat soon, I will have to eat you, my little gingerbread girl," with a grin, and put his hand on her furry mound, tickling the hair and making her wiggle.

She laughed, a sound as sweet as tinkling bells, and said, "Ah, I fear there is little nutrition in that --- though, I do love it especially….. Can you do it later? For dessert?"

He grinned at her and, with mischief in his eyes, offered, "I suppose, but if you love food better, maybe we should use a knackwurst next time….." He barely dodged the pillow she threw and hid behind the chair, lest he become victim to another of her shots, then peeked over it and saw that she had given up and was dressing, so he began to make himself street-worthy, as well.

At 2'o'clock, they left the pension and met Nick outside. Leaving Nick's cab in front of the building, the three of them walked to the restaurant down the street and, finding it empty at that hour, had their choice of tables. As he often did, the proprietor sat with them for a bit, recommending the fried brook fish, which always came in fresh on Thursday, while they decided what to eat, and praised their choices, when they had made them --- the fried fish with potato dumplings and cucumber salad all around.

Seeing the question in Nick's face, Liz began, "Franz has remembered some things, but not everything. He will remember more as time passes, I believe --- I hope --- and he remembers me."

"Ah, good!" Nick blurted out, then said, "Oh, I didn't mean to be rude."

"Oh, Nick, I know you wouldn't be rude. You're just happy for us, aren't you?"

"Yes, yes, of course!" he said, then added, softly, "Marie will be happy, too."

"Eventually, we will need to go to the U.S. Legation," Liz said, "They think that you're a defector, Franz. Do you remember anything about that?"

"Yes, I remember a man coming to the cellar. He rescued me, but left me to get out of Europe by myself with identification from someone who had died and some money."

"Then," she continued, "You went where?"

"I was near Bonn, so I tried to go to a man I knew, named Froehlich, in Koln. We spoke and he helped me with more money. I was going to Brussels, maybe Amsterdam, to try to get out of Europe. I thought you were dead so, when the train was stopped by the battle, I sneaked off, not wanting to be interred --- and having no reason to go back to Illinois.

Then, I was wounded in my leg by a fall and I headed for Luxembourg, walking and hiding --- lucky I didn't die. I don't know how I was wounded on my head --- I don't remember it --- probably shrapnel --- but maybe one of the times I fell from the pain in my leg..... My identification said I was a Luxembourger, I remember that, but I lost it somewhere after a couple of years. The man even looked a lot like me --- Henri Bruckner. Sometimes, I know I was in a hospital and I had problems with my memory --- it comes and goes --- when it was good, they would let me work there. My leg healed pretty well and I don't often feel pain in it."

"The scar on my eyebrow," he said, feeling it, "Is from one of the falls when I escaped into Luxembourg, but the one on my lip is from a Nazi interrogator's fist. I'm lucky that's all I got --- they wanted me to work for them very much --- and voluntarily at first. They kept me confined in that cellar for about 9 months. Maybe they hoped that I might still capitulate --- or were glad that, at least, I wasn't working for the other side. They fed me, but not very well."

At this point, the lunch was served and, after the usual interaction with the waiter vis-à-vis beverages and requests, they began to eat a bit before he continued.

Liz asked, "What did you do when you came to Luxembourg?"

"That's when I was in the hospital a lot. Taking me for a native son, they treated me well and, since my surname was Germanic, they didn't bother me once they saw I was not fit for fighting. I have not used English until now, holding it locked inside for fear of discovery, at first, and then falling out of use of it. When I was in the east of Luxembourg, I spoke Luxembourgish and when I was on the west or south, that or French. I avoided German, because there are bad memories with it for me --- and for many Luxembourgers."

They ate in silence for a bit, then Nick asked, "How did you live when you weren't in the hospital?"

"On the road, in ruins, working when I could find work and living indoors when it was available. I even slept in a park a few nights ago in a place called Hesperange," whereupon Liz and Nick looked at each other quickly, then back at Franz.

He continued, "Some of the past is very vague, like a haze, and some is clearer. I remembered Liz still might have relatives in Heffingen, but I was afraid of going to them and possibly drawing them into my problems. By the time the war ended, I just didn't bother. I thought there was no more Liz and this was as good a place to exist as any."

At this point, another customer entered and the proprietor spoke with him for a moment, then asked Liz if he might join them. Thinking it might be the all-knowing Desautels, she said it would be all right, but was very startled to see, when the man came over, that it was Mr. Henri. Strange, she thought, that he is so open here.....

He greeted her, then proceeded to greet her companions, as well. Nick smiled at her, saying, "Sorry, Liz, I was helping Mr. Henri --- but in your best interest."

She turned to look at Franz as he said, "Good to see you again, d'Croixville. Thank you for getting me out of that

J. Matheny

cellar --- I'd have starved if you hadn't, I think. They were giving me less and less food and coming less often."

Liz, for once, stunned into silence, looked from one man to another, not knowing what to ask or think first, then finally let out a "huumpphh" and went back to her lunch, leaving the men to chat.

Eventually, however curiosity got the best of her and she asked of d"Croixville, "Why didn't you tell me more?"

"Don't you think that you did quite well on your own?" he asked, "After all, you found him when I could not."

Liz thought for a moment and, having to agree with him, nodded, then said, "Well, you could have told me that you were d'Croixville!"

"What would it have solved, ma cher?" he asked.

"So many men with so many secrets! And they say women are deceivers! Hah! And, now, what do we do? Franz has no passport from any country and our families are in America!"

"This is why I am contacting you today, ma cher," he said. "He will have to go to the U.S. Legation and tell them who he is and how he came to be here. There will be hospital records and my account, as well. Now that the Germans are at bay, they will be all too glad to tell all and admit such a small thing --- it's the perpetrators of big transgressions who are lying and trying to escape punishment. It may take some time, but he will have a passport eventually. Meanwhile, Luxembourg will be happy to have one of its own sons live

300

here and, after your long wait, I suspect that a second honeymoon is in order," he said, winking at Liz.

Liz blushed and Nick tried to hide his smile, saying, "Yes, by all means, and I know the very place."

Liz knew, too, and looked at Franz, who realized immediately what was meant. Only the mysterious and enigmatic d'Croixville was left in the dark --- for once.

After a few hours of sitting in the restaurant and visiting over their late lunch, Nick asked them to adjourn to his home, where Marie would by now be preparing the evening meal. Liz and Franz looked at each other, wanting to get back to the pension, but they knew Marie wanted to be part of this reunion, so Liz reached under the tablecloth and squeezed his hand when he said, "Oh, we must honor the Rachmaninoff of the kitchen, your Marie, with our humble appetites."

They walked the block back to the pension and Liz and Franz fetched their coats, and came back rather breathless, though not from the stairs, the others surmised.....

Once his passengers were inside and comfortable, Nick started the car and they were off to the celebration.....

Marie had a difficult time restraining her enthusiasm when she saw the lovers reunited. She hugged Liz over and over again, wiping stray tears from her eyes with the corner of her apron hem. Liz went with her to the kitchen to help, leaving the men alone with a bottle of wine and talk of world events.

Over the preparations, Marie asked Liz how she knew he was really Franz and Liz, smiling, asked, "Would you forget Nick --- or the way he makes love to you?"

Marie, blushing, admitted that she could not and Liz smiled, lifting her hands and tilting her head, as if to say 'see'.

They worked on the meal, enjoying each other's company, talking of things other than Liz and Franz. Sometime during their conversation, Liz asked Marie, "Would Elena like to go to the country for a visit in a month or so?"

"Where?" Marie asked.

Liz began the story of Heffingen and Grosstante Anna. She made Marie laugh with the story of Frau Dachdecker, and Anna's assessment, and they began to plot on Emmalina's behaof, as well.

Nick came to the door eventually and asked what had been so funny. Liz answered, "Frau Dachdecker." Having been privy to that bit of conversation, he chuckled and nodded, then asked, "When will we eat?"

"Oh, you impatient one!," Marie said, turning to Liz. "He is always hanging in the kitchen waiting for treats --- like a pet puppy.....

"Yes," he said, quite merry with the wine, "*Your* pet puppy, who loves to lick your.... .....hand!"

Marie blushed, laughed and said, "Give me 15, no, 20 minutes more --- and put the plates on the table --- oh, and please remember the silverware....."

He bowed and retired to the parlor, where Franz and d'Croixville were still talking, poured them all another glass of wine and announced, "We must lay the table, or we won't be fed." It was not exactly what he'd been told, but he didn't have to do it alone.....

The meal was delightful --- Marie had outdone even her own stellar cooking and the braised vegetables, creamed spinach, pates and croquettes made a festive addition to the roast goose with stuffing and fine Luxembourg wine. This was quite an occasion for them all --- one worthy of celebration, and they made merry until past 9 in the evening. Nick imbibed more than was safe for a driver, so Marie went to a neighbor, who also drove a taxi, and asked him to take the guests to their homes.

Franz collected his knapsack before they left and when Liz and he were back in their room at the pension, he stowed it under the bed. This night, he and Liz began their lovemaking at a different pace --- slowly, and deliberately, building to a supremely passionate forte --- and sleeping soundly in its wake.

ᕼChapter 43 - Luxembourg, The U.S. Legationᕫ

They awoke late, the wine and lovemaking having allowed them to sleep well into the morning. Liz went to the window and saw Nick's taxi out front and remembered that the U.S. Legation was on their schedule for the day. She went to the bed and began kissing Franz awake, then reminded him that they must go to the Legation to start his paperwork so that he could go back to America.

Sleepily, he grabbed for her, catching a breast and holding it. It felt wonderful to him --- and to her as well, but she knew that they needed to get going and told him that Nick was outside waiting. This bit of information finally fired up his boiler and got him moving, Liz noted. In less than 10 minutes, they were downstairs and getting into the taxi.

Franz insisted they must have breakfast first and they stopped at the café they so often patronized, ate more quickly than usual, and headed for the legation.

Once there, Franz was interviewed behind closed doors by more than one person, as Nick and Liz waited and waited. At one point, d'Croixville came into the Legation and was ushered into the room where Franz was being interviewed. Eventually, he came out and assured them that all was going well and the staff of the Legation was merely trying to have

Franz remember as much as he could of what he had experienced --- for the records.

While they waited, Liz thought about the path that she had traveled in looking for her husband, the still unexplained notebook, the many people she had met along the way, and the question of whether the U.S. Government would press any charges against the soldiers who kidnapped, detained, and abused Franz. She pondered all of it in that somber setting and, knowing that what mattered most to her was Franz, she let it all go as if it had never been. Questions don't always need to be answered.

It was dinnertime when they finally released Franz and said that it would be no less than a month before he would have a passport and that it could take as long as six months, maybe more. Meanwhile, he could not leave Luxembourg. This was no hardship, Liz thought, since they already had plans right there --- in Heffingen.

When they were done, they invited Nick and d'"Croixville to join them over dinner in the little restaurant. Both accepted, and soon the taxi was on its way.

When they arrived, there was a surprise waiting within --- Desautels had booked a table for five and had already been seated. Each looked at the other, wondering who had asked him, and seeing their consternation, he broke the silence, saying, "Relax, lady and gentlemen, I am a medium --- I know these things....."

The conversation was delightful, as was the meal --- this time they left the fried fish for other patrons, ordered the lamb stew --- and went easy on the wine. At 8:15, Liz and Franz said good-bye and walked back to the pension, leaving the others to visit and finish the dessert tray the proprietor had provided.

On the way up the stairs to their room, Franz, lagging behind Liz put his hands on her bottom and, when she stopped and turned, enfolded her in his arms and kissed her, right there on the stairs, then lifted and carried her up the last flight to the door. Fishing in a purse for a key is not easy in a supine position, so he set her down and, when she had opened it, lifted her up again, walked into the room, stood her on the chair at the writing desk and took off her coat, then lifted her skirt to see if she had underclothing on. He was in luck, or perhaps it was she, for she was naked under that skirt and he bent his head to kiss her furry mound, and then her bellybutton, and, undoing the buttons and zipper at her waist, let the skirt fall to the chair. Next, he unbuttoned her blouse and began kissing her breasts until the nipples stood up proud and erect --- as if they'd been carved out of ice. He teased them gently with his lips and teeth until Liz shivered over and over and began to undress him as well.

Off came his shirt --- it was all she could reach without bending --- and then he lifted her in his arms and took her to the bed. It took but a moment for him to release his belt and undo the buttons, allowing his trousers to fall to the floor, and leaving them where they lay, he began to attend to his quarry --- Liz, all of Liz.

She lay there waiting, not knowing what to expect, and he gave her the unexpected. He sat on the bed and, lifting her to face him on his lap, had her straddle him with her legs on the bed. He began to kiss her deeply and, as he did, they could feel his member grow, pressing against his belly and hers as it grew up between them --- larger and harder with each kiss until, finally, he had to do something more.

He lifted her up by the waist, saying, "Put your arms around my neck and, as I lift you, I'll put this piece of wood inside you. Doing as he said, she put her arms fully around his neck and, when he straightened himself there was enough room beneath her for him to hold his saber tall and straight as she let herself down onto it. When she was sitting there, feeling its fullness deep within her, he put his muscular hands on her waist and began lifting her up and down on himself --- not high, just enough to make the friction work --- a few inches was all it took. He could feel her wetness dripping onto his thighs and the sensation spurred him onward. Though this was quite enough for arousal, the sounds, as they made love, were erotic as well --- the low moanings, as their muscles flexed and the nerve endings felt the friction, the squishy sound of her flowing juices, lubricating their passion, and making it possible.....

Finally, he began to shudder as his orgasm overcame him and, feeling him finishing, Liz lifted herself off of him and, rolling to the side, was able to get off the bed and bend to hold him in her mouth as he finished, sucking gently and amplifying his orgasm as he fell back onto the bed. While he finished, she licked him ever so gently on those tender places and gave him an extension of the pleasure as it subsided. When it was completely over, she lay beside him and said, "I think you'll need to get up on the bed entirely, Franzl, or you'll have a sore back tomorrow."

He realized that she was right, and besides, he had more work to do..... He laid her on the covers and knelt between her legs, giving her what he'd promised that morning. He sucked gently on the little button hidden within her furry mound until she was at the edge of screaming with pleasure, then slid two fingers inside of her as he continued to lick and suck on it up to the point when he could feel her orgasm beginning to be strong. Then, he entered her with his resurrected member and, lifting her hips to meet his, continued plunging into her recess until her orgasm had completely subsided. When she was still and her breathing had returned to normal, he got up and pulled the blankets out from beneath her and covered them both as he lay at her side, his arm over her waist.....

☙Chapter 44 – Back to Heffingen☙

Days had passed, days of lovemaking, walking in the parks, and exploring the small towns of Luxembourg, as well as Luxembourg City, itself. Franz had telegraphed his parents and they would be arriving in a month, but, in a day or so, Liz and Franz would be going to stay with Tante Anna in Heffingen to begin the renovations to her home. This time, instead of working with the crew he had sometimes found work with, he had contracted for them to work under his direction to bring her house into the 1940's from the 1800's. Two of her bedrooms were useable, but the other two needed work and, when they were done, she could have visitors any time she wanted. One big issue was better indoor plumbing….. Franz had ideas for a better chicken coop, as well…..

Thus it was, that, two days later, Nick took them to Heffingen with only some of their luggage, for they would continue renting the pension room as a home base.

Nick and Franz took the feather bed from the best guest room outside and shook it well, then, did the same for the feather comforter, while Liz shook the pillows. In a few hours, everything there was fresh and ready for them to sleep that night and Nick and Franz turned to some other heavy chores --- Anna's bed needed a good shaking, also, and so did her comforter. She beamed as she saw the work they were doing for her and praised them at every turn, feeling blessed to have them there. Ah, she thought, watching their youthful strength, if only I could have youth again!

Liz had explained to her what they were hoping to do, in bringing her people to make her life less lonely --- so that she could stay in the country, in her own home --- and to help her with upgrading her house. The ideas they had spoken of excited her and she began doing little chores she had put off time after time, energized by their productivity and their dreams for her.

She made them a lunch and brought it outdoors, to a table in the garden, where they were discussing all of the possibilities. The men were to arrive with their truck, the following day, and would help further with the renovations, but they would need a list of alterations, so that parts could be purchased. A list of chores would be necessary, as well, since there were many things that had been put off for lack of strength --- tree trimming, the chicken coop repairs, fence repairs, and others.....

By the time they had finished eating, they had a plan and Tante Anna felt like a queen, thinking of the new things that were coming.

It was at this time that Liz thought of Emmalina and decamped for half and hour to call on her. She found the address easily, for Heffingen was tiny, and knocked at the door. Emmalina answered and her face lit up when she saw Liz. "Oh, I thought you had forgotten me!" she said. "Come in, come in!"

Liz followed her inside and into the country kitchen. Apparently, this was the time of day that Frau Dachdecker napped, so they were able to visit quietly without interruption. Liz told Emmalina about their plans for renovating, as well as for the future, and mentioned that a group of men would be coming to work on the house. She gave Emmalina a pointed look when she said this, and when the hint was lost on her, said, "Some of the men are unmarried and they have skills and a job. You could do worse."

At this point, Emmalina understood her point and blushed, then asked, "Do you really think that one of them might..... might be interested in me?"

"Of course, Emmalina! You're pleasant, you laugh, you're kind, and you're a hard worker," Liz replied.

"How long will they be here?" Emmalina asked.

"Oh, on and off for a month or more, I think."

"Should I just come by when grandmother is sleeping?"

Approving of the idea, Liz said, "I think that would be excellent." Then, hearing someone stirring in the direction of the bedrooms, she said, "Go, now, I'll let myself out." And, as Emmalina disappeared toward the sounds, Liz eased herself out the door.

Back at Tante Anna's, Liz busied herself with sweeping and tidying. She knew it would have to be done again, and often, what with the workmen coming soon, but it gave her a sense of accomplishment. Eventually, she called her aunt in from the garden to supervise preparation of the dinner for that evening.

Tante Anna was amazed at what had been going on while she listened to Franz and Nick talking and planning in the garden. It had been so interesting --- she felt as if she had magically entered a man's world and eavesdropped on what went on. They talked about such interesting things --- not babies and grandchildren.....

Now, she was back in the woman's world and, at least, she had a pleasant companion to share it with. Together, they made the preparations for a dinner of roast chicken with garlic cloves stuck beneath the skin and rosemary leaves sprinkled over it. Liz filled the vent with many kinds of vegetables: shallots, carrots, parsnips, celery, and winter squash, then added various nuts, some prunes, and a sprinkle of salt on the skin, as well as inside. Then, covering the roaster, slipped the bird into the wood-burning stove. She washed and oiled large dark-skinned potatoes and slipped them into the oven next to the roaster after pricking the skins, then, pulled Tante Anna into the other rooms to show her the progress that had been made.

Her aunt was delighted and told her so. She could see how happy Liz was to be there, with Franz, and active with something other than searching. Impulsively, Liz hugged her aunt and kissed her cheek, drawing tears to Anna'a eyes. Liz, seeing them, asked why Anna was crying and Anna said, "It is the first time that anyone has done something so nice for me."

Liz smiled at this lady, her great aunt and, remembering that she was the family anomaly --- a woman who didn't marry after her sweetheart died in a farm accident, said, "Tante Anna, it gives us pleasure to do these things for you, because we know that you have a beautiful soul and have done these things for others when you were younger and able."

"Yes, I did," she said, "I took care of my mother and father when my sister and brothers got married and left Heffingen for America and for the cities. This was our house when I was a child and now I live in it as an old lady. None of them wanted it, so here I am."

"It's all right, Tante Anna, you will soon have friends coming to visit, and enjoy being with you. In your old age, you will be popular. You will visit them in the city, too."

A joyful chortle escaped her aunt's throat, reflecting the pleasure she was anticipating.

Then, Liz told her about the visit to Emmalina and her aunt's chortle nearly choked her with delight at the thought of Frau Dachdecker's granddaughter finding a beau right under her nose and getting out from under the old dragon's thumb. "You will have worked a miracle," she told Liz, then, whispered conspiratorially, "But, don't say I told you."

It was all Liz could do to maintain a straight face, but the thought of the work still to be done came to her aid.

By dinner, much had been accomplished. The men had planned every detail of the renovations and laid out a plan of action vis-à-vis the supplies. Liz and her great-aunt had inventoried everything in the house and made a list of what they must purchase in order to restock the bedrooms with more suitable linens for guests. The thought of a shopping trip in Mersch --- or perhaps even in Luxembourg City had Tante Anna all a-twitter --- she had not been on a shopping trip in decades. The older country folk had stayed in the country during much of the war and. before that. her linens were not so threadbare.

In truth, the end result was to be a small private country inn where friends and relatives of Tante Anna could come and relax, enjoy her company, share her life for a few days or weeks, and help her with the chores and responsibilities of a house and property, thus keeping her independent and improving her life, as well as allowing them to enjoy the benefits of spending time in the country --- on the land.

At dusk, Liz left Tante Anna in the kitchen, basting the chicken as it cooled, and went to call the men indoors. They were already putting the chickens away for the night and came in as soon as they had gathered their papers together. Nick had filled his handkerchief with nine eggs they found in various places and Anna showed them how to tell if they were fresh, by seeing if they floated in water. All of them sank, bringing a smile to her face and she gave a self-congratulatory raise of the eyebrows and a nod to the men, as if to say, 'see, this is how it's done'. Everyone giggled at her antics --- even Tante Anna, who knew she was a character.

After dinner, Nick left for home. This was one of Marie's late nights, but she would be home by 9:15 or so and he wanted to tell her about his wonderful day in the country and all of their plans.

Liz wrote a note for him to deliver to Paul Tischler in the morning, inviting him and his wife to come up one day with Nick during the renovations and to come and visit Anna when the bedrooms were in good order. She wrote another for Elena, Marie's mother.

Not long after Nick left, Tante Anna began nodding and Liz and Franz adjourned to the kitchen to clean up from the dinner. After about an hour, her aunt came wandering in and asked why they hadn't awakened her to help. Liz answered, "Because we wanted to play like newlyweds....."

Her aunt laughed and winked at Franz, adding, "Better watch out if she's got you drying dishes! Next thing, she'll have you changing diapers."

Franz smiled meaningfully at Liz, who ducked her head and blushed at the decidedly erotic thoughts which came to mind.

Finally, Tante Anna, feeling as though she'd at least made an appearance in the kitchen as the duenna of the house, gave in to her body's demand for rest and went off to bed, leaving Liz and Franz to finish their work.

It wasn't long before they were done and, lifting her onto the counter, Franz put his arms around her and began to kiss her deeply and thoroughly. With her legs wrapped around him, she squeezed him tightly and, breaking from the kiss, whispered in his ear, "Let's go to bed, Franzl."

He didn't have to be told twice. Carrying her in his arms, to the bedroom at the farthest end of the hall from Tante Anna's, he laid her on the bed, then went to the door and closed it. He took off his clothes as she watched, then undressed her, lingeringly, savoring her as much as he had savored the dinner she prepared. Allowing his fingers to trail along her arm or shoulders, so lightly that it sent little chills through her, he brought her to an aroused state and, then, laid down beside her to continue the arousal with kisses, touching and squeezing.

It didn't take long before they were both writhing on the bed, which thankfully didn't squeak, breathing heavily as their passion arose and touching and kissing everywhere they could reach.

Unable to bear it any longer Franz rolled atop her and wiggled himself between her legs, spreading them open and revealing the treasure between them. His saber found its scabbard without him touching either, like the prehensile appendages of some fish and creatures without legs --- or without the ability to reach their sex organs.

Feeling him enter, she arched her back and moaned her ecstasy at that filling of her need, then thrust her hips forward to meet him energetically, with passion. There, in that thick-walled, old country house of Liz' ancestors, they gave their bodies free-rein and acted out their desires and fantasies as seldom before. And, when they had finished they slept, curled together like two kittens from the same litter, as sated with mother's milk as these two had been satisfied with their more adult activities.

After a long while, Franz moved a little and, putting his hand over her furry mound, slipped a finger into her secret recess for one last skinny dip before sleeping, eliciting an 'mmmm' from Liz as she put her hand down to hold his where it was. Her hips began to rotate and grind forward as his lips found hers, and they began all over again.

❧Chapter 45 – Luxembourg, Country Days❧

The days went by without much variation --- renovations had begun and were well under way. Paul and his wife came up with Nick one day and kept Anna occupied while the work was going on, as did Marie and Elena. Wonderful things were happening at the old Kayser homestead. Anna bloomed with all the attention and company, as well as the house.

Finally, it was time for Liz to take her shopping for linens and things for the house. The ladies went back to Luxembourg City with Nick one night and stayed in the pension. The next morning, he picked them up and took them shopping at all the most up-to-date stores. Their purchases filled the roomy trunk and the front seat beside Nick --- with a few packages occupying the ample knee room in the back seat. Then, too tired to shop any further, they set out for Heffingen with a large box containing a variety of tea sandwiches and desserts to share --- and bottles of mineral water.

On arriving back in Heffingen, Nick brought all of their packages in and left them in the newly refurbished bedrooms under Liz' direction. The following day was Saturday and she would open everything and put it all to rights, with Marie's help, when they arrived.

The days passed and guests and workers came and went. Emmalina came faithfully each day, too. She had caught the eye of more than one of the workers, but one in particular pleased her. He was a lanky fellow, quite a bit taller than she, and something about him moved her the way Franz moved Liz --- well, perhaps not that passionately --- but, certainly more than any others she met. It had come to the point that he took his lunch whenever her grandmother fell asleep for her nap and they sat together, in Tante Anna's garden --- so close that one could not have slipped a sheet of paper between them. Liz watched from time to time, hoping that something would come of it.

The time for Franz' parents to arrive grew closer --- only ten more days if their connections all worked well and they decided not to tarry. They had already reached London, where they were visiting friends and planned to take a smaller ship to Le Havre, France, then on to Luxembourg by rail via Paris, Reims, and Metz. His parents had friends in Paris, as well, so this seemed a logical itinerary.

The property improved day by day and Tante Anna did, as well, seeming to grow younger with each guest and each renovation. Her step became livelier and she smiled even more than usual --- perhaps looking forward to seeing Franz' parents.

Then, one day, Liz saw the foreman talking to her and the look on her face when he walked away told all. Liz didn't know whether this was a reciprocal feeling or one-sided, but she didn't want her aunt hurt, so she talked to Nick to get his, more objective, opinion. Used to sizing up people in his taxi, Nick got the lay of the land very quickly. The fellow wasn't after her house --- he had property and money --- it just seemed that he liked Anna, herself. He was no spring chicken, though his muscles and strength from the years of physical exercise made him appear younger. Nick advised Liz not to worry and to let it go where it may.

Satisfied, she stopped hovering and looked more at the possibilities of the property. It had a long garden and backyard as is so often the case where people in villages wanted to keep animals near, but not so near that one could smell them all day and night. At the very end of the property, there were still old pens and shelters --- nothing so grand as an American barn, but shelters for goats, or perhaps a horse, in days gone by. Here, she knew she would find old manure for the garden and the garden could also be enlarged to incorporate more varieties, perhaps she could even send produce to the city with her guests.....

Meanwhile, Liz wrote to all the friends she had met along her pathway to Franz, telling them of her ideas and her happiness, and inviting them to come and visit Luxembourg --- and Tante Anna. She smiled, as she wrote, envisioning her aunt as an international hostess of the back country --- unless she got married and went traveling herself.....

In time, it all came together and the work was finished. Days had melted into weeks, and the weeks into over a month. In a few days, Franz' parents would arrive on the scene and be Tante Anna's first official guests in the totally renovated property. Everyone seemed to be holding their breath.

Then the day came..... Nick fetched them at the station in Luxembourg and brought them to Tante Anna's --- after stopping at the pension to unload their excess baggage. Franz' mother wept at the sight of her son and hugged him over and over, then held Liz, saying, "You did it; you did it; you found him. What would we have done without you?"

His father, more stoic, hugged him, then sat down with him to talk and to ask the questions parents ask. He seemed concerned when Franz didn't know some answer about what happened to him, but made certain that his engineering schooling had not been forgotten --- not one bit of it. He could still run the company some day..... Franz' Dad was a good man, and a good Dad, but business was business to his mind --- as it was to many of that age.....

After they had chatted awhile, his parents began to notice the house and the apparent newness of it. Liz took them out into the garden and showed off the improvements there, as well, pointing out innovations that were Franz' doing, proudly, and smiling at her husband.

Dinner was perfect. Everything, except the flour in the bread and the goose they had roasted, had come from Tante Anna's wonderful garden. Over dinner, Liz talked about what she wanted this to be for her aunt and, after a glance at each other, Franz' parents agreed that this would be a wonderful thing for her --- as well as family members and her friends. A place to rest and revive one's spirit..... A retreat.....

❧Chapter 46 – To England at Last❧

For a few days Franz' parents were content to rest and relax, but eventually, they got bored from not having things to do and people to see, and went off to Luxembourg City to shop and see who they might know.

It was through their leaving, that Franz' passport came through. His father found he had known the second-in-command at the Legation years earlier and was able, with his help, to speed up the process considerably. Life really works this way and, more often than not, it isn't what you know, but who you know.

Franz and Liz stayed on in Luxembourg for a few more months, shifting between the pension and Tante Anna's house, and enjoying their life together. He showed her parts of Luxembourg she had not seen and they met with friends, like Nick and Marie, for dinners.

By this time, the workers had, of course, gone on to another project, though Emmalina received mail from her beau at Tante Anna's address --- addressed to Anna, lest the postman in a small village let the secret slip. At times, the foreman slipped a letter in to Tante Anna, as well, and, when they had projects in the northeast, he and Emmalina's beau were certain to show up on their day off to sit in the garden or play cards at the kitchen table --- until, of course, Emmalina had to attend to her grandmother   Startlingly, Anna married the none-too-young foreman two days before Liz and Franz left and Liz and Franz signed the register for them as witnesses.   Later, they received the news that Emmalina became engaged to her beau a few weeks later.

Franz and Liz then retraced her path of discovery back to all of their friends --- though that is another story --- and ultimately, to a ship in Genoa, bound for England.   They relived their honeymoon on that ship, walking the decks in a daze of love, dancing as though they were the only two people on board, and having passionate physical encounters at any hour of the day. The other passengers remarked that it seemed as though they were the only two people in the world, so focused were they on each other. It was supposed that they were honeymooners.

When the ship docked in England, they went immediately to the house of the friend who had lent it to them for their honeymoon, for he had offered it again --- Ponce he heard the news from Franz' parents. As before, they very much enjoyed it's charm.

A few weeks after his parents had returned to America, there came a time when Franz drove down to London to meet with clients of their parent's company and Liz stayed at the country house, not relishing the thought of being one female in a group of men. Then, missing him after two days alone, Liz took pen and paper and began.....

"My dearest love," she wrote, *"I miss you dreadfully."*   A small blob of ink blurred the words and she had to blot.

Surveying the damage, she decided to begin again and wadded the paper to toss it into the refuse basket, then tilted her head to one side as though listening. Forgotten, the crumpled paper slipped from her hand onto the small writing desk as she rose and hastened to the window. Looking into the distance, she could see a bit of dust rising from the road and now she was certain she heard a motorcar.

First, a quick look in the mirror, then hurrying downstairs, she paused for a moment to regain composure and walked seemingly serene across the drive into the water garden to sit by a fountain with a white marble woman holding a vase above her head which dripped water down onto her invitingly nude body. This was Franz' most favored piece of all the statues on the grounds. He so loved the upward tilted breasts and the trickle of water pulling the eye to each curve of the comely maiden.

The sound of the car was nearer now and Liz seated herself on the lip of the fountain, gracefully draping herself in a manner she knew Franz would like. She was not ingenuously oblivious to his sensual fantasies, rather, she enjoyed providing him with opportunity for increased arousal. It was a game they played.

She watched as the dragonflies hovered over the water, iridescent wings reflecting beautiful colors. It brought her quickly to a state of torpor and, when the roadster pulled up, she was a picture of the languid lady on a summer day.

Franz sat there for a moment looking at her. The sun illuminated the colors of her frock and gave a glow to the scene. The very air seemed to glisten. He was struck by the beauty of it and aware of a certain tightening in his trousers. When she trailed her finger in the water and lifted it high to allow one sparkling drop to fall back into the pool, he felt an incredible urge to take her in his arms and make passionate love to her. He paused in that fantasy for a few moments longer, then climbed out of the roadster without opening the door, walked to the fountain and said, "Any room there for me?"

Liz, who had been genuinely entranced for a moment by the drop of water on the tip of her finger, shuddered slightly, then, turned to him saying, "What is the password?" a smile playing on her lips.

Franz, for his part, was beyond ready to participate in the game which was afoot. His manhood was already throbbing and straining at the confining cloth of his trousers.

He opened his mouth, hoping inspiration would step in and give him the word she sought, and someone or something said, "Beautiful." The smile on her face was answer enough for him to know that he had spoken well. He felt as though all the light of the sun was coming out of her face and he wanted to hold that energy to him closely and feel its warmth imprinted on his skin forever. He took her in his arms and held her as though he would never let go. It was something beyond sex, but it continued his arousal nonetheless.

He began to kiss her, this glowing being, deep hungry kisses full of his longing to penetrate her inner recesses. Their lips met, then parted, then, as though one kiss was insufficient, they met again, tenderly, skin against skin, slowly bringing every nerve fiber into readiness. Liz pulled back to catch her breath and allow him the space to catch his, then said as her head tilted skyward, "It would seem this would be a day to be out of the sun….." Franz took her meaning and, happily taking her hand, was led into the house.

She continued to lead him and they did not stop until they were in that selfsame upstairs room where she had pulled back the drape to see the road.

She seated herself on the chaise longue and Franz sat next to her, giving her tiny nudging kisses. His hands touched her body, little vague, trailing touches that were far more arousing to her than a firm grip would have been. The slow sensuality of it was causing their hearts to pound, but they allowed that to abate, so that with each step their arousal would be higher and more compelling.

Franz kissed her neck and she whispered in his ear, "I was writing you a letter to tell you how much I missed you." His lips found hers and they kissed, tenderly at first, then with a hard passion that left them breathless.

"What do you want?" he asked.

"You know what I want," she said, her hips moving back and forth with her need.

"Say it," Franz countered.

"Must I?" she answered.

"Yes, you must. I want to hear it. I need to hear you say it," he replied.

"I want to feel you sliding in and out of me," she said, with a deep breath, then, "I want this," as she squeezed his bulging trousers, "stuck up between my legs as far as it will go."

"Ah, you say that now," he teased, "But will you say that when I'm doing it?"

"Try me and see," she bantered.

"I believe I'll simply be forced to accommodate you, madam, in order to ascertain the veracity of your ardor," came the reply, and with that he began to remove her hairpins and undo the fastenings of her clothing as her tiny hands struggled with the buttons of his shirt.

Soon his hands were stroking soft, naked flesh --- as were hers, as well. Quiet for the moment, each savored the feeling of the other's skin --- and the feeling of being touched. Liz trailed her lips against his chest, then his stomach. Franz held her breasts, slightly pinching the nipples between his fingers, and rolling them as if he were dialing tiny knobs on a machine of some sort. A small moan escaped from her mouth and she threw her head back for a moment, but only a moment, then gasped as he ran a finger over her little button and slid it easily into her secret cave. Nerves in her lower torso and legs were going crazy --- her body twitched and spasmed as his eloquent finger had its say and she crooned, "Ooooh, oo-o-oh, ooooooooooooooh....."

Finally, the finger was removed and she was free to attend to Franz' body. Not one to be neglectful, she plied him with massage and teasing until, in a matter of minutes, he was aroused further to full proportion and ready for her. At first,

J. Matheny

she licked his rigid saber until he fairly seemed to be bursting out of his skin with each stroke of her tongue. Then, ever so gently, she took him into her mouth. His hips surged forward to meet her as she pleasured him. This sensation was wonderful, but there was more in store. As he lay reclined on the chaise, Liz left her ministrations and stood above him, then sat on his erect member, driving it into herself to the hilt. Now, it was his turn to gasp. Liz had the advantage and she began to push herself against his loins as he bucked like a bronco seeming to be intent on bucking its rider off. His hands moved to her hips and he placed his thumbs together on her clitoris so that every time she moved, they pushed against it firmly.

Her own orgasm was not far in front of her, but she kept pounding her flesh against him, driving and urging him forward to his appointment with ecstasy.

He watched her bouncing breasts, as they made love, and reached for one of them and began to squeeze and knead it, then held the other as well. As Liz put a hand down to massage her clitoris in the absence of his thumbs, he could feel the contractions begin in her tight little haven and his own orgasm began to relieve itself as well. He almost lost consciousness with the force of the energy that rippled through every fiber of his being, and for at least a while he had no recollection of anything but his throbbing, ejaculating member as it pulsed his juices into his Liz.

Liz' release came on the heels of his own, and she ground her pelvis into his with a fervor. As her body reeled with sensation, she began to laugh, a light joyous laughter with tinkling notes only he had ever heard. She collapsed onto him, then rolled sideways and lay next to him to savor the afterglow. The roadster sat alone and quietly in the drive a long time before they stirred again, but stir they did.

Ravenous as crows, they woke late in the day as the sun was going down and, after showering, they trailed downstairs swathed in towels to raid the larder. Liz brought out a roast of beef and fresh bread, while Franz found the plates and silver, as well as a long sharp knife for the meat. They uncorked a bottle of deep red wine, heavy and bold, and drank it from his friend's best crystal, sitting there on his terrace. in their towels, then topped it and the beef sandwiches with fresh fruit harvested from the trees in the garden only that morning. A feast fit for a king, they declared!

In the twilight garden, where they sat satiated in many ways, they talked of a variety of things: world events, progress and science, as well as the weather. Quite a lively discussion ensued between the two. Liz was the more liberal and sometimes fell afoul of Franz, but he, knowing that women often think with their hearts, forgave her this slight fault and, in point of fact, loved her all the more for it.

Eventually, the hour grew quite late and the lovers, having ensconced themselves in the large bed with canopy and velvet curtains, fell asleep in each others arms. Sometime in the middle of the night, though, they turned over under the thick feather coverlet and lay back to back as though each was protecting the other's blind side. Liz lay there thinking deep thoughts. This had been so like the time they spent in this house on their honeymoon, but it was a little different.

J. Matheny

This was not the Franz she had known, she thought, and, yet, it was. His hair was the same color, his smile was the same, his eyes could twinkle with secret laughter just as before --- even his hands touching her, and the look and feel his body, felt the same. Their intense passion for each other had not changed one iota. It was just that there was some tiny difference in him, not completely accounted for by the quirks in his ability to remember things or his scars.

Perhaps, it was that his trusting innocence had been destroyed along with those bits of his memory that seemed buried --- or missing.....

She loved him still with all of the glow and the passion, but it was as though someone new had come into her life and she had had to get used to having a partial stranger make love to her in a manner so extremely reminiscent of her Franz, and, yet, the tiniest shade off somehow, though she never let on to him and never would. As she thought that, she reminded herself, that this *was* her Franz. This *was* the man she had searched for so diligently and she would do whatever it took to see him through his healing.

For, theirs was a love that reached beyond the ordinary.

Theirs was a connection, an embracing .....of souls.

An excerpt from the next story by this author:

As they turned toward the house, her foot engaged a pebble and she leaned into John, almost falling. He caught her and, holding her in his arms and feeling their hearts pounding, he brought his lips down to hers and, parting his lips, kissed her passionately. Elisabeth returned kiss for kiss and passion for passion, pressing herself against him as firmly as he pulled her to him. Had there been a bed nearby, they would have made use of it, but only a stone garden bench availed itself..... Sitting there, they held each other, kissing and touching as much as they could reach. John lifted her skirt enough to run a hand up her leg and onto her thigh, then into the open crotch of her undergarment, designed to make necessities easier, but handy for lovers as well.....

Elisabeth gasped in her arousal, rocking her head back and forth, and feeling almost faint in the heat of that moment. Taking this for assent, John proceeded to explore with his fingers, the territory beneath that opening in her undergarment. It was very wet with a juice of some sort much like his of the night before and it made her body slippery. His hand probed further, finding a mound of fur, from which the juice seemed to be emanating. Yet, further, his long slender fingers encountered tissues not unlike lips and a crevice, into which he plunged his finger, then another, making Elisabeth gasp and moan. "Am I hurting you?" he asked.

"No," she moaned sensuously, "Please carry on," then placed her hand on the mound grown in his groin, eliciting a groan from him, as well..... He did carry on, running his fingers in and out of her and slipping them up to the risen button of flesh at the apex of her own furry mound, then finally, realizing that he could rub that with his thumb as his other fingers slid in and out of her, he experimented with her arousal. She reacted immediately with greater groaning, though he could see she was trying to hold it in, and finally, at the point that he thought he would faint away as more and more blood served his erection, she began to whimper and he felt the muscles of her interior parts convulsing on his fingers..... The tactile sensation was too much for him to bear, holding back, and his own orgasm rocked them both as it overtook him. He didn't have time to think more than a fleeting --- wish I could be free of my trousers --- and, suddenly, he was holding his fingers deep within Elisabeth and vibrating them to bring her to greater sensitivity and a more erotic orgasm.

Elisabeth held him more tightly than she had ever held anyone before, rocking with the force of the experience and kissing him deeply and with more passion than

331

she knew she could feel or, for that matter, express. It seemed as though it would go on forever in the dark of that spring garden, scented by flowers and lit only by stars.

When they finally sat there holding each other, but not intimately, he ventured, "I'm afraid I must depart for my rooms, ma'am, for my trousers have become damp. May I see you to the door of your study?"

Still holding the bulge in his trousers, she gently squeezed --- and he jerked as if shocked --- then, she squeezed again and he pushed forward into her hand, wanting to feel this contact with her again and again. Putting his lips to her ear, he whispered, "Tomorrow, dearest lady, tomorrow."

Then, he escorted her to the door of her study, embraced her, and kissed her soundly, then turned on his heel and retreated to his rooms.

Once inside, all he could think of was his need for greater release and, stepping out of his trousers, he lay in his bed with his towel, now rinsed and dry, to ease his need. Stroking his manhood, he began to bring himself to completion again. Up and down his hand slid, milking that stiffened teat and hoping for a bumper crop of release. Squeezing it, from time to time, as well, he finally erupted into the towel again, spent and satiated for the time being. As his thoughts flew to Elisabeth, he could feel it stiffening again, though, and began a gentle massage to relax it, but succeeded only in arousing himself again, due to his thoughts of her, and this erection took much longer to put down. His right hand was sore and his arm, too, before juice had sputtered forth from his member for the third time that day.....
What was this magic that she had --- to bring him to desire her so much --- he wondered, as he lay there nearly unable to move for the heaviness of his limbs.....

Left at the door, Elisabeth entered the study, crossed to the hall, then slowly ascended the stairway to her bedroom. She felt a languor, as though her limbs could not obey her and, undressing, she slid under the covers naked --- to touch herself and augment the actions John Bishop had performed. Finding the juicy slit between her thighs, she began to run her hands through the wetness and stimulated the sensory button he had so adroitly addressed with the mere touch of his thumb. It was very sensitive, very responsive, and she jerked with each touch to it, but she persisted and, eventually, she experienced yet another orgasm, this time arching her back and keening her pleasure. As she lay there afterward, she thought of him and let out a sigh, the sigh of a woman satisfied ---